"The joy and excitement of engagin dates back to the beginning of time. The for women, and the passion is no less pi illustrates the emotion of sport as it chronicles the journey of fathers, mothers, sons, daughters, grandparents, coaches, school administrators and students during the transition from pre-Title IX expectations to 20th century possibilities. You'll be inspired by the story!"

> —Jean Driscoll, Eight-time winner of the Boston Marathon,
> U.S. Olympic Hall of Fame

"The story that too often goes missing in today's athletic arena is that of the Title IX pioneers who made it possible for young women to compete on so many levels. *When Girls Became Lions* fills that gap. Though the story might be contemporary fiction, its characters are real and their experiences true, reminding us of the many women who endured so much because they just wanted to play their game. This novel is a winner for all of us."

> —Sue Semrau, Head Women's Basketball Coach, Florida State University,
> Athletic Coast Coach of the Year and President of the WBCA

"I read a lot of fiction and am thrilled that Val and Jo have given us *When Girls Became Lions*, a story with women athletes at the heart. I've looked for a novel like this for a long time to provide a window into the world of women's sports and Title IX's implications, especially to inspire—and inform—our younger athletes. I can't wait to give a copy to my players and friends!"

> —Jane Albright, Head Women's Basketball Coach, University of Nevada

"I've coached women's college soccer for over a decade and have seen first-hand the growth and advancement in the world of women's athletics. I am so thankful to the countless women and men who worked to bring equality and exposure for women in soccer over the years. *When Girls Became Lions* reminds us of the courage and joy of those pioneers, and helps us see how far our game has come in providing the opportunities that now exist for young women in soccer and in sports. For Val and Jo to bring us such a captivating story will not only be entertaining for soccer lovers, but will shine a light on the journey that brought the game so far. It's an important story to tell and so fun and meaningful that it is told so well."

> —Mike Friesen, Women's Soccer Coach, San Diego State University

"Too often the stories of early advocates championing the cause for sport equality aren't told. That's why a novel like *When Girls Became Lions* is so important: it tells one of those stories in a beautiful way. Authors Valerie Gin and Jo Kadlecek provide today's female athletes a glimpse into the lives of those brave souls who came before them and upon whose shoulders they stand. May those of us who have the privilege of working with young people remember those women and men who struggled so that we may enjoy and celebrate the opportunities we have today. This is a great read for anyone involved in the development and leadership of girls and young women!"

> —Samantha K Huge, Senior Associate Athletics Director/
> Senior Woman Administrator, Texas A&M University

First printing, September 2015

Cover and book design by Christine Richenburg
Cover image by Rachel Chang
Copy editing by Jennifer Beatson Martin
Special thanks to Sonia Weston

ISBN: 978-1-68222-180-8

Library of Congress Cataloging-in-Publication Data

when girls

became

LIONS

a novel

Valerie J. Gin & Jo Kadlecek

Dedication

To Val's Mom and Dad, Thank you both for teaching me that it is much more important to do and be my best than to be the best. I'm grateful for the selfless sacrifices you made to provide every possibility for me to play, learn and thrive.

and

For the greatest champion of women's sports I know, my big brother, Jim Kadlecek, who coached my college club team helping it become Division I, and who coached his daughters—my amazing nieces—little league and high school teams.

Prologue
2008

The memory of a strong woman is a sanctuary. When the storm comes, you remember how her arms anchored your frame, her words soothed your soul and her eyes—deep and brown and bold—hushed the fear.

She reminds a girl to hope.

That's what she always did with me anyway. It was as if hope rounded out every syllable of my grandmother's sentences. She couldn't help it; no matter how dark the sky, she'd never miss an opportunity to point me to the generations before us, those she called the "rudder on our ship." They were the people who'd made our lives better now because of their struggle then, and so were "helping steer our course across the waters."

I always thought it was a funny thing for her to say, considering my grandmother never once set foot on a boat. But I'd nod anyway. She was my MaeMa after all.

Born and raised in Cincinnati—where tough neighborhoods and the Ohio River separated her from Kentucky hills—Reyola Mae Wallace (or MaeMa to me) wanted better streets for her little girl and baby boy. She had bigger things to do while she waited for their daddy to come home from fighting in Vietnam.

He never did.

So she poured herself into the town of Claymont Falls, a thirty-minute drive from downtown Cincinnati, and raised my uncle and my mother through one troubled decade into the next. When I came along February 1, 1983, her small but solid house became my home too, mostly because my mom refused to move in with the "low-life crazy man" she called my father. That "crazy man" convinced Uncle Jimmy to move to Chicago when I was still in diapers and we didn't hear much from either after that.

So it was just us—MaeMa, Mom, and me. We went everywhere together—to the store, the library, and just about every high school game or concert or art show there was. The town revolved around that school—Home of the "Lions"— maybe because there was not much else for folks to do, unless they wanted to drive to the city. And most, including us, did not. The older I got, the more folks simply referred to us as, The Wallace Women.

But there was no mistaking the matriarch. MaeMa was the first African-American teacher at the Claymont Falls elementary school, back when my mom started kindergarten in 1968. In between teaching fourth graders and serving on the missionary committee at church, MaeMa was one of those people who never thought doors would close if you wanted them open. Possibility to her was as natural as our family picnics and bedtime stories, and just as easy.

I'll always remember how each night, she'd sit on the edge of my bed, read a few pages from whatever story we were exploring until my eyes would grow heavy and she'd close the book. Then she'd turn out the light and whisper words that became a familiar balm, "'Night, baby girl. Tomorrow needs your all good sleep now because you've got your best to give, not anyone else's, just yours." And near the fog of a dream, I'd hear her shuffle back to the living room and plop herself on the sofa to read until Mom came home from work and I'd be fast asleep.

If MaeMa gave me home and stories, my mother gave me my first shoes that mattered: cleats. The tiny rubber studs under my nine-year old feet felt as exciting to me as when I dressed up in her high heels. At youth soccer practice, I'd run faster than everyone else, I was sure, and kicked more goals because of those Pumas.

It didn't stop there. With each birthday, Mom somehow managed to buy me Nikes or Adidas, gloves, racquets or balls, and then find any sport possible for me to play in town. From tennis lessons and track teams, to softball, volleyball and soccer, she made sure my energy and abilities were put to good use while she worked at the school cafeteria during the day and Joe's Diner at night.

And I loved every last one of those games. Each chance I had to lace up those shoes, tie back my hair and wear T-shirts and shorts, I'd feel just as at home as if I were in MaeMa's kitchen. Each time I won a 50-yard dash, a team trophy or Most Valuable Player, MaeMa and Mom would pin those ribbons and awards on every wall and shelf in the living room until they spilled over into the hallway. Instead of paintings above the couch or photographs on the bookshelves, my medals, honors and trophies were displayed, rearranged and dusted. The Wallace Women liked to say they had a champion in their midst, and I'd never argue.

"You're becoming your best for everybody," MaeMa would proclaim as I walked off each field or court with her, holding her hand on one side and my mother's on the other. "You'll see, you'll see," my mom would echo.

What exactly "I'd see" was never entirely clear to me, no matter how many times they'd tell me, not even when I graduated from high school and played on a soccer scholarship at a university 600 miles away. I was too absorbed with my trophies and books and cleats.

Until, finally, I had to sit down, pay attention and remember. And that 'had to' journey began not long after I'd landed my first job: as a teacher and a coach in the same high school my mother and I both had attended, a career step that made her cry with pride, especially when she imagined out loud what the news would have meant to my grandmother.

If she'd been alive to hear it.

chapter
1
1983

"Girls? Are you kidding me?"

Bailey Crawford couldn't get the words out of his mouth quickly enough. And he certainly wasn't about to take the chair Harry Hanks offered him; the athletic director's office suddenly seemed too small anyway. So Bailey just stood there, fists and arms lodged across his chest. He shifted his weight to his left foot and studied the man behind the desk, sitting calmly, adjusting the cufflinks on his sleeves and glancing occasionally toward the window, like he, too, would rather be somewhere else—but for a completely different reason.

"You knew it could come to this, Crawford," he said, his voice a rhythm of ego and impatience. "We had to put the best applicant we had with a girls team to show we're in compliance with the new rules. You're our best."

"But I didn't apply." Bailey shifted again, this time to his right foot. He shook his head, lifted his baseball cap and ran his hand over his bushy black hair before returning the cap. He turned toward the table below the window, picked up a small but heavy trophy. It was a statue of a miniature quarterback with a football in his hand, frozen in a stance that suggested he was about to pass, with a small gold plate beneath that read: "Regional Tournament, 1st Place, Claymont Falls Lions, 1982."

Last year's trophy. Bailey tilted it sideways before replacing it as if he were considering its significance. He cleared his throat and turned toward his boss.

"I'm the best, huh? Who's the 'best' to coach girls?" he said. "Does Lars know? He was thinking I'd be his replacement. I've been his assistant for the past eight years, you know."

Hanks grinned. It was a wide grin that pushed thin lines across his face, making him appear older than he probably was. Too many days beneath the sun at baseball games and fighting the bitter Ohio cold at football practices had punished his face. As athletic director, he'd clocked in hundreds of hours at every game the school offered as well as overseeing the football program. Now a weary annoyance was beginning to form in his eyes as well. Maybe because, as Bailey thought, adding a girls team now meant he'd have to supervise it as well. He was running out of patience.

The athletic director withdrew the grin as quickly as he'd offered it, clenched his jaw and adjusted the stacks of paper on his desk as if he were tidying both his temper and his workload. He picked up a single sheet of paper, ignoring Bailey's question about Lars.

"Here's the contract. You'll teach your usual class load and we'll set up 10 or so games for this first season, you know, to see if they can handle that." He held out a ballpoint pen to Bailey. "Yes or no?"

"You're serious? Girls soccer?"

He shrugged and waited, still offering the pen. "It's the law of the land, like it or not, a thing called Title IX. We don't comply, we don't get funding for other sports. Plain and simple."

Bailey swallowed and considered. "Any equipment? Assistant coach?"

"Hmm, I did order new jerseys and balls for the junior varsity boys' team this year, so I guess the girls can have some of their old ones."

Bailey laughed at the thought. True, his daughter and her friends loved borrowing their brothers' oversized sweatshirts to roam the neighborhood or the malls. But it was one thing to wear a sibling's old jacket for fun and another to wear worn out uniforms—which probably wouldn't fit—for an altogether different purpose.

"Old boys' jerseys for girls? So much for equality," he muttered, looking his boss directly in the eyes. In a department already built on the emotional battlefield of competition, the comment was an easy button that now pushed Hanks into the irritation he'd been holding at bay.

"Shit, Crawford, I thought I was doing you a favor. You've got a kid who's been chomping at the bit to play the game and I'm giving you your . . ."

"I've got two kids, Harry, remember? Twins. Seniors. And one is a whole lot more likely to get a scout to see his talent than the other. You know as well as I do scholarships don't exist for girls." He was breathing hard, a small sweat forming across his forehead. He stepped closer to the desk and confronted his superior:

"Besides, fathers coach their sons, not their daughters."

The administrator now accepted the challenge, rose from his seat and leaned over the desk, a full five inches from Bailey, planting his cuff-linked wrists on the desktop as if the gesture prevented him from taking a swing at the coach across from him.

"Take it or leave it," he whispered, ire escaping the sides of his mouth.

"Who will coach the boys then? I'm next in line." He had to ask.

"What's it to you?"

What's it to me? The question stung. This was not how it was supposed to be. All the years he'd spent working with B.J., they looked forward to his son's last high school season together when Coach Lambert had told them he'd retire. But the school's athletic director wasn't offering him Lambert's job; someone else would be taking it, and Bailey realized his emotions were gaining a momentum he knew was not healthy. He composed himself. He took a half step back from his boss and gathered his courage before turning down the volume of his voice and shifting gears:

"As a father, I'd like to know who will be coaching my son. That's why it matters."

Instead of answering, Hanks simply pushed the ballpoint pen into Bailey's right hand. Then he shoved the contract in his other and waited, glancing at the clock near the door, his jaw grinding.

Slowly, decidedly, Bailey Crawford lifted his shoulders and filled his lungs. The contract felt like a hundred pound weight. After almost two decades of serving in the school district's sports programs, first as the elementary school gym teacher paying his dues, and then stepping into this position when it opened up at the high school. During his time working as Lambert's assistant, Bailey had helped build the program and prepare dozens of players to go on to play college ball at all levels. The international sport of soccer—or "futball"— was gaining popularity in Ohio, though it'd never catch up to America's version of football, Bailey knew.

Still, he'd helped develop young athletes and fully expected this was the year he'd step into the third most prestigious coaching spot— behind football and basketball—at Claymont Falls High: varsity boy's soccer. And this year, 1983, was the year his son and a dozen other solid players actually had a chance at a state title.

But girls? They were cheerleaders, maybe gymnasts. Yes, he knew of a few girls in his history classes who played tennis, but none he thought could handle a fast and physical game like soccer. Except maybe his own daughter who was a natural, but even she earned her share of bruises and scrapes whenever she kicked around with her twin brother and his buddies, so much so that they'd walk away teasing that she "played like a girl."

How in the world could he field an entire team of girls who played like, well, girls?

Hanks' offer to coach them seemed absurd. Then again, Bailey knew no one who actually wanted a team of girls to play soccer, and he'd never heard so much as a single speck of interest from any local girl or parent to have her daughter play. Now because of some federal law, he was being told to make a team from scratch and confront a whole way of thinking that, before today, he didn't imagine existed anywhere in the Midwest.

But he loved coaching soccer. Though he'd never admit it to his athletic director, he'd have coached the boys for free. Thankfully they paid him, because he and Cathy had come to rely on the extra income and routine. His family scheduled their calendars around seasons, and planned their vacations early in the summer so they wouldn't interrupt preseason training. What he'd earned from coaching, he knew could help at least one of his children, and hoped like crazy the other would get a scholarship.

That prospect wasn't looking so good now.

Coaching gave him a completely different satisfaction than he got from teaching history. Yes, it was particularly fulfilling for him to take teenagers through the founding of the U.S., encountering the Revolutionary, Civil and World Wars as if they were real battlefields, exploring the character traits of presidents, senators and radicals throughout each era.

Coaching, too, had become such a fixture in his afternoons, the smell of freshly cut grass, the inspiration of watching players improve, discovering new strategies, preparing for championships, recruiting new . . .

"I said, take it or leave it. Girls or nothing." The ultimatum jolted Bailey back from his thoughts. Hanks tapped his pen against the desk. "Listen, Crawford, we've got other coaches who know it's easy money. Hell, you don't even need to know the game to coach them."

That did it. Bailey shook the contract out in front of him like he was getting out the wrinkles, and read over the single page. Then he placed it on the edge of the desk, leaned over and scribbled his name on the line near the bottom of the page. When he finished, he simply set down the pen on top of the contract, turned around and walked toward the door. He ignored the sarcastic "Good luck!" as he turned the knob and didn't bother closing the door behind him.

But a few steps later, he spun around and marched back into the athletic director's office.

"You didn't answer me."

"What?"

"I'll find out soon enough who'll be coaching my son," Bailey paused. "My question is, will I get an assistant coach?"

"They're girls, Crawford. Not football players. I think one coach is plenty."

Hanks sat back behind his desk, a king returning to his throne. He slipped the contract into a manila folder and returned to fiddling with his cufflinks.

Just as Bailey Crawford was about to object, the phone rang and the king dismissed his subject with the brush of a hand, like he was swatting away a fly. Bailey glared at the gesture, then at his superior who had picked up his phone and swiveled in his chair toward the window, leaning back as if this were going to be a long conversation. And with barely a clue about what he'd just done, Bailey Crawford turned and exited the office. This time he pulled the door shut.

"Girls? Girls." He debated with himself as he hurried from the administrative area and into a hall lined with only a few students late to class.

Just as he turned, Bailey ran smack into a backpack. It had been hanging from the shoulder of a skinny girl with stringy brown hair. Her pack spiraled to the ground, two, maybe three books and a few pencils spilling out and sliding across the linoleum floor. The girl and Bailey both shot down to collect the items and thumped their heads at the same time. The collision knocked Bailey back onto the floor, his feet out in front of him, but the girl wobbled, caught her balance and shot up before zeroing back on her books like a bird her prey.

"I'm so sorry! I didn't see you," Bailey said. He picked himself up and bent to help the girl but she'd already gathered most of the contents and was shoving them back in. Bailey saw the bag had no zipper.

"Really, let me help," Bailey said, reaching toward her. The girl jumped back at his movement, almost bumping into another student who was sprinting toward class, but she shuffled sideways to avoid another collision.

"No, that's all right," she said. Her eyes avoided Bailey's and she stayed focused on her backpack, the floor, the ceiling, anywhere but Bailey. She was a student he didn't recognize. True, the school was getting bigger each year but it was May already and he'd thought at least he'd met most students before the year ended. This girl, though, with her worn out jeans, bleached white blouse and patched up backpack that looked like it had once belonged to someone else, must have been new to Claymont Falls.

"Well, at least let me introduce myself. I mean, if a clumsy oaf runs into you in the hall, you should at least know his name," Bailey said, smiling and offering his handshake. "I'm Mr. Crawford. I teach junior and senior social studies."

"I know," the girl said, shoving her hand in her back pocket before taking his quickly and yanking it back when the shake was official. She flung her backpack over her shoulder with her other hand and sniffed. "You coach soccer."

Bailey was surprised. He dropped his hand. "Yes, I do, but not sure why I've never seen you. Are you new this year?"

She shook her head, eyes still everywhere but his, and she began to chew on her lower lip.

"No? Guess I just haven't run into you before," he chuckled. She shifted her weight but not her expression. She still was not smiling.

"Bad joke. My mistake, Miss . . . ?" Bailey addressed students the same way they did him, formally. A mentor early in his career taught him that he'd earn respect from each child if he offered it first. But this girl hesitated. He pressed. "Miss . . . ?"

"Beaucamp. My name's Adeline Beaucamp." She said the name as if she were hoping some tenor of dignity would suddenly resound from it that she hadn't yet heard in her 16 or 17 years of living. But it never quite arrived and so she followed up with, "Kids just call me Kentucky. And I'm going to be late to class, Coach."

With that, "Kentucky" sprinted away from Bailey, weaving in and out of the few remaining students and teachers still wandering in the hall, and disappearing quickly around the corner a good 40 yards away. The class bell rang and Bailey tilted his head at the trail the girl had just left, wondering if he'd found his first recruit.

If, in fact, Claymont Falls High was ready for such a thing as a girls soccer team.

Bailey sighed and turned toward his next goal: fifth period American History with juniors. With only three and half weeks left before the summer break, he still needed to wrap up with Hitler and the Invasion of Normandy. He'd deal with Eisenhower, McCarthyism, Civil Rights and Vietnam first thing in August since he'd have most of the same students back for senior social studies. Then again, maybe he should just return to the country's beginnings.

Talk of revolutions never seemed more appropriate.

Instead, Bailey stuck to his lesson plans and by the time his last class ended, he'd almost forgotten the encounter he'd had with his athletic director. Almost. But as he began his end-of-day ritual, the exchange came back to him like a punch in the gut, forcing him to consider how he'd break the news to his family. He erased the chalkboard and thought of his son's disappointment. He returned a few texts to their shelves, reached for his coffee, now cold, and imagined how his wife and daughter would respond to his new coaching position. The blue and green mug with its Lions silhouette on it—a gift from last year's cheerleading squad to all the teachers and coaches—sat in its usual spot on his desk: between the ceramic soccer ball pencil holder and the miniature globe.

He picked up the mug, drank and considered how to communicate something he still wasn't sure of himself. It was not unlike the many times he'd sat here creating a game plan for another tough opponent, yellow pad nearby, cold coffee, pencil and eraser.

As the junior varsity boys' soccer coach, Bailey planned his own game strategies and practices but he always supported Lars Lambert at varsity games. When he was a young man, Bailey hadn't played much soccer; in this Ohio town especially, football reigned supreme but he was too skinny in those days for gridiron. A boys' soccer program only began his junior year at Claymont Falls High, so he played basketball instead. Years later, basketball helped his understanding of soccer; he could relate to the offensive and defensive strategies soccer required because of its similarities.

And that was what qualified him when Lars first approached him to be the assistant coach the year after Bailey was hired to teach history. It was a step up in the district he'd grown up in himself, where'd he'd taken the first job offered to him after college: as the elementary school gym teacher. That was his foot in the door when his kids were little, but he'd always kept an eye on returning to the high school.

A smart and patient mentor, Coach Lambert, the school's physical education teacher, had once run marathons and played "futbol" in Austria before immigrating with his family to the U.S. But these days, Lars was happy if he could walk to the field from the boy's locker room—his knees were a mess and after nearly a half century in Ohio schools, he told Bailey, he was ready to "pass on the baton and boots."

This was his year.

Bailey Junior was now a solid midfielder on the junior varsity team who expected his dad would move with him to the varsity team during his senior year. Almost every day since the fall season ended, B.J. had talked about how they'd bring the Lions its first championship ever. He'd even begun introducing his dad as the new coach.

The coffee's last sip was not only cold, it was bitter. Bailey washed out the mug, returned it to his desk and pulled his car keys from his pocket. He was going home empty handed this evening—he'd leave his grading for tomorrow's study hall. Tonight needed to be a time when he concentrated not on quizzes, book reports or upcoming lectures, but on his family. Especially his son.

B.J. was sprawled on the couch engrossed in a novel when Bailey walked into the living room. His leg dangled over the side, his bare foot just skimming the carpet as it swung back and forth. He was wearing black athletic shorts and an orange Cincinnati Bengals T-shirt that Bailey recognized as one of his own. His son's frame was similar to his at that age—boney, thin, un-toned—but B.J. had already passed him in height by a good inch. His curly brown hair was cut short and his face clean and void of but a few strangling whiskers. At 17, B.J.'s body was stuck at that stage in-between teen and man, but his face still looked like that of a second grader, especially when something exciting or big was happening. Wide-eyed and full of emotion, B.J. was a sensitive but confident kid, qualities Bailey was sure came from his mother.

"Don't get up," joked the senior to his son. B.J. responded with a wave of the hand and without a flinch of his head. "Where are your mom and sister?" The teen hand pointed to the kitchen, the toes still skimming the carpet.

Bailey smiled. He'd known the answer the second he'd walked through the front door from the smell. Lasagna maybe, and definitely one of Cathy's homemade loaves of bread, the aroma so welcoming he didn't mind B.J.'s non-verbal response. Besides, the last thing he wanted to do was interrupt a story absorbing his son. If there was anything B.J. loved almost as much as soccer, it was reading. Always had. And Bailey would sometimes tease the boy that if he wasn't careful with all those books, he might just grow up to be a professor.

"Thanks, Bud," he said. B.J.'s hand formed a thumbs-up in response and then dropped across his stomach as he brought the novel closer to his face with his other hand. He was near the end of the book, probably just at the climax, since his eyes had just stretched wide into his brows and his foot's pace picked up.

Cathy was taking out a pan from the oven when her husband appeared. He leaned into her and kissed her cheek before setting down his car keys in the tray by the back door. Cathy closed the oven and turned toward Bailey. Almost a foot shorter than he was, Cathy Crawford was the perfect opposite of the man she'd married. Where he often towered over people in size and presence, she looked up to them and moved behind the scenes. Where his hair was dark and curly, hers was blonde and straight. Where he was athletic and intellectual, she was a gardener and realist. Her soft blue eyes were always searching, sizing up situations and often noticing things few others did, a trait that captured Bailey the minute he'd first met her. Though she was two years older than he was, they complemented each other.

"Good day?" she asked. Her voice was smooth as she paused from her dinner preparations. His wife was the type of woman who, when she asked a question, genuinely waited for an answer, giving the full care of her attention. She leaned against the counter, her arms resting on both sides as her red flowered dress—the one Bailey watched her put on for work that morning—hung neatly to her knees.

"Uh, interesting. Yours?" Bailey deflected, opening the refrigerator and reaching for the jug of orange juice. He also pulled a bottle of Coors, given the news he had to share, and decided beer was best reserved for moments like this.

He wasn't a big drinker, just a bottle of beer with dinner or for just watching a Reds doubleheader on Friday night.

"Busy, busy," Cathy said. "All sorts of meetings and projects, projects and meetings. Could hardly keep up." She grinned and watched Bailey pour his beer into a frosty mug as she waited for him to catch the joke. The froth was just forming at the top when it finally registered.

"Wow. Great. Business is finally picking up, huh?" he teased back.

She laughed. As the secretary of First Baptist Church and the only other employee besides the pastor, Cathy's days were quiet and dull compared to Bailey's. Nothing much happened in her office besides paying bills and typing sermons or letters, which was fine with her. She only worked Mondays, Tuesdays and Thursdays anyway, and the pastor made it clear when he hired her that she and her family did not have to attend services just because she worked at the church. That was six and a half years ago. They'd been glad for the freedom and the part-time income ever since, and had joined the congregation most Sundays anyway.

"Grueling," she responded. "Guess you'll tell me about yours over dinner, which is in about two minutes." She began tossing a salad.

"Guess I will," Bailey said, gulping the beer and setting the mug on the table. He looked out the kitchen window and saw his daughter in the driveway with her neighborhood friend, Tricia. They were laughing and talking non-stop, in-between tossing a basketball every which way toward the backboard, trying to see who'd spell P-I-G first.

Bailey noticed, as if he'd never before seen it, his daughter's fitness and form as she shot the ball.

"You know, she's pretty good at that," he said.

"Yes, she is." Cathy was setting the plates on the kitchen table and putting forks and knives out as well. "And she's good at setting the table too though we'd never know it. Call her inside, okay, Hon?"

Bailey stepped outside into his driveway just as a basketball ricocheted off of the hoop, spiraling right at him. His reflexes kicked in, and he caught the ball, swiveled, then went up for a layup.

"Oh! Crawford puts in the game-winning basket, just in time for dinner!" As the ball dropped through the net, he caught it and cradled it between his elbow and hip.

"Hey, Dad!" Mandy hollered. Every inch a tomboy, his daughter nonetheless had a sweet prettiness to her. Long brown curls outlined her face and shoulders, and she was as thin as her twin brother, almost as tall. Her arms had slightly more muscle tone than B.J.'s, or perhaps Bailey was just noticing it for the first time, in much the same way he could see whether a returning player had worked out over the summer. But Mandy's tank top also showed off her 17-year-old figure, her shorts a little too tight for a father's liking, and he suddenly was thankful for baggy uniforms.

"Shoe's untied," he said. She looked down just as he tossed the ball at her, but she recovered, grabbed the basketball and put it back up to the board in an instant. All three watched as it banked off and into the net.

"Ah . . . Crawford ties the game!" Tricia exclaimed, using her best imitation of Howard Cosell, the sports announcer. "That girl's the best there is. Can't keep her down. I will tell you, the last time I saw a shot like that, well, I've never seen a shot like that. Nobody can do what she does! Ladies and gentlemen, we have got ourselves a game."

The three laughed as Tricia scooped up the ball, dribbled it a few times—or tried to, since her eye-hand coordination was not quite as quick as her facility with words—and then she tossed it back to Mandy, who dribbled it low to the ground, alternating its direction between her left and right hands, and in and out of her legs. Tricia, who watched admiringly, was much shorter than Bailey's daughter, round in the body, though her arms and legs looked more like broomsticks. Hers was an odd shape, topped by sandy brown hair tied back in a ponytail, yet with several strands refusing to stay in place. Her Ohio State sweatshirt hung to her hips, above her fluffy jeans and Converse shoes. Though they looked like they had nothing in common, these two girls had been best friends since anyone could remember.

"Ah, shucks, Howard, we've run out of time tonight," Bailey said. "Time for dinner at the Crawford court."

"All right then. The team's gotta get their strength. They'll need it for the playoffs as they're up against the roughest, toughest boys in town. That's it for now, everyone. Well, see ya later, Coach," Tricia mused, still Cosell-like as she turned toward her house across the street and a few doors down. "I'll call you later, Mandy. See ya!"

Father and daughter walked inside for dinner, washed their hands and joined mother and son around the table. Helpings were dished as bread, butter and salt were passed in typical Crawford family-style fashion.

But when Bailey cleared his throat, took a gulp of his beer and announced his new position, his wife, son and daughter each dropped their forks and stopped eating at exactly the same time . . . for entirely different reasons.

chapter
2

2008

My journey began with an open casket, though from where I was sitting in the pews I could not see the face of the man lying inside. Not that I wanted to. He was a stranger to me, and I was an outsider invading his sacred departure from Earth. As the lone representative from the athletic department of Claymont Falls High, I'd been sent to pay respects to a coach who—before this very moment—I never knew existed.

I did not want to be sitting in a church, preparing for a service of sad good byes when I had never even said hello. It was a spectacular Tuesday afternoon, perfect for anything but a funeral. The sun was stronger than it had been all week, and only a few wisps of white clouds pushed their way across the sky. There were no ominous skies anywhere, not a hint of the torrential rain I'd come to expect at funerals where people dodged puddles and hurried under umbrellas to mourn and weep and agonize over their loss.

It had poured the last and only time I'd attended a funeral. MaeMa was gone and the weather pummeled, matching the emotions of the day. That day there was no sun, no warmth, no invitation to do anything but sit with my mother, already paralyzed from a loneliness reinforced by an ache everywhere.

I missed MaeMa every day.

This funeral, though, had a slight and certain breeze to it along with a stunning blue sky. It was weather that shouted life, telling women like me to get outside, to move, to celebrate and to feel my muscles and bones working in one steady motion. On my way to the church, I'd rolled down the window of my car, breathed in the crisp autumn air, and imagined a hundred other ways I could take advantage of a day like this.

Instead, I was staring at a casket, when I could have gone for a run. Or lined the soccer field. Or painted the fence behind the goal, which I'd wanted to do since I first saw it. That chipped white paint needed serious scraping and definitely new colors, solid blue and green, the colors that mattered. I could have practiced some shots on goal. Or I could have sat under a tree in the park with a good book, completely absorbed in a Walter Mosley mystery, not even noticing the sounds of people on picnics, because "Easy Rawlins," the private investigator, was about to nab a thug even the Los Angeles police department couldn't catch.

It was that kind of day for me, the kind that really should not have been spent indoors, much less in a church full of strangers gathering before the embalmed body of the man they'd come to honor, the man who'd been father, friend and coach to them.

This was depressing.

An organ played, but my mind again wandered, this time to the district league meetings taking place across the county, as well as to the lesson plans I needed to be working on before school started on Thursday. Harper Lee's To Kill a Mockingbird was assigned reading for my freshmen, and introductory paragraphs to be dissected for my essay-writing sophomores. During my other classes, I'd have to go back to the district curriculum. Plus, my players would be coming in at 3 o'clock for conditioning, so I created a mental list of sprints, obstacle course exercises and paths around the sports complex. Since my team didn't yet have the skills for a successful soccer season, my girls would at least be fit. So fitness and strength was the only strategy I knew to get them to the place they deserved to be: competitive.

The organ swelled, and my mind returned to why I was at this funeral in the first place. I'd been ambushed this morning at our athletic department meeting. My athletic director had made the announcement that Bailey Crawford's service was today, and then waited for a volunteer. No one offered, though all the coaches agreed someone should go. Some representative from the high school staff should attend this funeral, and it might as well be the newest coach at Claymont Falls High.

"Reynalda Wallace?" Preston Hanks had proclaimed my name, as if he'd just drawn the winner from a hat and I was the proud recipient of a million bucks. I pretended not to hear.

"Yes, you," he pointed. "Reynalda Wallace." He seemed to love saying my name, as if it gave him more authority as my boss, as if anyone could mistake who was in charge here.

The man was 6'4," with thick arms and a wide full grin he used only when he wanted something. A former linebacker who'd also come up through this very school, and the son of the previous athletic director, Preston Hanks had played at Ohio State before returning to his alma mater as head football coach and athletic director, just like his dad. He'd lost most of his hair since his return 16 years ago, long before I was a student here and, more recently, as a coach in his office. His balding head alternated between pale white and pink-red depending on the weather and if he wore a cap. But he liked to joke that winning so many close games would do that, especially in a town where no other sport mattered.

The organ grew louder as people filled the church, lining evenly on both sides with few places left to sit. I shifted uneasily in the pew at the memory of Hanks' demand.

The other men in our meeting had nodded at me, as if that would help confirm my decision. There was no other woman coach at the table for me to look to for solidarity, not even another African-American or Latino to side with, so I'd focused on scribbling some new ideas for defensive drills in my notebook, clicked my pen on, then off, then on again and concentrated on the page.

"Coach Rey?" Hanks spoke again, this time with a lilt of sarcasm as he used the name of familiarity my athletes had given me last year when I started this job. Which wasn't fair of him. As I looked up, my boss tilted that big head of his, and grinned.

I exhaled. "I'm not sure why I should go since I never met the man and . . ."

"It's your sport. Good PR opp. Besides, I've asked nicely, haven't I?" He leaned back in his chair and tucked his arms behind his head so that his elbows stuck out above his shoulders. The other coaches chuckled at his sarcasm and kept staring from me to Preston, waiting for the ground to swallow me up if I disobeyed.

I straightened my shoulders and tried to return the attitude: "Well, since you did ask nicely, I'd be honored to go and represent the exemplary coaches of Claymont Falls." I resisted rolling my eyes. "Now, who died again?"

I stared at the photo of the program I'd been handed when I walked in the church, organ music coming to an end, and Hanks' words echoed in my head: "Crawford coached here, before your time. It's a shame the cancer came so quick. I'd go myself, but with so much to get done before school starts, I just can't afford the time. You don't mind, do you, Coach Rey?"

He did not wait for an answer. He took off his glasses, wiped them on his sweatshirt, and then returned them to his nose while glancing around the table. "Anything else, guys?"

Heads shook. The dozen or so men pushed out their chairs, grabbed their notebooks and coffee mugs and scattered toward their respective offices or classrooms. Meeting adjourned.

Of the full time coaches at Claymont Falls High, I was the youngest at 25, which alone wouldn't have been a strike against me had I not also been the only woman on the coaching staff, and had I not happened to have two other strikes against me as well: I was African-American and an English teacher.

I'd never understood how history and biology could produce so many football and basketball coaches.

That staff meeting—only three hours ago—nagged at me now as I was standing with others, hymnals open, watching a procession of robed clergy approach the front of the church. They were followed by 10 or 12 middle-aged women marching down the center aisle toward the casket and into the second pew. The women were striking in their differences, each wearing business suits, designer dresses or casual slacks, each a taller height or wider shape than the other. Yet they walked arm in arm, as if they were sisters, as if they'd been together forever.

A tall man with round glasses walked behind them, an older woman clutching his right elbow and a younger version of her clutching his left. Behind them walked another woman holding the hands of three children, all slowly making their way toward the front row, just feet from the man in the casket. I pretended to sing as I stared at the dead man's family.

Hanks should have attended this funeral, I argued in my mind. Next time I'd be firmer if he called one of his spontaneous gatherings of the athletic department. Next time, I'd throw my fist into the air and proclaim my autonomy. I would not back down. I could be assertive, even if I was the youngest and the token double-whammy minority.

Okay, maybe I wasn't so good at asserting myself, but I could at least be assertive for my team—which should have held my focus this morning instead of my representing the coaching department at a funeral.

Not that it'd do me much good now. I was stuck. The church was stuffy with so many people and I sighed as we collectively took our seats.

The organ held its final chords, and I glanced again at the cover of the program, careful to avoid the elbows of the man and woman squeezed into the seats beside me. A black and white photograph of a man filled the top half of the page. It wasn't a formal photo but rather one that could have been taken on a family vacation: he was smiling, his face so relaxed I thought he might have been laughing as the picture was taken. He wore a baseball hat with a "C" above the brim, and his nose was long and thin, like that on a Roman statue. He might have been 45 or 50 years old in the picture, but his face had a distinct youthfulness to it.

Below the photo were the words, "Bailey Paul Crawford, 'Coach', August 3, 1945-August 13, 2008."

The organist released her hands from the keys, and perfectly timed, dropped them to her lap. The silence betrayed sniffles and sobs. I glanced across the sanctuary, and saw gray haired men in dark suits, and dozens of families with teenagers, toddlers or babies. I did a quick scan behind me—as I always did in these situations—and noticed only a few other non-white faces.

Not that I was surprised: Claymont Falls was a working class town, as much a reflection of Kentucky as it was a suburb of Cincinnati. But it was also my grandmother's town, the one where both my mother and I had grown up, where they taught me to navigate my way as a black girl through little leagues, sports camps, and town parades. It was familiar territory.

I flipped the page of the program. A short obituary about "Coach" was printed opposite the schedule of the service but I didn't have time to read it before the tall man rose from the first pew and walked to the pulpit. He pulled a small piece of paper from his tweed jacket, unfolded it and held it gently in his hand. He adjusted his glasses with his fingers and looked from the paper to the people in front of him.

"My father would be really happy to see you all here," he began, his voice a deep but soft pitch that neared the edge of emotion. "In fact, I can't remember a time when he wasn't happy; even these past few months when he struggled the most he ever had in his life, he would laugh. Tell us jokes we'd heard a million times. Remind us how great every single day was just because we were together, and how much the little things mattered more than anything big. My father was, as most of you here know, a man of principle and great enthusiasm. Whether teaching social studies at the high school, coaching us in the game he loved most in the world, or bringing our mother and my sister and me here most Sunday mornings, Dad always said we only needed three things in this life: character, enthusiasm, and of course, family. If we had those, we'd never need anything else."

The man cleared his throat and looked back at the paper. He smiled for a second, and continued, his face serious: "I'm proud to be named after him. Yes, now you all know that my real name is Bailey Paul Crawford Junior, not B.J., as most of you call me." He laughed and the relief prompted a few chuckles across the sanctuary.

"I'm also proud that because of my dad's almost obsessive love for the world's most famous game, my mother became the first official 'soccer mom' in the history of our country, long before the phrase was cool." At this the sanctuary burst with laughter. That got my attention, and I noticed the small woman sitting in the front pew wave her hand before returning it around the shoulder of the woman sitting beside her, whom I guessed was B.J.'s sister.

"Yes, I'm proud to be my father's son. To have watched him throughout his life stand up for what was right, for others who weren't as fortunate, no matter what it cost him. He knew how important it was to . . ." This time B.J.'s voice did crack and an awkward silence hushed across the pews as quickly as the laughter had come and gone. Someone coughed. Programs rustled. The fan hummed, though the air still felt warm and heavy.

B.J. took a full breath and as he did, his frame rose, filling out his jacket into a solid physique for a man who seemed to me to be around the same age as my athletic director, but with hair and muscular tone. He looked up again, swallowed and said, "On behalf of my family, thank you, each of you, for being here today, for supporting us in this time, and mostly, for loving my father almost as much as we did."

He folded his paper, returned it to his jacket and joined his mother and sister in the front pew. The minister rose to the pulpit and waved the congregation to its feet. The organ played the next song. Instead of opening the hymnal, though, I read the Coach's obituary:

Bailey Paul Crawford, or "Coach," is survived by his wife Cathy, his twins Mandy Renee and Bailey Paul Junior (B.J.), his daughter-in-law Ellen, three grandchildren, Bailey, Ryan and Rebecca, and hundreds of students and athletes who have grown to become his friends. He taught and coached at Claymont Falls High School for almost thirty years. A popular U.S. history teacher, he coached boys' soccer under the legendary CFHS coach Lars Lambert and, in 1983, Coach Crawford led Claymont Falls first girls soccer team to a state championship. They won county, district, regional, and the state titles, all first place achievements for the first team. He retired from the public school district in 1993.

What?!

I stood with the congregation and brought the program closer to my eyes, trying to make sense of the words: state championship in 1983. The year I was born. Though others were singing around me, I was re-reading the obituary, in case I had missed something.

How had this happened? I'd been an obsessive student of the sport I'd fallen in love with as a girl, the one that, with enough Wallace determination, helped me get the education my mother had hoped for her only child. And with the full scholarship to the best Division I school in the country, my grandmother's prayers had also been answered.

But I hadn't stopped there: I studied the world's game as diligently as I studied for my American literature and secondary education classes. Ask me anything about players like Pelé, Beckenbauer or Maradona, Mia Hamm, Julie Foudy or Michelle Akers, and I could give you stats and details for each. I even knew the names of the coaches from those first women's World Cup teams, their strategies and records, and, of course, everything there was to know about goalkeeper Briana Scurry, another inspiration for me.

"The first girls coach of my own high school? And a state champion? 1983?" I said out loud. The man next to me glanced up from his hymnal suspiciously.

I smiled toward him and, thankfully, the singing ended. I fell back into the pew, but felt like running straight out of the church and into Hanks's office to ask him why no one had bothered to tell me about this coach. And I might have, too, if the woman who'd earlier led the procession of other women to the second row wasn't now standing behind the pulpit.

The minister walked over to adjust the microphone for her. She looked to be about the same age as B.J., but about half his height, though wider in frame. She nodded her thanks, adjusted her bangs and began to speak. Unlike B.J., she used no notes.

"I'm Tricia Woodring Johnson and I can't think of any greater honor than talking with y'all about Coach." She shook her head and her hair bobbed. She pointed at the second row of women, the group just behind the Crawford family. They sat closely together, a few dabbing their eyes with tissues.

"Where in the world did the time go, ladies? Doesn't it seem like just last week we were flying high from that great first season with Coach? That was a sweet time, one we won't ever forget; we worked harder than we ever thought we could. Though I think some of us haven't exactly kept at it, if you know what I mean!" She widened her eyes, pinched a roll of flesh above her hip, and shrugged her shoulders before adding a "tsk, tsk" to stress her point. The women's faces lightened and Tricia laughed before continuing her speech.

"I'm not sure how I got to be the one up here today out of all these other great girls, except that everyone knows I'm good at talking. I've always been a talker, and every one of you knows—if you're honest—that I was a much better talker than I was an athlete, let alone a soccer player. But Coach, he seemed to think I could help you girls and add something you didn't have, and well, here I am." Her voice softened even with the microphone and I leaned forward to make sure I could hear.

"You know what? He was the first person who ever told me there was something I actually could do. Besides talking, that is. And that has made a difference for me the rest of my life. This man who smiled all the time, even if we were losing, who reminded us to have fun even when there wasn't much fun in working so hard, and who told us—like he told you, B.J.—that all we needed was a little enthusiasm to conquer anything that came our way. Coach always said enthusiasm was putting belief into action. And that has made the difference for us, hasn't it, ladies? It has kept us together all these years, still friends long after that final game—and that's one of the greatest gifts he gave us."

I was staring hard, back and forth, from this woman to her former teammates in the second pew, amazed by what I was hearing. Each woman nodded in response to Tricia's claim as if it was the truest thing they'd ever heard. Her eyes filled up but she caught herself, cleared her throat and turned her gaze away from the row of women toward the Crawford family in the front row.

"Coach Bailey Crawford was one of the best men this town has ever known. He made just about everyone who knew him want to be a better person and a better friend just because, well, that's who he was. Mandy, it's been an honor to be your best friend all these years and watch how much your daddy loved you, to see your family stick together in spite of . . . everything. Mrs. Crawford, you be sure to tell us whenever you need anything, okay? And B.J., well, for heaven's sake, don't be so much of a stranger! Bring those gorgeous kids of yours around here more often."

They laughed together again as Tricia just about leapt from the pulpit and into the arms of the woman next to Mrs. Crawford. Then she squeezed B.J., his wife, their children, and Mrs. Crawford, before bouncing to the row behind them to hug every woman she'd been talking to, all of whom had apparently once gathered around a high school sport and had remained friends since.

Not that anyone told me.

The minister stood and stepped toward the pulpit. But when he saw two other women from the second row hurry toward the microphone, he returned to his seat. One with sandy hair stood tall like she had royalty in her blood. She looked familiar to me, although I wasn't sure why. The other, with jet-black hair and a tiny, scrappy build, was her exact opposite. The shorter stepped forward and spoke clearly into the microphone:

"I'm Gina Martinelli, or Nelli with an 'i,' and #1 on our team." She smiled and looked at the other woman before addressing us again, as if they knew her more by her number than her name. "These days I run Martinelli Real Estate, but I wouldn't be doing anything good if it'd hadn't been for Coach and I just had to say so today. My first two years in high school I was having a little too much fun, if you know what I mean. I'd always been quick—especially quick to get in trouble—and lucky for me, Coach noticed me sitting in the principal's office one afternoon, waiting to pay for all that quickness. He made a deal with me that same day: if I agreed to try out on the team for a week, he'd help me get out of the tight spot I'd put myself in. It was the best thing he could have done." The tall woman beside her patted Nelli's shoulder as she paused. Then Nelli glanced at Tricia and the Crawford family before speaking directly to B.J.: "Your dad—and Coach Lars Lambert, remember?—they both helped me put my quickness to good use, and after that first week, then the second, I knew I was all in, adding my own brand of fire to the team while they, um, kept my fire in check off the field. It was a win-win for all of us." A few women chuckled from the pew but listened intently as their friend continued.

"I didn't know these girls before that season, but I think we all know that we became family after that, and I'd go to hell and back for any of them. Hell, I have gone there with some of you, and others, thank God, I even helped you find your dream houses. But you know why? Because Coach had the guts to tell me I could actually help people. I don't know how he did it, but . . . I'm sure glad he did."

She brushed her eyes and stepped back from the microphone so the woman standing beside her could speak. "I'm Annie Knudsen, #00 on the team, and now I run Knudsen's Bakery." Ah, the coffee and pecan rolls. That's where I knew her. "As many of you know, my mom was diagnosed with MS when I was in fourth grade so I had to grow up real fast to take care of her, babysit my little brother Wally, and help my dad with the bakery. But Coach saw potential in a shy, tall, gawky kid, and made a goalie out of me. Somehow, he convinced my dad to let me play and recruited Wally as our ball boy, so it'd be easier for us all."

She stopped, as if public speaking was not an easy task for her. She tapped on the pulpit, glanced at the carpet, and then looked up to find the right words: "To this day, I'm proud to have stood with each of you, where we learned first from Coach Lambert how to play in gym class, then on the field, mostly to fend for each other . . . like we still do. Even if the school or the town or no one else ever recognized us as champions, we knew who we were: winners. And better still: friends. We have Coach to thank for both."

Annie and Nelli, an odd contrast of toughness and grace, embraced and walked arm around the other toward the Crawfords. I watched another round of hugs between family and friends but quickly forgot who was who. Then a few more women rose to the microphone to offer their own words, each with a vastly different story but a message that was always the same: because of Coach, their lives together mattered.

If the reverend of First Baptist gave a spiritual message at that point in Bailey Crawford's funeral, I wouldn't have known. I sat staring, hearing his voice, but distracted by the Crawford family, the women behind them and the man whose photograph was on the front of the program. Each time I tried to listen, I'd look again at the family, the women, the photograph. I liked to think of myself as a quick study in most situations, but this coach, these women, this history, none of it made sense.

The organ snapped me back to the service, but I couldn't bother. I just listened, to the voices, the harmonies, the sounds of sobs and comfort. The feeling from the music captured me, as music always did, but the song brimmed with years and years of genuine love for a man whose life I had only learned about a few hours ago.

"The best this town had ever known," one woman had said of him.

When the singing ended, the minister reminded us that they'd be heading next to Claymont Grove Cemetery for the burial before returning to the Crawford home for an informal reception. All were invited.

I smiled at no one in particular and joined the line for the guest book in the church lobby. As I waited, I listened to portions of conversations about "Coach" before they were interrupted by emotions or hugs or other memories and stories. When it was finally my turn, I picked up the felt-tip pen and wrote: Coach Reynalda Wallace, Girls Soccer Coach, on behalf of Athletic Director Preston Hanks and the Claymont Falls High School Athletic Department. And as I finished, I watched families and children and older folks lingering in the lobby and sanctuary, talking with one another, shaking hands or embracing or just standing.

I glanced back toward the group of women, that first team of state champions, for Pete's sake, who were still standing together toward the front of the church. No one seemed ready to move on.

Suddenly, I felt myself wanting to go to the burial, but I also knew if I did, I wouldn't make it to practice on time. It was already 2:35 and though I felt pulled toward the crowd of families and friends, theirs was a grief that did not belong to me. Even if it felt strangely like it did. Or should.

So I dropped the program into my purse, smiled awkwardly again at no one and hurried to my car around the corner. The fresh air was a relief, a familiar comfort contrasting with the foreign experience I'd just had. But the walk in my new pumps pinched my toes and, although the sky was still perfectly blue, I was reminded of why I hadn't wanted to come here in the first place.

Now I could not stop thinking about all I'd just heard. I drove back across town, processing the words, the faces, the stories I'd just experienced. I flipped on the radio and turned onto Main Avenue. I turned up the volume, a trick I'd learned in preparing before key games when I was the starting goalkeeper. No team member had ever been able to get me pumped up to play the way songs could.

The station was stuck on the same Motown oldies I'd heard earlier, because "Nightshift" was playing—again. The words now felt like much more than merely an another old song: "Oh, I'll bet you're full of pride, Gonna be a long night, It's gonna be alright, on the nightshift . . . Oh, You found another home, I know you're not alone . . .."

Before I realized it, I had turned into the school parking lot, punched off the radio and, as if I had never wanted to know anything more than in that moment, I heard the sound of my own voice question out loud what Annie Knudsen had said in her speech: "Even if the school or the town or no one else ever recognized us as champions . . ."

I repeated it: "no one else ever recognized us as champions . . ." How was that possible? How could a championship team be so . . . invisible, as if they never existed at all?

chapter
3

1983

There weren't many quiet evenings in the Crawford household. At least none as quiet as that night.

Mandy was no longer on the phone with her friend Tricia or tapping the soccer ball back and forth against the stairs with her foot. B.J. was not playing his stereo. In fact, the last sound from his room had been the slam of his door after he'd pushed his chair away from the kitchen table. Away from the news his father had just delivered to their family. Away from the reality he'd have to live with his senior year of high school.

It was a double portion of bad news for him: B.J. would no longer be playing for the only coach he'd ever had but he'd also have to live with the humiliation that his dad was now coaching girls. Girls. The topic alone was sure to fuel a steady stream of mockery from his friends.

Bailey had tried to wait through two helpings of lasagna, and a second piece of bread, strategizing that maybe the news would be easier to swallow with a scoop of ice cream. Maybe a tub of Rocky Road, bowls and spoons full, would make the news less dramatic.

But he couldn't wait that long. He'd never been good at waiting. He swallowed the last of his beer, set down his napkin and described what had happened in Harry Hanks' office earlier that day.

His family's reactions were simultaneous:

"But who's going to coach us?" B.J.'s voice was the loudest, his eyes narrowing on his father.

"You mean I really get to play and you'll be my coach?" Mandy's eyes, full of energy and wonder, bounced from her father to her brother to her mother and back again.

"Well, it's about time," Cathy said firmly, pushing her fork back into the lasagna on her plate for another bite, as if the news flavored the taste.

Bailey didn't know which remark to answer first, in part because he still wasn't sure what he thought about his new coaching position himself. He studied his son, then his daughter before glancing toward his wife for help, but Cathy only shrugged and took another bite of her dinner.

The look on her face signaled that she knew what he was thinking: though their son and daughter were twins, they'd never been alike in anything but competition. As if he were born with a book in his hand, B.J. was as serious and deliberate as a philosopher or statesman. He needed time to study and adjust to every change or new challenge that came his way. His sister, however, had all but danced her way out of the womb as if she were Ginger Rogers, always hoping her brother would be her Fred Astaire. Yes, he was the older—by three minutes—but she, a perpetual spark of life and spontaneity making it difficult for her brother to keep up, was the one who set the pace in their day-to-day routines. Or tried to.

Even so, B.J. had been the child who was given the opportunities, Bailey suddenly realized as he sat in the tension that hung over the dinner table. From Little League baseball and soccer to Boy Scouts and paper routes, B.J. had taken advantage of every extra-curricular activity their community afforded them.

When Mandy, on the other hand, wasn't with her friends at the mall, she was on the sidelines cheering for her brother at Saturday games or practicing with him during the week. She'd never pestered her dad or mom about playing youth soccer because there was no league for girls. Sure, she played Little Tykes up until fourth grade when the competition ended for girls and most went on to cheerleading camps or Girl Scouts. But Mandy hadn't been much interested in those other activities, only in whatever her brother was doing. Her face now was filled with all the affirmations she'd hoped to hear but never had as a child in perpetual motion.

Bailey turned to his son. "You're on the best team the school's ever produced, B.J., so any coach you get will already be at an advantage," he said, forcing a smile as he picked up his fork and set it on his plate. The clink against the ceramic startled him. But so did his son's response.

"No way. You're the only one who can get us to state, Dad," B.J. retorted. "You've got to go back to Mr. Hanks and tell him that . . . "

"I signed a contract, Son," Bailey said solemnly.

"You what?"

"Well, why shouldn't we get Dad to coach us?" Mandy interrupted. Her brother rolled his eyes.

"Because you're girls, and girls can't play soccer," B.J. said.

"We can try."

"No way."

"We can too. You should know."

"What's that supposed to mean?"

"It means you'd never be as good as you are if I didn't help you in the backyard all the . . ."

"You're crazy!"

"I am not. It's true. You'd never have scored at all last year if I . . ."

"That's enough, you two," Cathy intervened as her children's voices rose and their dinner went untouched. "Your dad's worked hard. He deserves to get a chance like this."

With that, all three Crawfords stared at the woman who'd just cooked their dinner. A chance like this? No one moved. B.J. and Mandy actually looked alike for the first time that night, frozen in their stare, their heads tilted just so at their mother, and their father's resemblance not far off. Cathy, however, swallowed her last bit of supper, licked her lips and tossed her fork on her plate triumphantly.

"We'll figure it out," she said, smiling.

Her son's face thawed and turned back to his father. "Dad, you've got to go see Mr. Hanks and get him to . . . "

"I said, that's enough," his mother responded. "Now go wash the dishes, your sister will dry tonight and then I expect you both to finish your homework. Got it?"

"But . . ."

"Right now there are more important things in the Crawford household than soccer seasons," she commanded, "like chores."

B.J. rose slowly from his chair as if a great burden weighed heavy on his back, groaning for dramatic effect. He stacked the plates and headed to the kitchen sink. As he began to fill it with soap and water, his sister bounced behind him with silverware and glasses. Cathy wrapped the left over lasagna and salad, humming as she did. And Bailey simply made a cup of coffee.

He'd known breaking the news to his family would be the toughest part.

No one said much to each other the rest of the night. Cathy retreated to the garage to finish painting the antique chairs she'd found at a garage sale last week. Mandy had managed to get her mom to agree to a phone call, which she made immediately after she dried the dishes. Her friend Tricia would never forgive her if she found out from someone else at school tomorrow that there would now be a girls soccer team at Claymont Falls High, its first ever. And B.J. stomped to the couch, picked up his book, and stomped toward his room, making sure everyone heard the door slam behind him.

Bailey read the Claymont Falls Daily Register. Or tried to. This was not how he'd imagined the evening would go; then again, he'd known when he left school that tonight would not be easy. He folded the Register, reached for the phone and dialed the one person who would know what to say about this.

A voice still rich with a German accent answered.

"Hi, Lars, this is Bailey. Got a second?"

If there was anything Lars Lambert always had, it was time. He was a man who stopped whatever he was doing whenever someone walked into his office or the gym, which was his classroom. To him people mattered more than tasks and schedules, even more than games.

"Of course."

Bailey scratched the back of his head as he spoke.

"Maybe you've heard the news already from Hanks?"

"Which?"

So Hanks hadn't bothered to talk to Coach Lambert. Bailey sighed.

"I didn't get the job as head boys' coach."

Bailey pushed the phone closer to his ear, hoping to hear more than Lars breathing. The silence between them felt long. Granted, these two men weren't much for social conversation; because they had worked together for years, they communicated in ways that often made words unnecessary. A look, a gesture, a shrug, each had a meaning the other understood. But those were hidden over the phone, and so Bailey tried to wait.

He glanced down at his newspaper, but just as quickly looked at the chairs in the living room and prodded.

"Lars, I said I didn't get the job. I won't be head coach."

"Yes, you will. You'll be a fine head coach," Lars said softly.

"Maybe I'm not being clear here. Hanks has given the position to someone else and . . ."

"But he gave you the girls," he said.

Bailey's head shot back. So Hanks had talked with him about the change of positions. How long had he known?

"And Bailey, I am glad. You will treat those young women as they should be treated. With respect. Dignity. As you do all your young people."

Lars's voice was so soft Bailey wondered if he was hearing correctly. He sat forward on the chair, considered his coffee but decided against it. This was also not what he had expected to hear from the man who had taught him all he knew about the game; this was turning into a very confusing day.

"I know already about this because I recommended you to Harry," Lars said.
"What?"

"I did. Those boys will be fine because of what we have already built. But why not give the girls a chance, too, with the best?"

"You mean you were . . . "

"I mean when I told Harry I was done coaching and he said they had to fill a new team with a coach, I said they should put you there," Lars said, his voice clearer now in Bailey's ear. Bailey shifted uneasily in his chair as the elder coach continued. "Many years now I tell him we need girls to play the game too. It's the law. Now finally they can."

"Are you serious?" Bailey answered, blinking from the reality of what he'd just heard.

"I am serious. Why can't they play, huh? Other schools in other states, even colleges, give girls a chance to play now. The Title IX law passed 13 years ago so they could," he said. "I bothered Harry so much that now they can. And you're ready."

"You . . . you're behind this? But you never once said a word about this to me, Lars."

"I never knew if Hanks would actually go through with it, so I thought, why get your hopes up?"

My hopes up?! If Bailey hadn't been so stunned by what he was hearing, he might have recognized the soft little chuckle on the other end.

"Besides, your girl, your Mandy, she's a player. I see it in her eyes. All these years we coached together, I've seen her eyes. And I think, why doesn't she get to play too? So I pushed the principal and athletic director to do right. Each year, each season, each meeting I had with them, I say, these girls should get to play. Why not? I push and push, and finally, the state tells them they have to make a team or they don't get their other funding. See, I know this, Bailey, and I told them you'd be the best coach for them. You're ready, yes?"

"No! I mean, I don't know the first thing about coaching girls, Lars. How could I be ready?"

Bailey had never in a million years imagined something like a girls soccer team coming to his district, let alone coaching it. Now he was shaking his head, completely unsure of what to make of this news, more dumbfounded than he had been earlier that day in Hanks' office.

"We'll talk more tomorrow, my friend," Lars said. "I must go now. You are ready. Guten Tag."

Though Lars had hung up, Bailey sat holding the receiver, staring at it as if he really had not heard right, as if he'd missed some spectacular secret. He wondered how, after all this time working with Lars, he had not once anticipated something like this.

He slouched lower in the chair and stretched out his feet in front of him. Maybe he'd get another beer. Or maybe he'd just sit and think. He recalled the few conversations he had had with Lars about taking over the boys' team, and suddenly saw the elder's face in his mind. Each time Bailey had brought up the idea, Lars would smile, shrug, and simply say, "We'll see. We'll see." Bailey had taken it as a challenge to maintain his work ethic, and figured that Lars expected all along that he'd be his replacement when he retired. Now nothing was clear, and Bailey suddenly wasn't sure whether to feel betrayed or honored.

He hung up the phone and went to the garage. Cathy had to hear this. But the lights were off and the back door locked so he hurried toward the bedroom. She was slipping on her nightgown when he walked in.

"You won't believe this," he said.

Cathy crawled into bed, and turned on the lamp as she picked up her novel from the nightstand.

"Believe what?"

"Lars has been behind this whole thing, this girls team, this coaching position, this . . . whatever the hell this is! He's been the one to push Hanks. Can you believe that?" Bailey was pacing now, back and forth between the closet and the bathroom. Cathy set the book on her lap and grinned.

"I've always liked that man."

Bailey snapped. "That's not funny."

"It wasn't meant to be," his wife said. "Why wouldn't he support something so important? What's wrong with that?"

Bailey stopped his pacing. "What's wrong? For one, I'll be the laughingstock of the department, maybe the entire school if this thing . . . "

"That's never stopped you before, Hon. I mean, think of all the crazy ideas you've had for teaching history. What's the difference?"

"The difference is I'll have to start over completely, and to be honest, I don't know if they can even do this."

He started pacing again, as if the movement would inspire some new argument and resolve that would fix this problem. "Besides, it's unprecedented here. How in the world can we build a new team when these girls have barely even run around the track? Soccer isn't like going to the mall, you know; it's tough. It can be a really physical game, brutal even. They might get hurt. Who knows how much they'd be able to handle."

Cathy folded her arms across her chest and tilted her head forward, her jaw grinding. "That's the best you can do? That these girls might not be tough enough?"

Bailey now turned at the closet and headed back toward the dresser. He glanced at his face in the mirror and turned around again. "You've watched B.J.'s games, Cath. You know how rough it can get."

"And?"

"And I just don't know if they can handle it."

"But that's the point, isn't it? To give them a chance," his wife's voice was soft but firm. "I wish I'd had the chance. Now your daughter does, and I think you and I both know she'll be able to hold her own."

She looked down at her book, opened it, and then closed it and returned it to her nightstand before staring directly at her husband, a look that both drew him close and challenged him further. He'd seen this look many times before over 18 years of marriage, and if he was honest with himself, it was the primary reason he'd married her in the first place. They'd been young, but those bright, penetrating brown eyes, the curved shape of her nose, the way her lips curled slightly to the same side her head tilted, each conveyed a trust, respect and intimacy that at once softened him every time he saw it.

This woman knew him, understood him, sometimes better than he knew himself.

Her voice now was almost a whisper: "Maybe, Bailey Crawford, maybe the girls aren't the ones who can't handle it. Maybe you're wondering if you can."

He sat down on the edge of the bed, his back to his wife, and put his hand through his hair, stopping every now and then to massage his scalp. Bailey let her words sink in.

"But guess what? I know you can," she continued, her hand finding its way up his back. She leaned forward into her husband's neck, her lips moist against his skin. Her arm rested on his shoulder as they sat close, listening to each other's breathing. He took her hand and then felt her mouth next to his ear: "I think they got the best there is."

Bailey turned to his wife and brushed a strand of hair away from her face before leaning in to kiss her. She reached toward the lamp, turned it off, and fell back onto her pillow, her husband following her invitation, the tenderness of unity a gift neither took for granted.

Eventually, they fell into a sound, peaceful sleep, her head nestled against his heart, his hands shielding her back. A steady song of cicadas beneath their window merged quietly with their breaths.

At breakfast the next morning, Cathy smiled gently toward her husband as he came into the kitchen. She handed him a cup of coffee and nodded to a bowl of oatmeal on the table. Two other bowls sat untouched across from

Bailey, the chairs empty. Cathy turned to the refrigerator, pulled out a loaf of bread and slices of turkey and began to make sandwiches. Bailey picked up his spoon, admiring his wife's ability to maintain routine regardless of the events of their lives. She was a steady calm for him no matter what new challenges blew through their home. A fortifying armor whenever he entered a battlefield. And today he was about to.

"Morning, everybody!" Mandy announced as she appeared in the kitchen. She wore a denim skirt just above her knees and a green floral blouse with matching earrings that dangled beside her cheeks. In one constant motion, she tapped her father on the back, hugged her mother from the side before dropping into her chair and instantly popping back out again. A blaze of excitement, she skipped around the table to give her father a hug before whirling back into her chair and grabbing her spoon.

"I mean, good morning, Coach!" she blurted out across to Bailey, unable even to say the word without an expansive grin across her face. Her eyes sparkled at her father, showing the same expressive light her mother had had when he first noticed her. But now their daughter, with her soft brown hair curled just so around her face, suddenly seemed much older to him.

Even though she was finishing her junior year of high school, Bailey still thought of her as the little girl riding her pink Stingray bicycle in the driveway. Until now. Suddenly, he saw a young woman sitting across the table from him, gulping her orange juice with the same enthusiasm as she had approached everything throughout her life. And as she dabbed her mouth with a napkin, he saw a maturity he hadn't before noticed. Or perhaps hadn't wanted to. As much as he was usually able to share in his daughter's exuberance, whatever the occasion, the term "Coach" coming from her this morning was an unfamiliar mix of sweet and bitter for Bailey.

Mandy inhaled her breakfast, bounded from the table and set her bowl into the sink. "Gotta go. Trisha's picking me up for school," she said, grabbing a brown paper bag from her mother and clicking on her shoes. "Don't worry, Dad. We'll start recruiting today. Trisha's got a plan. It's going to be great. See you later!"

And before either parent had time to respond, she was out the door at the same time they heard Trisha's car, her horn and muffler announcing her arrival. Cathy smiled, shook her head and returned to the lunches. Bailey pushed a glob of oatmeal around in the bowl with his spoon, then stopped and pushed again. He wasn't much interested in breakfast. His coffee was as much as he could handle.

He did manage to look up from his bowl, though, as B.J. wandered into the kitchen wearing a blue hooded sweatshirt and jeans. His baseball cap tipped back on his head, like he wasn't exactly ready for a game or much of anything for that matter. He collapsed into his chair, hoisted up his spoon as if it weighed a hundred pounds and poked around his oats like he was looking for something. He sighed and reached for the brown sugar and milk. Except for the clink of their spoons, father and son sat silently over breakfast, neither looking up or acknowledging the other or eating much of anything. The kitchen clock ticked loudly.

"Really, you two. You'd think you were going to a funeral," Cathy said, interrupting the gloom as she leaned against the counter. "Maybe we should just cancel . . . everything." Neither Bailey nor his son smiled at the joke, or moved at all. Cathy took a big breath and rolled her eyes. "I know, I know. Life's not fair. Well, now you know what it feels like."

That got B.J.'s attention. "Mom, this was supposed to be the year we went to state, the year the college scouts would come to our games, the year . . ." his face was getting blotchy. "The year Dad was supposed to coach us. Now we'll probably barely make it to playoffs and I'll have to live with the embarrassment that my own father is coaching girls because he didn't fight to keep his team."

"That's enough, young man," Bailey said. He'd tried to infuse some authority into his own voice but he knew it hadn't worked. He wasn't convinced himself about what he'd been asked to do, and he certainly wasn't sure how he'd work this out. Lesson plans and lectures on history, he could breeze through. Coaching strategies and drills for boys' soccer, he'd come to see as second nature. But girls? Maybe his son was right—he should have fought for his team.

"One of those girls happens to be your sister, Bailey Junior," Cathy was standing over both of them now, like a referee at a game about to throw a yellow card. "And your daughter, Bailey Senior. So how about if you both try to think of her for once? I have to go to work. Don't forget your lunches."

She grabbed her purse and car keys, leaned in to give both husband and son perfunctory kisses on their cheeks and walked out. They watched her leave, sitting paralyzed in their chairs when she closed the door. Neither ate. Or moved. They just stared at the door. The silence loomed. Bailey picked up his coffee cup and set it down again. B.J. drank his juice.

"Look, son, I'm disappointed too. More than you know but—"

"Then go see Mr. Hanks, Dad. You have to."

"I'll talk with him. I promise. But a contract is a contract. And unless something else happens, well, your mother might be right. We might have to accept this . . . for Mandy's sake," he finished his coffee. Finally.

"No way. It's ridiculous, you know that," B.J. said, his emotion leveling. He stood from the table and retrieved his lunch. "She can't play."

They had twenty minutes to get to school so Bailey decided not to push it any further this morning. Besides, he wasn't altogether sure B.J. was wrong about whether girls—other than Mandy—could even kick a soccer ball, let alone form a team. Mandy was one thing; Lars had noticed that in her, even if her own father had never thought twice about her skills. But other girls? He had his doubts.

The car was hot and the ride quiet. Once in the high school parking lot, B.J. emerged from the passenger seat, flung his backpack over his shoulder and quickly greeted his friends who'd pulled up in an old Mustang a few spaces away. Bailey had never quite gotten used to having his own children attend the school where he'd worked these past several years. Sure, he was glad to see them more, to keep an eye on them as they navigated the uncertainties of teenage life. Even so, it was unsettling every time he watched them wander off with kids he had had in class or had heard his colleagues talk about in the teacher's lounge.

"It's called growing up, Hon," Cathy would say, trying to soften the blow of reality's sharp edge. And he'd nod obligingly, willing to concede—again—that his wife was right, even if he wasn't entirely ready for their only two children to become adults.

He watched B.J. disappear into the crowd of students before adjusting his tie and locking his car. He moved slowly toward the school office to collect whatever memos or notices were in his teacher's box. At 7:55, he had five minutes to drop into the cafeteria for an extra cup of coffee before heading to Room 211 for his first period American History class.

But as Bailey turned the corner of the hall, he interrupted a lively discussion between an assistant football coach and two basketball coaches. His presence stopped their conversation. Students stared as they strolled toward class.

One of the basketball coaches tossed out the challenge: "Say it ain't so, Crawford." The coach was new this year, more height than common sense, Bailey had thought. A nice enough guy though, for the life of him, Bailey had never been able to remember his first name.

"Say what?"

"You're not really going to coach girls, are you?" the coach asked. Students stopped. A teacher glared.

"Who told you that?" Bailey asked, adjusting his tie again for something to do.

"Who didn't? Seems like just about everybody knows."

"That'll be a good source of entertainment in the fall," the bulky coach said, laughing as he dug his hands into his pockets. "Not much else to do, except of course watch football, and that can get so dull when we win all the time." He winked at the others.

"I don't know why they didn't just drop soccer altogether, like it's even a sport," Coach Tall said. "But now girls too? That's one helluva a good joke!" The men erupted into laughter, slapping one another on the backs and mimicking an attempt at a pirouette.

Bailey took in a deep breath, watching the mockery of these men, tilting his head like it was a joke he'd heard before but had never quite thought it was funny. His shoulders tightened.

The humor stopped instantly, though, and Bailey's face turned grim when he looked across the hall and saw a group of girls standing there, listening to the coaches.

Mandy was in the center of them, and Bailey had never seen his daughter look as pale as she did at that moment. Their eyes met.

"How you gonna do it, Crawford?" one of the coaches teased. "I mean, better get some easy drills so they don't hurt themselves. Wouldn't want to see them break a nail . . . or two!"

"Or mess up their hair! Oh, this is gonna be a good one!"

"How in the world . . .?" One of them couldn't finish his sentence, the idea too hilarious. And the other coaches, even some older boys walking by now, snickered as well, provoking each other with gestures and jabs and ridicule.

But the sound of them and the sight of Mandy and her friends still standing there, listening to this, moved Bailey deep inside, as if something that had been cold and dormant in his blood was beginning to thaw and grow as it did. His heart pounded. His pulse quickened. He swallowed, dropped his hands at his side, and took a step forward, straight into muscle and height and arrogance.

"I'm going to coach those . . . girls . . . the same way I'd coach any player—to be the best they can be. You got a problem with that?"

The coaches' laughter faded quickly into a few snorts and grunts. One shrugged his shoulders. "I think you're the one with the problem, Crawford. Good luck."

The bell rang but the first lesson of the day had already begun.

chapter
4

2008

I slipped off my dress, hung it on the back of my office door, hopped into my sweats and cleats, and bolted through the locker room. I hated being late almost as much as I hated losing.

Granted, attending the funeral of a coach I'd never before heard of was at least a respectable reason for arriving six minutes after my team's practice began. Never mind that going to the funeral at all had felt like an unexpected shot on goal, a quick strike out of nowhere from a boss with an ego as big as the district stadium. I knew as well as anyone that I'd been on the end line that morning when Hanks hurled his decree my way.

But a goalkeeper's survival is her lightning reactions, and Hanks could kick a hundred tasks my way that he claimed were "for the good of the department." I could handle it. I'd trained for moments like that, to be ready to set the record straight for any player or coach who dared to challenge my ability.

"That child's born ready," my grandmother used to say to anyone sitting beside her and loud enough for me to hear as I ran onto the field during little league games.

What I hadn't expected was to be blindsided by a history lesson that betrayed every hard-won experience I'd had as a player and now a coach at the same school I'd attended, where Baily Crawford had also worked. Whoever was responsible for sending a championship team into virtual obscurity was either a serious egomaniac or just plain mean. It stung.

After all, wasn't the story at today's funeral the stuff of legacies? Of school lore passed on to the next class, and the next, building institutional pride as well as magical identities that made every kid in the state want to play there?

I should have known. I'd spent three years on the same field, one of the few honored female athletes in the school's hall of fame, so someone could have told me about Coach Bailey Crawford and his state championship team of girl soccer players. If I'd heard of him before he was being eulogized and buried, it might have made a difference.

But I hadn't. Instead, I'd simply had two small black women hollering for me from every sideline, which mattered of course. The idea, though, of an entire cohort of champions cheering me from history's games, inspiring me and empowering me each time I walked onto the field, well, that was what pushed good players into great ones.

Now, I couldn't help wondering how a winning first season went missing from the pages of a school known more for losing records than victories of any kind. I mean, if it had been my team who claimed the top honor for the entire state, I would have insisted on plastering every player's name across the billboards around the stadium, maybe even the town. Or at the very least, I would have demanded a banner outside of the gym reminding all who entered they were in the presence of champions.

Everyone would know who the winners were. That's the way I was raised.

But I hadn't had time to ask anyone at the funeral what had happened or how this man was laid to rest without proper recognition for his championship—at least that I'd heard of. And signing the guest book in the foyer on "behalf of the entire Claymont Falls High coaching staff" suddenly felt as if I'd joined some town conspiracy, helping the bad guys hide some big secret.

I was now late to practice as well, defying my personal coaching mandate that punctuality was the beginning of success. It was the first of many in a series of obstacles for a team to overcome. If I didn't model it to my athletes, then I could hardly expect any improvement from last year's dismal record. Little things mattered in building winning attitudes.

The team was warming up in the center circle of the field by the time I sprinted toward them at 3:10. The afternoon, thank goodness, had maintained its autumn brilliance and the sky's blue was the perfect complement to the rich green of the freshly-cut grass.

My two seniors—Kate Podurski and Maggie Lee—were leading the players through stretching exercises. Kate shouted a greeting toward me that I couldn't quite make out; her thick legs twisted in a figure eight as she bent over, her head turned upside down and sideways, her arms dangling toward her cleats. I waved anyway.

Though she wasn't a natural athlete, Kate was one of those players who knew how to work. It might have been because she was also one of the few students at the school who was bussed in from the rural area near the Kentucky state line, a farm girl who was not intimidated by sweat or dirt or discipline. She would have been my first choice for the captain slot even if we'd had dozens of seniors. Even so, I decided to make the only other senior, Maggie, co-captain.

There was strength in numbers.

Kate's freckly skin and perpetual brown braid down her back ensured her low wrung on the ladder of popularity, but she had heart. Some of her friends had played basketball or volleyball so at least knew how to practice. But a few too many girls seemed to think joining soccer was like going to the mall or the movies; it was another way they could be together with their friends. And from the way some of them practiced, it was about as strenuous as shopping.

That was the first of many challenges I knew I was inheriting when I took the job. I didn't expect to be fielding a team of natural athletes, let alone intense competitors—or anything that remotely resembled descendants of a state championship program. But I did expect that they'd try hard for the standards I'd set.

So I didn't mind that girls like Kate kicked a soccer ball like she might a cow paddy; she was at least agile and I knew from day one that her enthusiasm alone might inspire a team lacking skill, pride and players.

That was okay—if I believed they could improve and grow, I figured they would too. Eventually.

The other interviews I'd had for coaching and teaching jobs after graduating never made me regret my decision. There'd been something about coming home, about being near Mom and MaeMa that I couldn't argue with. They'd kept me up to date on my alma mater (and how mediocre the team had been) since I left. They said I'd be a good fit for those girls, that it'd be a good match. Plus, it was no secret they had ulterior motives.

So I'd said yes to that first district interview, then to Preston Hanks, heir to the infamous Coach Harry Hanks of football fame. And Preston went from being Mr. Hanks—the athletic director who'd once called me the school's "best girl athlete"—to being my boss.

I knew it wouldn't be easy building a winning program in a district better known for football than for anything else. But that was exactly the challenge I wanted.

"Okay, hustle in," I said when I reached the center of the field, shifting gears in my head. Kate and Maggie hustled, a few others followed their lead and ran, while the others simply skipped.

"Sorry I'm a little late—Mr. Hanks asked me to go to a memorial service."

The girls looked confused and I answered their silent question: "A former coach from our school passed away. A girls soccer coach, in fact."

As if the thought of coaching soccer could kill someone, two sophomores took a step back. One squinted at me. Another let out a hiccup.

"He was the school's first girls soccer coach about twenty four, twenty five years or so ago, which was before my time, if you can believe it," I said. No one laughed. "Anyway."

We paused for an unofficial moment of silence. I re-tied my cleat. Kate did the same.

When I stood back up, I noticed a few girls watching the football players. I rallied. "Let's talk about what's next," I said, clapping my hands and outlining a quick preview of practice—the drills we'd do and the reasons behind them—before sending them off for four laps around the field, pushing into motion silver soccer balls just inches from their toes as they ran.

It was a routine we established a few weeks ago as our season began. Everything they did at practice, even laps, had to include a soccer ball. The ball was their "new best friend," I'd said, explaining how much they needed to get used to its feel. Eye-foot coordination wasn't easy for most of them, some playing the game for the first time, so constant contact would be crucial. Familiarity would gradually build confidence.

I ran parallel to them as they circled the field, some girls moving quicker than others, a few wobbling around the sidelines as they chased after their balls. I considered whether to cut practice short. Any other day, not even the best excuses—two inches of snow, cramps from "that time of the month," heartbreaks over boyfriends— nothing was reason enough to keep me from using the full two hours allotted by the district. Every time we stepped on our field, I figured we had an opportunity to make some progress. And I scheduled practices the way I planned my classes: expecting as much from my players or students as I myself gave.

Today, though, no matter what drills we did, my mind raced back to Coach Bailey Crawford and the women at that funeral. How had he managed to build the school's first team? What miraculous strategies did he use to motivate his players to take on powerhouses—like County Day Academy—and win?

I wished I knew, especially as I watched my own players stumble back toward the center of the field, where we moved on to sprints and passing games and shots on goal. I only had one season under my belt with these players, and I was determined to build on it, to shake things up in the Claymont Falls High athletic department.

Besides, I had turned 25 in January, and given my experience with the game at high school to Division I college ball, I expected respect.

"Coach Rey," Kate interrupted my thoughts. "Coach, you want us to do 2v2s?"

I glanced at my watch, exactly one hour and 35 minutes after we'd begun today's practice, and made a decision.

"No, Kate. Everyone, come back in." The team gathered in a circle.

"It's time to think about what we'd achieved so far." The girls stared at me. Kate scratched her braid.

"I mean, most of you have worked pretty hard this week, and good practices win games," I said. Maggie guzzled her water bottle. "Our first game against Lake Ridge is in two weeks. We have lots to prepare for mentally and I don't want you to burn out even before the season starts. See you tomorrow at 3 o'clock sharp."

Kate nodded emphatically and began collecting balls and drill cones. A few teammates helped her while others gathered their bags and walked to the locker room, chattering and laughing as if the movie was about to begin.

When Kate and I locked up the equipment, I jogged back into the school. The clack of my cleats on the tile floor echoed throughout the halls. Most teachers were gone for the day and only a few custodians were mopping or painting in preparation for the first day of classes next week. It smelled like a combination of ammonia and turpentine.

I clipped past the school entrance, directly under the photos of athletes that greeted students and visitors near the wide front doors. I tried not to look but never could restrain myself: there I was—that is, the seventeen year old version of me—hanging in the direct line of vision from the doors, an embarrassing photo taken toward the end of my senior year that had been hanging there ever since. Beside a dozen or so other students who'd set some sort of school record in the past twenty years, mine was the only brown face on the wall and one of only a few female faces. The gallery was a glossy school history meant to inspire all who entered the building. The Hall of Inspiration, the principal called it.

I rolled my eyes every time I passed that picture; my hair was frizzy and my right collar poked up just so above my shoulder while the other hung flat. I shook my head as I passed, still disturbed by how ridiculous I looked. I knew I was supposed to count it an honor that I'd been photographed at all. Only two other athletes—both white boys—had earned first team, all district awards in three sports as well as academic honors the year I graduated, 2002. And their pictures hung beside mine, lining the wall with those of other athletes, from team shots to individual sport stand outs, dating back fifteen or so years.

But that picture of me? Pathetic.

"Who cares?" my mother said, repeatedly, beaming over that photograph every time she saw it, as if her daughter's face had been carved on Mt. Rushmore. She wouldn't have cared if my head had been bald or if there'd been tiny strands of spinach in my teeth; that photo represented the year I became more than just "the black girl" in town. That was the year her daughter had lived up to her own mother's dream, becoming only the second Wallace to earn school honors and the first to earn a scholarship for college.

"Your grandmother was beside herself when they hung that photo," she'd say, a look in her eyes clouded by both regret and pleasure. She had never gone to college, though my grandmother—who had been the first Wallace to attend— had always hoped she would. Instead, Mom met my dad and never quite got around to studying . . . or to the altar. She'd been at the elementary school ever since—first as a cook, and now as the assistant cafeteria manager. But she never hesitated to tell everyone she knew how I'd lived up to the family name, how impressed the North Carolina coach had been with her Reynalda, how proud MaeMa Wallace was, and would be still.

I sprinted past the teacher's lounge and the counseling center, and was about to turn the corner for the library, when it suddenly hit me. Team photos! I spun around and ran at full speed back toward the Hall of Inspiration. My eyes jumped from picture to picture on the first wall, then to another, and finally to the hall where the "oldest" team photos hung. There was the 1986 county champion football team, the district baseball team champs the next year, and a few other lone runners and wrestlers up until 1995. This was the "oldest" section of Claymont Falls High athletic history, but every photo I saw—every single one—was of white boys with adolescent faces, stubby mustaches, and weird haircuts. Not a single girl—much less a team of girls—anywhere.

I looked again, just to be sure, grunted and turned toward the library. Positioned in the middle section of the campus, near the biology labs and the computer science center, the library always seemed the last place in the school to get upgrades. I swung open the door and headed toward the reference section, my cleats quiet atop the same old carpet that was there when I was a student.

With the image of Coach Bailey Crawford and his now-grown team in my head, I scoured the shelves from top to bottom and then the next. There, beside dozens of old Britannica's on the second-to-top shelf were several copies of the Panthera—the aptly named yearbook with the school's blue and green colors decorating the spines. A tiny face of a lion was printed above the numbers as I read them left to right: Panthera 1976. Panthera 1978. Panthera 1971. Panthera 1982. Panthera 1962.

Were the librarians so busy they could not keep yearbooks in their proper order? How hard could it be? My finger collected a chunk of dust as I scrolled through the numbers, passing Panthera 1981, which was next to Panthera 1970 and Panthera 1987. I did the same on the next shelf, sighing and cursing under my breath until finally I spotted it.

The Panthera 1984 was tucked several inches back from the edge, angling beside Panthera 1995 and Panthera 1990 in the corner. I grabbed it, flipped the pages and landed on the senior class photos, slightly embarrassed by the hairstyles and outfits of twenty-five years ago. Underneath each student's picture were words to songs or poems, clubs and activities the students had been a part of, which boys were the most likely to play in the National Football League, which girls would become Miss America. I noticed only a few Asian faces, one Indian-looking kid, and a solitary African-American girl named Phoenicia Jones. Her bio read: "Motown Queen, Jazz Band, Theater, Will One Day Win an Oscar."

I studied the picture and wondered if Phoenicia's family had also come to Claymont Falls around the mid-1960s when my grandmother had. MaeMa had been told the schools here were better than in Cincinnati and figured she had nothing to lose. With a newly-earned degree from Oberlin College, a husband in Vietnam, and two young children in tow, she officially "integrated" Claymont Falls school district as the first black woman to teach in the elementary grades. Which, of course, meant her own children—and their children—would also stand as official symbols of the Civil Rights struggle that moved the nation in community after community—even in Ohio.

I flipped from Phoenicia's page to the Ks and spotted a younger version of Annie Knudsen, one of the women who spoke at the funeral, whose father owned the bakery. She looked serious and rushed, as if sitting for the picture had been an inconvenience she didn't have time for. Underneath her name read, "Home Economics, Honors Society, Girls Soccer State Championship Team. Quote for life: 'You don't have to be the best to do your best.' Thanks, Coach!"

A few pages later I landed on a very young-looking Gina Martinelli staring with sass and mischief straight at the camera. She wore one of those shoulder-less halter dresses, her dark brown hair piled high on her head. "Nelli: Most Fashionable. Homecoming Queen Runner-Up. Italian Club. Girls Soccer State Championship Team. Quote for life: 'You don't have to be the best to do your best.' Thanks, Coach!"

A few pages later, I stopped on the Ws and spotted Patricia Ann Woodring's photo captioned: "Tricia: Gossip Girl Extraordinaire, Choir, Music Ensemble, Girls Soccer Championship Team Co-Captain, and Editor, The Lion's Mane Student Newspaper. Quote for life: 'You don't have to be the best to do your best.' Thanks, Coach!" Her face was thinner, her hair brushed into curls that framed her face, but there was no mistaking her. This was the same person who first greeted the mourners at the funeral earlier that day, the same woman who talked directly to the Crawford family themselves before her former teammates made their way to the microphone.

"Find what you were looking for?"

I about jumped onto the shelves. A lean man with square glasses and straight brown hair that hung just above his shoulders suddenly stood a few feet from me. He wore pressed black jeans and a paisley print shirt that he left un-tucked. I'd seen him before at faculty meetings but hadn't had a reason to interact with him, until now.

"You know, you could let people know when you're about to . . . you could ask people if they want help," I suggested before continuing, "and yes, thanks, I'm fine." I looked back at Tricia's photo.

"Good. Because we're closing," he said. He stood about an inch shorter than I was, though I took him to be a few years older, perhaps pushing 30. He peered over my shoulder at the open yearbook, nodded and then glanced at his watch: "Hmm. The old days, eh? Sorry, but it is 5:13 p.m., you know. I should have left at five and if you need something else . . . well, we're open tomorrow." He held out his hands to his sides, like it was a common occurrence in his day to remind athletic coaches about library hours, long after everyone else had gone home for the day.

I shut the yearbook. "Mind if I take this with me?"

"Nope." "Great, thanks, I'll—"

"Nope, you can't, I mean. It's a reference book," he said, tilting his head. "Can't check those out, you know. Crazy rule, but that's how we keep things around here for students."

"I'm not a student. So how about teachers?"

"Same applies to teachers, I'm afraid."

I resisted a quick roll of the eyes but asked: "Do you really think someone's going to want to check out a yearbook that's 25 years old?"

The guy didn't blink. "You did."

I took a deep breath, didn't feel like arguing and pushed the yearbook back on the shelf, near as close as I could to where it belonged. I pointed.

"Those are all out of order, you know," I said, turning toward the door.

"Tell me about it," the librarian answered, suddenly walking beside me like an escort. "So are the old movies, the school newspapers, the art catalogues. But at least the fiction is right. Alphabetical by author. Hemingway is next to Hughes and Hurston, just as they should be." His voice was smooth but cheerful as he continued.

"Welcome to my world. We've been trying to digitize most of our archival resources so some things have sort of taken a back seat. Or in this case, a high shelf." He smiled, pleased at his own joke, and bumped my elbow as we turned down another aisle of books before nearing the magnetic bar of the library's entrance.

"I'm Will McCabe, by the way, assistant librarian and head technology geek for all things audio and visual," he said in front of the magazines. I nodded but didn't respond. What did that photo caption say again?

"Nice to meet you too, Rey Wallace," he said. "I'm a huge soccer fan. Caught most of last year's games. How's it look for this year?

"What?"

"The season? Your team? You know, girls soccer? Don't you have your first game in a few weeks?"

I snapped to. "Oh, yeah. Lake Ridge. Won't be easy."

"They never are," the librarian said while fishing his keys from his pocket, ready to lock up. He swooped down toward the desk to pick up a laptop computer and canvas bag. "What were you doing were the yearbooks anyway, if you don't mind my asking?"

I glanced back toward the section, my curiosity taking over my senses, and rattled off what my day had been like, the funeral I'd attended as a representative of the athletic department, the coach I learned about for the first time in my life—thank you very much—and the championship team I'd never heard of.

"I even cut practice short to come and see what else I could find out," I said, processing the whole thing out loud.

That was all that the librarian needed. He dropped his bag, pulled me back into the library, and stomped back to the yearbooks, pulling 1984 off the shelf again. He tossed open the book and went with expert speed to the back pages where the athletic team photos would be displayed. Football, wrestling, basketball and baseball, all had two, three and four page spreads which included team photos, records, individual shots of coaches, captains and Most Valuable Players in action.

Then he plopped his index finger on a single page that represented the entire girls athletic program: a tiny picture of the volleyball team on the top, the track team in the middle, and the soccer team on the bottom.

"There," he pointed, his fingers tapping the small print beneath the team photo of the girls soccer team. They wore what looked like boys' uniforms, and a dark-haired man stood in the back row on the end. The first row was comprised of only seven girls, including Tricia and Nelli, along with a small boy kneeling, each holding a soccer ball; the back row included seven girls with Annie in the center, and the coach on the right side. Some things hadn't changed much—the soccer program still wasn't very big. My own team had 16 players, if they stayed healthy, inspired and kept up their grades.

"Hey, look at this: 'District—first place. Regional—first place. Ohio State Champions. Coach Bailey Crawford, 14-0.'"

The librarian read the words with increasing emotion, then interrupted himself and looked straight at me: "14-0? Who does that?!"

As if on impulse, we both turned the page to see if there was anything else or any additional information. But the next page of the yearbook was the first in a section of school clubs, which began with a large photo of the all-boys debate club. We turned back to girls sports, and stared at the team photo.

I read the caption again, out loud, as if he'd not gotten it quite right: "District—first place. Regional—first place. Ohio State Champions. Coach Bailey Crawford, 14-0." It still didn't make sense. I poked my nose in close to the photo and studied the picture. The coach looked like the photo on the program at today's memorial, and the girls actually did resemble some of the women who sat together in the church.

"Someone should have told me," I whispered. "I should have known, I mean, wouldn't you want to know if you were a part of a program that had once boasted state champions? And in their very first year?"

"Heck, yeah," he said. "That's amazing. 14-0!"

"It's not right."

"I had no idea, and I do sort of pride myself on Lions history," the librarian said, shaking his head so that his hair bounced on his collar. He snapped the yearbook shut at the same time he seemed to have an idea: "Hey, wouldn't they be in the Hall?"

"What did you say your name was?"

He stayed the course. "Will McCabe. And I'll bet they're in the Hall."

"Right. Will. No, I looked already. Nothing."

"Are you sure?" He crammed the book back up on the shelf and hurried out the door anyway.

Within minutes, I was standing next to Will the assistant librarian in the Hall of Inspiration, which by now smelled more heavily of ammonia. Will searched the photos on each wall, mumbling about the "absurdity of football" as he did, before pointing to a few tennis players, baseball and basketball teams, and even an ice hockey team from three years ago when the new sport was announced. He came to the individual players and looked at the boys who'd set school records in track or baseball or football. Then he came to the few girls photos and without saying a word he glanced from my ridiculous photo back to me.

"I told you their picture wasn't here."

He nodded and pointed. "How about the trophy cases? Did you look there?"

There had to be a trophy since Bailey's team had won the state championship. Why hadn't I thought of that?

Will smiled and bounced toward the glass-enclosed case below the photographs, a long, wide wooden frame with windows protecting the prizes inside. His eyes roamed across the golden miniature footballs, bronzed baseball players, you name it, and dozens of small banners and pennants that hung behind them or lay beneath them, each sport organized by the season. There were newspaper clippings carefully placed in frames set beside trophies for fall sports, basketball nets that dangled off of a few large gold-framed bowls for winter, even baseball gloves, tennis rackets and ribbons pinned to the corners of the prizes for spring.

It seemed the boys at this school had won something in just about every athletic event possible, but no matter how much we looked, Will and I could not find anything for the fall of 1983, not a girls soccer championship mention anywhere, or anything else for the class of 1984. Or for many other girls sports accomplishments during the 1980s for that matter.

"It's as if they don't exist," Will said quietly, his face pressed against the glass, his eyes still searching for any clue that would confirm what he now knew to be fact. "That is not right."

As soon as he said it, some switch inside me flipped on. This was not right. This first girls soccer state championship team did exist, with a stunning 14-0 record in the fall of 1983, and a state title to match. Yet, there was not a ribbon or trophy or mention anywhere to vouch for it. Something had to change.

chapter
5

1983

Bailey Crawford sat at his desk, pulled the turkey sandwich his wife had made from his brown paper bag and unwrapped it. It was only 11:40 a.m. and he wasn't really hungry, but his spring class schedule meant he either ate during the first lunch hour or not at all. With two advanced placement courses, a remedial social studies class, and sophomore world history, Bailey's classes demanded his energy from 12:05 until 3:30, more than his two morning sessions of junior level U.S. Democracy.

Today, though, he opted to avoid the teacher's lounge and ate in his classroom. He just didn't feel like getting more jabs and jokes from other coaches and teachers about a girls soccer team.

Word spread quickly around the halls as it often did in a school this small. During the faculty divisional meeting an hour ago, even some of the female teachers questioned what a man could possibly know about coaching girls, and they didn't mind saying so. Only Delores Winston, the other physical education teacher who'd been at Claymont Falls High longer, it seemed, than the town had existed, even longer than Lars, stopped by to congratulate him on his "success."

Bailey ate half of his sandwich, looking out at the 30 empty desks that lined his classroom. He tried to ignore the teachers' comments, knowing they too often grew into school gossip that never did much good. He was more concerned about what his family said, and so far it was only 2-1 in favor of his new appointment. He preferred anonymity.

Bailey ate while he graded quizzes on the three branches of government. These were the kids who really needed his help, the remedial students who couldn't quite keep up in the regular classes. Sure, he'd heard his share of stories from other teachers about these "delinquents," but Bailey Crawford rarely seemed to have a problem with them. Maybe it was because he was the same age as their fathers, or maybe it was because he was also a coach and knew how to motivate even the biggest troublemaker, but in 16 years of teaching he couldn't remember more than a handful of discipline problems.

He reached into the brown paper bag for one of Cathy's brownies and had just taken a bite when the door to his classroom flew open. Mandy, Tricia and about seven other girls, most of whom he'd had in one class or another, marched in, their hair bouncing back and forth, their collective enthusiasm suddenly ricocheting off the walls and bringing the classroom to life.

"Dad, we have to talk with you," said Mandy, pulling up a chair beside him. No one could miss the family resemblance: her deep-set eyes and rounded cheeks were feminine versions of her father's.

"Yeah, Mr. C, it's really important, you know," Tricia said, following her friend's lead as she pulled over another chair. Within seconds, all the girls had formed a circle around him, watching him as he finished his brownie, wiped his mouth and sipped his coffee. Their faces were serious, their postures eager. Mandy scooted in closer to her friends.

"Let me guess: you want to memorize the Declaration of Independence, right? Or maybe the Gettysburg Address, which is a little shorter, you know." Bailey smiled as he finished his lunch. "Well, you've come to the right place."

Tricia was quick to meet Bailey's attempt at lightening the mood; the other girls nodding their support. "Yes, exactly, Mr. C," Tricia responded, her eyes bright. "We are declaring our own independence and we want to thank you for helping us address the first girls soccer team Claymont Falls High has ever had. You won't regret it. Now, we were thinking, Coach—can I call you Coach?—that we have here almost enough players for the team but it's only June, and by the time the season starts next fall, we—"

"We would have at least enough to be ready for our first game, because we'll spend the summer working really hard—" Mandy continued her friend's sentence before Tricia picked it up again, the other girls nodded at each point.

"Since we'll be training in the summer and doing whatever you tell us to do. See, we've all agreed to do whatever we need to, even though we've never exactly played before, except in P.E. with Mrs. Winston and Mr. Lambert. But, then again, there's Mandy, who's played with B.J. so much that she could probably make the boys' team, if you ask me! But, anyway, we won't let you down because—"

"Hang on, Tricia!" Bailey said. Tricia sat up straight, her curls bobbing above her shoulders. She nodded her obedience and folded her hands together on her lap.

"Listen, this all just happened, girls," Bailey said, "so there's a lot still to work out with Mr. Hanks and Coach Lambert."

Bailey swept the brownie crumbs across the table with his hand and into a small metal trashcan, which he then pushed back underneath the desk in one swoop. "I mean, this is a very new development," he mumbled, "and we haven't really thought about how we're going to make it work. I mean, I'm just not sure yet how, uh, or what a girls team can do."

His daughter's friends shifted in their chairs and Bailey tried to imagine them on a soccer field, running sprints or using their feet to pass the ball. Mandy was one thing, but he'd watched some of these other girls attempt softball on field day, or play in a powder puff football "game" for homecoming. Those events were more entertainment than serious athletics. Besides, he'd still not gotten used to the idea that he would be coaching a team of players other than his own son and his friends. He straightened the pile of quizzes he'd been grading.

The girls said nothing. Tricia, for once, was silent. They simply sat staring, his doubt of "what a girls team can do" reverberating into the question mark that had hung over their heads their entire lives. They'd been taught since they were born that they were mere observers of life, bystanders in just about everything, second class citizens because of their gender. They'd never imagined anything different.

Until now.

Bailey caught them staring at him, wide-eyed and hungry at the very idea of possibility. He read their expressions, and as he did, he realized he'd seen this look before: on the faces of his remedial students or his second string soccer players, the agony that they'd been told for so long what they could not do much or how they would probably never accomplish what other students would. Eventually, their hardened faces softened a little each day under his encouragement. Each day they began achieving one thing more than they—or anyone else—ever thought they could.

Now, these girls sitting around him, including his own daughter, expressed the same pained determination that came with one simple word: opportunity.

Tricia broke the silence. "See, Coach, we think this is just the beginning. Annie's cousin," she pointed to a girl with brown streaks in her hair, "her cousin has been playing already in a Cincinnati league for two years. And some of our other friends know of a few other schools that started teams last year. So why shouldn't Claymont Falls High have one?"

"And why shouldn't we be the first to play on it?" Annie said quietly, as if it was the bravest thing she'd ever said. The other girls stared at her, surprised at her question, but empowered by it as well. Then one by one, they took turns affirming it themselves, until the question built to a crescendo and a proclamation bordering on a rally cry:

"Yeah, why shouldn't we?"

"Why not us?"

"Who else could?"

"Most of us have been friends since kindergarten, so we could do it!"

"We all went to YMCA camps together—"

"And played powder puff—"

"And have the same classes—"

"So we could do it . . . together!"

"Yeah!"

"Yeah! We could!"

The noon bell rang, interrupting their spontaneous pep rally and causing them to jump from their seats, though Bailey wondered if it was the bell ringing that moved them or their team spirit. Nonetheless, he had honors students coming in a few minutes for class, including Tricia and two other girls already in the room. The rest of the girls needed to get to their own classes or to the cafeteria for lunch. So Bailey rose from his desk and approached the chalkboard. He picked up a thin piece of white chalk and wrote in the upper right hand corner: "Girls Soccer 1st Team Meeting: Friday, June 14, 3:30 p.m., Mr. Crawford's room."

He turned toward them. "Let's talk then, okay? I'll find out more from Mr. Hanks and we'll see what we, well, let's just see what we can do." The girls cheered and hugged each other, shouting in unison, "Thanks, Coach!" as most jetted out the door, talking and laughing while the honors students entered.

Bailey blinked at what he'd just witnessed, but just as quickly turned his attention toward Roosevelt's New Deal and spent the next several hours in the past, not the future. Apart from a few male students snickering about the announcement on the board, reminding him of his new fate, Bailey managed to focus on social studies. He'd learned a long time ago that if he didn't concentrate on his immediate challenge, that is, teaching and motivating juniors and seniors, he'd get sucked into the emotion of the next game or the challenges of the next practice.

Coaching could be a world unto its own, cut off from all other parts of life, and if Lars hadn't taught him how to keep it in perspective, he'd imagined himself swept away by the game itself, consumed by the sport. He loved soccer, but by this stage in his life, he knew it had its place.

He had to admit, though, the spirit of those girls at lunch distracted him.

As his final class ended, Bailey left his classroom and walked with the students down the hall toward the athletic department. Lockers were slamming, friends were gathering, and notes were being passed. Janitors were pushing mops in buckets down the hall, and teachers were talking outside classrooms. Bailey nodded at a few and looked toward the windows. Outside, spring was descending into summer, and students and parents were crowding onto the steps and parking lots of the school, symbolizing both the end of the day and the anticipation of a break. The close of the academic year always evoked an energetic buzz on campus rarely seen in winter or fall.

Harry Hanks was not in his office; in fact, no one occupied the athletic department desks, not even the secretary or assistant coaches. Bailey wondered if he'd forgotten about a coaching meeting, but when he saw it wasn't yet 4 p.m., he realized most had other duties around the school, monitoring the halls or greeting buses or diverting fights. Spring athletic seasons had ended a few weeks ago, so the staff was called on as reinforcements to handle the end of the year chaos. With only three days left in the spring semester, extra bodies in and outside the halls meant increased control.

Bailey was considering his options when a firm hand slapped his back.

"Ah, Crawford, the man of the hour." Freddie Smith was the assistant athletic director, head baseball coach and assistant wrestling coach. A former shortstop in the minors, Smith's once lanky build had grown flabby through the years; the busyness of organizing teams left him little time for anything else, like exercise, and middle age had caught him around the waist. He always looked as if he'd forgotten to shave and had long ago lost his comb, but he was never far from a good laugh or a cheer of encouragement. Bailey saw in Freddie a good coach, one who cared about kids but would never be the type who'd run the athletic department. Freddie didn't seem to mind either.

"Hey Fred," Bailey said, watching Smith toss two baseball bats against the wall before picking up a clipboard on the edge of the secretary's desk.

"My tools for maintaining order in the halls," he grinned, pointing toward the bats. "You might want to borrow one to knock a few heads together around here. Sheesh, you'd think folks never saw a girl working out or kicking butt. Well, you know what I say to that? Good for you, Crawford. Someone needed to step up and give these kids a chance."

Bailey leaned against the wall and let the words sink in. "It wasn't exactly my idea."

"So what? You got the job, didn't you?" Smith finished jotting something on the clipboard and glanced up at Bailey. Smith smiled. "Listen, don't let Hanks or the other idiots get to you. Before you know it, everyone will think it's all normal anyway."

"Normal?"

He shrugged. "Why not? I mean, it is 1983, for God's sake. Didn't the libbers do anything right? It's about time, if you ask me." Freddie punched Bailey's arm for good measure and turned toward his office. "If anybody can do it, Crawford, it's you."

"What does that mean?"

Smith spun around, belly jiggling. "It means Lambert and I convinced the old guy you were the right man for the job. Knock 'em dead." He waddled toward his desk and sank into his work amidst the clutter of newspapers, baseball gloves, and bags of Oreos.

"I'll take that as a vote of confidence," Bailey hollered. Smith waved, laughed and shoved a cookie into his mouth. The sight of such playful but certain support boosted Bailey in a way he hadn't expected. And though he wasn't quite sure what to make of it, he felt for the second time that day something undefined stirring within him.

So much so that by the time he found Hanks at the football field talking with a few maintenance men and pointing at worn out patches in the grass, he was energized. Hanks saw it too as Bailey stomped toward him.

"Harry, got a minute?" Bailey asked, catching his breath and looking from the field to the athletic director to the crew and back to Hanks. Hanks didn't answer. The other men shifted awkwardly and stepped toward a bald section of the field.

"Okay, about the girls team . . ." Bailey started.

"Too late, Crawford. You signed the contract. You can't back out now," Hanks said, his voice laced with irritation.

Bailey took a step back. "That's not why I'm here."

Hanks tilted his head. "Uh huh. I'm kind of busy. I'm sure it can wait."

"I'm sure it can, but I'd rather get a few things cleared up."

Hanks turned over his wrist to look at his watch. "Like . . . ?"

"Like practice times, jerseys, equipment, that kind of thing. If we're going to do this, I'd like to do it right."

"So would I, Crawford," he said. "But let's talk about it in my office. Check with Ellie to set up an appointment next week, after school's out."

"We really need to talk before then, if we could."

"Why?"

"So I can let the girls know what to expect."

He grinned. "Oh, sure. Good idea. Check with Ellie to see when I have an open meeting." Hanks walked to the center of the field like he owned it, the crew following him as servants would their king. Bailey jogged back to the athletic department office, the hot, muggy air against his face producing beads of sweat across his neck and forehead by the time he arrived inside. This time, he found the secretary in the office, along with a handful of other coaches and teachers, who stopped talking when Bailey walked in. Freddie was still stuck behind his desk, though the Oreo bag was now in the trash.

"How can I help you, Coach?" Ellie said. She was clacking away on a typewriter, glasses on the tip of her nose and her short hair clipped around her ears.

"Need to set up a time with Harry," Bailey said, dabbing the sweat off his forehead and nodding toward the others, who shrugged and resumed their conversation.

Ellie grabbed a thick appointment book and opened it.

"Hmm. This week's all filled up. How about next week?"

"No times at all this week?

She looked at Bailey as if his hearing was bad. Then she sighed. He leaned forward and steadied his hands on the edge of the desk.

"I know you're probably ready to head home, Ellie. I am too. But I need to meet with Harry this week. Please."

She pushed the glasses back up her nose and scoured the book. "Well, if you don't mind 7:15 Friday morning, he's usually here then. Otherwise, it's next week."

"I'll take it."

"Okay then, Coach," Ella said, scribbling his name on Friday's page and turning back to the typewriter.

Bailey thanked her, collected a few homework assignments and books from his classroom and drove home. He wondered how the conversation over dinner would go tonight. He found the house unusually quiet when he arrived. B.J. was working an extra shift tonight at the pizza shop—probably to avoid his old man, Bailey thought—and Mandy was at Tricia's, working on homework and planning, she'd told her mom, how to recruit players for the team. Cathy greeted Bailey with leftover lasagna, a salad and a kiss.

They talked little of the day or the new coaching position, though Bailey did recount to Cathy the lunchtime enthusiasm of Mandy, Tricia and their friends in his classroom. He told her how he was impressed by their eagerness and surprised at their excitement. He recalled each girl in the room, their names and year in school, what each said during their conversation, and even their movement out of the door as the bell rang. Cathy smiled as she cleared the dishes. Then she started to laugh.

"What?" Bailey asked.

His wife turned around from the sink. "Ha! Don't you see?"

"See what?"

"You're talking like you do before each season, sizing up your players, getting a read on what they need and what they can offer the team," she said. "Bailey Crawford, like it or not, you are the new head coach of the first ever girls soccer team at Claymont Falls High!"

The words stung—but only for a second as they settled over Bailey with a warmth that signaled to him this was the right thing to do. It was the next step, a decision no longer in question. And he began to laugh, too, the kind of laugh that rose from his gut all the other times in his life when he'd let go of a tension or an insecurity and took on a challenge knowing it would lead to something better. He had no idea what this "something" was, but that was part of the adventure, the joy, the reason for laughter.

The next few days were so busy, Bailey felt like he was barely bumping into his family as each came and went. Between end-of-semester school projects, papers and quizzes to grade, errands and pizza jobs, their conflicting schedules were the typical of the demands on family time as the school year closed. In the middle of it all, Bailey compiled a list of questions for his Friday morning meeting with the athletic director.

He arrived at school by 7 a.m., armed with a few apple fritters and donuts from Knudsen's he'd picked up on the way. He figured they might help the conversation. But when Bailey walked into the athletic department's office, the lights were still off. He switched them on and found a chair while he finished his coffee. And he waited.

When Harry Hanks blazed in at 7:20, coffee cup in hand, he looked confused to see Bailey sitting there when no one else was in yet. He said nothing as he unlocked his office door and tossed his briefcase on the desk.

"Brought you some of Knudsen's best," Bailey said as he stood in the doorway.

"Already had breakfast," Hanks said, taking off his jacket and plopping into the leather chair behind the desk separating the two men. "Sorry, Crawford, but I've got a meeting in a few minutes."

"Yeah, it's with me," Bailey said taking the seat across from the desk. "I scheduled it with Ellie after I saw you."

Hanks pulled his calendar from his briefcase and thumbed through it. "Nope, nothing in here about a meeting with you."

"Hmm. That's strange," Bailey said. The pause hung palpably in the air. Bailey shifted in his chair. Hanks glanced at the clock.

"Well, since you're here, I've got about 10 minutes." He leaned back in his chair and adjusted his cuffs.

Bailey called up the list he'd made in his head. "Let's talk about the practical issues first: jerseys, equipment, practice schedules, you know, that sort of thing."

Again, Hanks looked confused. Bailey reminded him. "For the girls soccer team?"

"But it doesn't start until the fall, Crawford. Don't you think it can wait?" Hanks gulped the rest of his coffee and decided to dip into the bag from Knudsen's after all. "Surely, we can get to this in July or August, can't we?"

"No, Harry. I'm meeting with the girls today after school and want to report to them on what they can expect."

He picked up a fritter and licked his fingers. "Okay." Hanks smacked his lips and explained to Bailey that there was nothing to worry about. It'd all work out.

"I'm sure it will," Bailey pressed on. "But they deserve to know a few things before they go away for the summer, like when—"

"Hell, Crawford, it's not like the summer is going to make any difference for these girls. What's the rush?"

"As I was saying, they deserve to know a few things like when and where they'll be practicing, equipment, jerseys, etc."

Hanks sighed. "Okay, then, let's make a decision right now. Since the boys' soccer team uses the football practice field after we have it, hmm, well, I guess they could have it after them."

"When it's dark?"

"Good point. Hmm. Oh well." He picked up a pencil and a yellow pad of paper. Bailey didn't respond. "Wait, maybe they could have it at 6 a.m.—nope, that's the marching band. Helluva way to wake up the neighborhood. So maybe you can find someplace else around town."

He looked up from his desk and went on: "They can have the old junior varsity jerseys but you'll have to work it out with the new boys' coach what equipment you'll share since our budget has long been spent. I'm not sure what the Booster Parents are going to contribute this year yet. Anyway, I'm sure there are a couple of old balls floating around somewhere. You don't need much more than that, right?"

Bailey couldn't help himself. "And who is the boys' coach?"

"Don't know yet. Still figuring that out."

"How about a trainer? And where are the girls supposed to change?"

"What's wrong with the bathroom or the girls P.E. locker room? I'm sure Delores won't mind. And there must be a spare first-aid kit around here somewhere. If you find one, it's yours. But like I said, our budget is gone so we can only afford trainers for football," Hanks said. "What else, Crawford?"

Bailey knew that he was being pushed out of the office as Hanks stood up from his desk, but he didn't budge. "What about our schedule? How many games can we expect? And I'm assuming you'll be arranging the buses and referees and concessions?"

Now his boss was growing impatient. "Not sure which part of 'no budget' you didn't understand but we cannot afford buses or referees. Any extra funds we get come from the concession stand, which is open at football games in the fall, when there's a crowd and we might actually make some money. We'll work on getting some volunteer parents or someone to referee—unless the district supplies one, which they probably will since they're mandating this damn thing in the first place. We're required to have 10 games for the season. But . . ."

Hanks cleared his throat, still standing and expecting his coach to do the same. Bailey finally obliged, now squaring his shoulders opposite his athletic director. "But those 10 games don't include district playoffs for the state tournament."

Bailey blinked. He hadn't thought that far ahead. "A state tournament?"

Hanks shook his head. "Insane, isn't it? The thought of giving girls a state tournament! But that's part of the law."

Ellie knocked on Hanks door. "Your 7:30 appointment is here."

Hanks looked at Bailey. "We're done here, right?"

"Sure. Thanks." He turned toward the door and saw Freddie Smith smiling as he walked into Hanks' office. The two exchanged greetings and the door shut behind Bailey, his mind racing at what that conversation might be about, how his day would unfold and what he would tell his daughter and her friends at their first meeting afterschool. Maybe they would forget about it entirely and just start their weekends early.

They did not. Bailey looked up when Mandy, Tricia, Annie and a handful of other girls marched into his room, occupied the desks nearest the chalkboard and looked as serious as if they were expecting to take an exam. No one said anything. They simply waited for him to give them the first talk they'd ever had from a coach.

Bailey leaned against the desk and rested his hands in his pockets. He smiled and looked each girl in the eyes just as he would with his boys' teams at the start of a new season.

"Enthusiasm is belief put into action," he began. "Let me say it again, girls, enthusiasm is belief put into action. And do you know what happens when you do that?"

No one answered.

"You win games." It was the line he'd always used with his players at the start of a season and at the beginning of each match. He was not about to change now. They sat up like arrows. "No matter how the odds are stacked against you, no matter how good the other team's record is, or what others might say about you, if you hang onto that enthusiasm, that belief, you walk away a winner. Period."

The words might as well have been music played by a world-class orchestra because Bailey instantly saw something he had never seen with his other teams: change. It was as if the rhythm of his sentences swept up the girls and carried them to that magical place that songs can take you, that world of inspiration where anything is possible. Confidence suddenly danced in their eyes. And the more he spoke, the more they listened like there was nothing else happening in the world, like no other voice mattered as much the voice of this man standing in front of them. Their faces believed.

"It's not going to be easy, you know," Bailey sang. "Challenges never are. In fact, I think this may probably be the hardest thing you've done yet in your lives. But together we'll do more than we ever could alone, and together we'll achieve more than we—or anyone else, including me, for that matter—thought possible." Their shoulders straightened. No one looked away. "This is an amazing opportunity. Do you know that?"

"Yes!" Their voice was one loud firm chorus. Bailey smiled again. And he forced himself to keep smiling, especially because he knew what he needed to do next: confront the reality of what they were getting into. He relayed to them his morning meeting with the athletic director, hoping they wouldn't quit before they'd begun.

"We won't have much. Limited equipment, old jerseys, and we'll even have to practice before school starts, as in 6 a.m., perhaps off campus somewhere." He waited, expecting complaints, anger, or both.

But no one said a thing. They just sat in his classroom as if this was the best news they'd heard all year.

Bailey looked across their faces, expecting someone to move or challenge or leave. No one did. So he handed out to them a summer schedule of exercises they could do on their own as well as a list of times they'd meet for summer practices at the local park.

"We'll need to recruit a few more players by the fall. Think we can do that?"

"Sure, Coach," Tricia said. "How many do we need to play?"

Bailey swallowed. "Eleven players at game time on the field." She did a quick count in the room.

"We've got 11!" Tricia exclaimed, as if she'd just earned an A+ on her final test.

The smile stayed on Bailey's face. "Yes, Tricia, but we play for 40 minutes non-stop each half on a big field so we'll need some good substitutes. And we have a schedule of at least 10 games, plus playoffs."

The girls gasped.

"So we'll need to be in really good shape," Mandy announced, thereby declaring herself a leader helping her new teammates refocus. The girls nodded.

Bailey discussed the process and the importance of discipline, explaining a few exercises and strategies. He asked if anyone had questions. But just as he did, the door opened.

Coach Lars Lambert walked in. He carried a huge bulging bag over his shoulder and wearing a Claymont Falls High soccer T-shirt and matching blue shorts.

"I heard you might need an assistant coach?"

The girls let loose a unified scream that forced the retiring coach to drop the bag and plug his ears. A few hugged him before he herded them back to their seats.

"Lars?" Bailey said.

"I found a few old balls in the back of the shed and wanted to make sure you got them before anyone else did." He opened the bag and handed the girls their own soccer ball.

"You're going to have to share. But you can take them home with you today. Get the feel of the ball with your feet, in your yard, on the sidewalk, when you get together or walk home. Kick it anywhere but in the living room. We don't want to make mothers mad, right, Coach?" He winked at Bailey.

"Right!"

The girls received the soccer balls like they were trophies and carefully placed them at their feet. "One more thing. You girls listen to Coach Crawford, yes?"

"Yes!" They exclaimed.

"Maybe I can join you for summer soccer?"

"Yes!" The echo ran across the room and sang again of possibility. As the girls rose to leave, Mandy stood beside Tricia and Annie, and then looked at Lars.

"But I thought you were retiring, Coach?"

Lars smiled. "Almost. Since your dad helped me for so many years, I wanted to see if I could give something back, if it's okay with you, Bailey?"

Bailey's smile broadened. "Of course, Lars. I'll take all the help I can get. But I thought—"

Lars interrupted. "Everyone deserves a chance to play the greatest game in the world."

And this time he did not hold his ears when the girls cheered and screamed and all but skipped from the room, leaving an empty bag at his feet, and a grateful but dismayed Bailey Crawford watching his new team begin their season.

chapter
6
2008

The light on the glass case scattered shadows across the shelves. The way it jumped and hid, for some reason, sent the image to my mind of the glass display cases in the Claymont Falls Public Library. The first time my grandmother took me there, I was six years old, maybe seven, and reading was an altogether new adventure for me. It was as much of a thrill to follow words through a story as it was for me to ride my bicycle—without training wheels—through the neighborhood, though MaeMa and I both knew I spent more time pushing my feet against the pedals than I did my eyes across a page.

That's probably why she squeezed my hand as we climbed the steps to the second floor, stopped in front of a wall filled with photographs of old white men and town leaders, and looked at the typewriters and rare manuscripts on display in the gleaming glass cases. We stared for a while before sitting down at a table where MaeMa pulled a long, thick book from a nearby shelf. Magically, the faces and words of pioneers journeying across prairies, of abolitionists speaking in town halls, of black children walking into schools, all these came to life before me, my grandmother's finger pointing to each, her voice whispering their stories and grounding me in the tender truth every child needs to know: I belonged. To the stories, families, and ancestors who made this place ours.

"Their struggle then made our day today possible," she liked to say, her eyes smiling at the very idea.

The memory of sitting beside her flooded over my being while I stood staring at nothing in particular in the Hall of Inspiration. Over and over, she had read to me tales that shaped my imagination until they became my stories, my adventures. She'd pointed out yellowed photos and weathered speeches, artifacts of a history that meant little girls like me mattered. The trail they forged was a trail for me, MaeMa said, one that meant I could walk and run anywhere I wanted and, eventually, forge not only my own way, but one for others as well.

I breathed in deep. I suppose the sweet sting of that memory had surfaced this moment because, no matter how I looked, or longed to hear their voices, I could find no details that linked the past struggle of Bailey Crawford's team to today's high school. Nowhere was there so much as a whisper of the legend of a man I'd uncovered at his funeral that morning. No medal or plaque, no prize or banner. Not even a framed award hanging on the wall. Nothing but a tiny photo in a dusty yearbook captioned "1983 Ohio State Champions."

Now I felt not only bewildered, but offended. I'd been slighted by a collective oversight that relegated all sports—except football—to second-class status, one that denied the power of the past to affect the present.

So I kept looking, scouring the display cases, in case I'd missed it, or perhaps some shinier award was blocking it.

"How could a team that won every game they played be so . . . invisible?" I sighed. "So forgotten?"

"Girls." Will startled me again. I'd been so absorbed in my thoughts that I'd forgotten he was there hunting the trophy cases with me. He stepped away from the glass, shook his head, and then quickened his stride back toward the library. The hall was empty. I skipped after him.

"Wait." I marched, past shiny lockers and push buckets. "What do you mean?"

Will's pace was more intense now, his hair bouncing lightly off his neck with each step. He tucked a few strands behind his ears and adjusted his glasses. "Just what I said: Girls. That's the reason we can't find any trace of the team. Small potatoes compared to the beefy jocks of this place."

I struggled now to keep up with the librarian. I stared at the saggy seat of his pressed pants where his slight buns hardly moved with each step. His shoulders, however, swung slightly back and forth, propelling him forward. For someone who spent his days with books and technology equipment, he had a tennis player's frame: sexy, smooth, lean.

I dismissed the thought with a grin and returned to his comment. Following him through the library's entrance, I shouted to his back: "Just because they're girls doesn't mean—" Will stopped instantly, then spun around. "Are you kidding? This place is all football all the time. It has been ever since the infamous Harry Hanks was the A.D. And trust me, it will be long after, at least as long as his son's in charge. Please tell me you noticed!"

"Well, I—"

"Girls sports matter to Preston and the rest of your department about as much as what happens in the library. And you have noticed all the renovations in here lately, right?" He waved his hand toward the shelves and walls.

I glanced at the tables and magazine rack, the decades-worn carpet, the dated computers and dust-covered catalogues. He had a point. The library was old and tired—most of it remained exactly as it had when I was a student here six years ago. I nodded. Will took off his glasses, breathed on them and wiped them on his shirt before pushing them back on his nose, as if the mere act helped him regain his composure.

"I hate seeing things this way and will use any means necessary to challenge the establishment." He stopped himself. "Okay, that might be a little dramatic," he said scratching his chin. "But you should be crazy, insanely furious over how your team gets zero attention. I guess it's just par for the course considering how a championship team was treated—or rather not treated."

"I am ticked. I mean, no one—not Preston or my own coach or anyone else for that matter—ever told me a single thing about a state title," I said. "Don't you think that would have made a difference for me as a player? And now as a coach?"

Will took a step back. "Seriously?"

"Seriously. Winning records inspire more winning records, you know."

Will pressed his lips together tightly, and his jaw began to gnaw back and forth. Then, in an instantly quiet but firm voice, he said, "In case you hadn't noticed, there weren't any girls sports in that trophy case, let alone the team that most deserved it, the championship team you said you were investigating." He turned toward the office, his voice building to a challenge: "News flash, Rey Wallace: not everyone gets to do what you did."

I'd grown familiar with the range of insults I'd received over my 25 years—as an African-American, as the "smart" kid, as a female, as an athlete—so much so that they no longer bothered me much. But this comment caught me off guard. I stepped sideways then gathered back my hair and reconfigured it, considering my next move.

He shifted as well. "Whoa. More drama," he said. "Sorry. I just get so sick of these guys taking over, at the expense of everyone who's not, who's not . . . them." He studied his watch. I glanced at it as well—5:35—and noticed how white his skin was.

Will popped around the circulation desk, grabbed his laptop computer and tucked it into what I now saw was a canvas messenger bag. He zipped it, then tossed it over his shoulder and reached for his keys to lock the office, whisking me out with him as he did.

"Look, I shouldn't have said that," he said, his breathing loud, his hand tight around on the doorknob.

"No, I'm the one who just barged in here wanting to snatch the yearbook, spouting off my mouth and taking up your time," I countered. "It's just been a weird day."

The library door latched shut behind us.

Will jingled his keys. The clicking of our shoes against the linoleum floor was suddenly embarrassingly loud in the hall. By the time we reached the school's entrance, I'd mentally tallied the count of every locker and window. Will sighed, and then turned toward me. "Tomorrow I'll see what I can find out, if you want. I can probably get access to the district archives."

The florescent lights in the hall suddenly seemed way too bright. "No, that's fine," I said, shifting my weight and wishing myself out of these stupid cleats. "I've got enough to go on already from today's service. I can take it from there."

"Tough luck—you've got me curious now," he insisted, and turned toward the door without looking back or waiting for an answer. "See you tomorrow after practice. Then we'll compare notes."

The heavy glass door at the main entrance thumped against its hinge as Will left, and I noticed daylight just pinching the evening. I didn't want to make it another late night. So I ran back to my office, kicked off my cleats and picked up one file, then another for each of my players: permission slips signed by parents, copies of physical exams, transcripts and academic records and medical details I'd need to know, just in case. A pile of district bus requests for away games could wait until tomorrow.

The television was loud as I walked in the front door and I knew instantly it was a cooking show, one of Mom's favorites, probably "America's Best Chef" or some such program. I set my bag down on the bench by the door and peeked at my mother on the couch in the living room, still in her school cafeteria uniform with her "Jocelyn Wallace" nametag, her worn-out slippers dangling on her toes.

"Is that you, Rey?" she said, not turning from the television. I chuckled.

"Nope, it's the Boston strangler."

"Chicken's on the stove for you."

It hadn't been easy moving back in with my mother after college, but I didn't complain the nights she kept dinner warm. I wandered into the kitchen, dished up a plate and joined her in front of the TV. I'd convinced myself that living here was the best way to save money until I'd have enough for a down payment on my own place, a condo downtown or in one of the converted old houses around the corner.

Or until some hunky jock asked me to move in with him—which would probably be never.

Besides, this was MaeMa's house; my mother had grown up here, before I came along. And Mom wasn't going anywhere when we lost MaeMa. So in a way, these walls and rooms were daily remnants of the woman who'd anchored us both.

Still, I'd been away at college four years, so on more than a few occasions I'd have to remind my mom that I wasn't a teenager anymore. Whether she acknowledged it or not, I'd done a lot of growing up. I didn't need to explain where I was going or when I was coming back, nor would I ask her permission. She'd nod and look away, her face tightening into a look I'd seen a hundred times growing up, one that carried the conflict of change she'd rather not confront.

So I'd put my arm around her and console her that I didn't go out much anyway. Where else would I go, except to the school or soccer field, the movie multiplex or Knudsen's Bakery? My days might have been longer than my mother's, but they were just as scheduled and predictable. No surprises. No secrets. No social life.

Even our nightly interactions had settled into a routine. I'd walk in the door, and she'd asked me the same question, usually during the commercial break from her program. Muting the sound on the television set with her remote control, she'd smile, look up and say, "Anything interesting happen today?" I'd shrug and return the question. Then she'd recount for me her day until the show—and the sound—came back on.

Tonight's version deviated.

"I went to a funeral today," I initiated, a mouthful of chicken muffling the words, even before she'd asked. Grief pushed slowly across her eyes and I instantly regretted the comment. Funerals were not on the list of answers for the day's interesting events, not for her—or me.

We both missed MaeMa.

I chewed and diverted. "Ever hear of a guy named Coach Bailey Crawford? He passed last week and apparently he was the . . ."

"Cancer. I saw his obituary in the Register but some of the cafeteria ladies told me before that," she said. She glanced back at the television, then at me. "Bailey and Cathy Crawford, they good people. They don't deserve that. I met him, with MaeMa."

I set down my fork. "You knew Bailey Crawford?"

"Well, just a little. MaeMa knew him more."

My mother sipped her coffee, reflecting, it seemed, over the sound of such names in the same sentence: Bailey and Cathy Crawford, MaeMa. She leaned back into her pillow and rubbed her eyes. Most nights she was in bed by nine, just after her shows were over because she had to be at work so early the next morning. Losing MaeMa wore on her every day, a heavy burden that never seemed lighter no matter how many days passed.

The commercials ended and my mother pushed the sound button on her remote control as a pudgy chef in a white uniform came into the picture. I stared at her as she stared at the screen, nodding at the chef like they were old friends. I picked up my fork again; sometimes I hated television for this very reason. It had ended almost every conversation I'd tried to have with my mother since coming home. I'd learned the hard way not to interrupt her before commercials.

By the next break, I had a list of questions ready. But Mom picked up where she'd left off.

"Like I said, he was a good man. Why did you go to his funeral?"

"No one else would and Preston said someone needed to."

"I'll say. That man did a lot for you girls."

"He did? How come no one told me about him? I felt like an idiot, and now I wonder what else I've been missing about—"

"Tricia Woodring there?"

"You know her too?"

"She's one of the editors at the Register." The commercials ended and my mother's attention returned the culinary show. "Finally. Tonight he's giving his secret to barbeque ribs—let's see if he's got it right!"

I chomped impatiently. My mom laughed at the chef on the television and jotted down notes in a tiny spiral notepad, something I'd watched her do many times before. It contained recipes or tips for getting the best meals out of the bulk orders of foods she had to prepare at the school cafeteria. I glanced occasionally at the show, in between irritated bites of my dinner.

Five minutes later, the music swelled, the chef said goodbye and Mom switched off the TV. She rubbed the back of her neck, then her temples. I knew what that meant.

"Okay, tell me real quick about Bailey Cra—"

"Reynalda, I need some sleep." She stood from the couch, like she had a 50-pound sack of potatoes on her back, and began to shuffle toward her bedroom with weariness in each step. "I been on my feet all day."

"But just a few—"

"He was a fine man. And tomorrow I'll tell you more. Tomorrow, I promise," my mother said, the energy evaporating from her voice as she reached her room. "'Night, baby girl."

"But—"

"Rey. Tomorrow, please."

"Okay, night, Mom."

I finished my dinner and flipped the TV on, then off again. Everything in me wanted to go knock on Mom's door to get the rest of her story, but she'd signaled the conversation's end with her usual bedtime farewell. I had no memory of a night in this house when I was not called "baby girl" before heading off to bed, except the one two years ago, when we lost MaeMa. That night, my mother just stared, her eyes brimming with sorrow, afraid maybe that if she said anything at all, expressed even the slightest tinge of affection, a flood would open that she could not stop. That night she just switched off the lights.

Every other night, though, I was "baby girl." It didn't matter that I was now twenty-five years old, not five.

I reached for my computer, skimming through the day's news and the sports section of the Cincinnati Herald. I moved to the Daily Register where the headlines announced the start of the new school year, a city council meeting and a new owner for Joe's Diner. All things Claymont Falls.

I clicked the "About Us" section and scrolled through the photos of the newspaper's editors. Tricia Woodring Johnson—whose picture had obviously been taken a few years ago—was listed as the managing editor. A phone number and email address were listed below.

I took a chance. Tricia answered.

"Night desk, Tricia Johnson here."

"Oh, hi. Yes, this is Reynalda Wallace. I'm the girls soccer coach at Claymont Falls High, and I heard you speak today at Coach Crawford's memorial service."

She sighed before responding: "Is that good news or bad, Sugar?"

I could hear the tattering of keyboards in the background as well as people talking and what sounded like a radio with static signals in between voices.

"Neither. It's just I'd never heard of Mr. Crawford—or your team—before today, so I'm wondering if I could find out some more about both."

She paused before she answered and I wasn't sure how to interpret the silence. Then she spoke: "Why?"

"As I said, I'm the new girls coach at the high school and thought it might be helpful for us. For me."

"Preston Hanks never said anything?"

"No. But I—"

"I guess he wouldn't. That man. What the —?"

I heard someone call her name. Then she came back on: "Just had an accident on the interstate and I need to get a reporter there. What's your number? I'll call you back when things slow down here."

I acquiesced and hung up the phone. Instinctively, I surfed a few soccer web sites before closing my laptop and scooping strawberry ice cream into a bowl. Then I filled the sink, scrubbed the dinner dishes, and wrapped the leftover chicken. I reached for the towel to start drying the plates when I heard the phone. I grabbed my bowl and hurried to the living room.

"Hello? This is Rey."

"False alarm. No accident after all. Thank God. Just a car with a flat tire," Tricia said. "Now what did you want to know about Coach Crawford, besides the fact that he was the best man this town's ever seen?"

"That sounds like a good place to start," I said, plopping onto the couch where my mother usually sat, as if I were about to enjoy a show as well. But I didn't need the visual of a television set to note how relaxed and smooth Tricia's voice was. I imagined her kicking back in her chair, feet propped up on the desk, cradling the phone between her ear and shoulder and using her hands to animate each detail. She explained how Coach Crawford had been appointed to the position, and how she couldn't get over how far the program had come since that first season.

"You girls even have your own locker room now, don't you?" Tricia asked, but never slowing for a response. "Not us. Not even a storage room or a bus. It wasn't without trying either. Coach seemed to know which battles to fight and figured if he could just manage to get access to something that at least resembled a field, you know, working around the football and marching band and boys soccer team schedules, that'd be enough. Back then, the school only had one field."

"How did you compete if you had nowhere to practice?"

"Exactly, Hon. But that was fall of 1983 and we were the first girls team so we felt lucky to get to play at all. And we were resourceful. Sometimes we'd run sprints at the park or do passing drills in the parking lot."

Another part of my education solidified with this detail. Though I'd never heard of the championship team before today, I'd also never thought about the fact that there had been a time when a girls soccer team at Claymont Falls High did not exist. I'd come up through this school, had played on the girls field just opposite the boys' soccer field, and complained with the rest of the athletes about how rundown our locker rooms and showers were. I couldn't imagine being in high school as a student—or now as a coach and teacher—without these elements Tricia considered luxuries.

"Believe me, it was Coach who made it happen at all. We didn't even know we could play, I mean really play, until he told us we could." Tricia paused, as if the thought had struck an emotion she wasn't expecting. She sniffed before continuing. "God, he was a good man. It was a great time together. And you know what? Most of us are still good friends because of it. Some of us even raised our kids together. Holy cow, that was almost the entire starting lineup sitting together at today's service, right there behind Mandy's family. I was supposed to speak on behalf of the team, but you saw it: everyone had to say something."

I remembered. They'd donned a blend of professional suits and casual dresses, but they'd reflected something else altogether that had drawn my attention, and even now I couldn't quite put my finger on it.

"Listen, hon, he made a big difference for all of us. You know, you could probably talk with some of the others if you wanted since most live around here," Tricia said. "Hang on, Sugar."

I overheard Tricia talking with a reporter about getting another source or she'd kill his story and the need to call someone at the council to confirm his facts.

As I waited, a gold Most Valuable Player cup on the bookshelf across the living room caught the light. My mother still had not rearranged many of the ribbons and plaques I'd won as a girl. I picked it up and remembered the ninth grade softball honor when I'd won the shiny cup for my quickness as catcher. I'd thrown out 13 players trying to steal second base that summer. I smiled at the memory, just as Tricia came back on the line.

"Sorry about that," Tricia said. "The news can't wait. Now, anything else?"

"Just one question: why isn't there anything at the school about your team?" I pushed the phone closer to my ear as I set down the softball trophy. "I mean, if I'd won, or my team won, I'd put it all over the school and town and then—"

"Are you kidding? We were thrilled to get a team picture in the yearbook," Tricia laughed.

"But you were champions. State champions. Why wouldn't you deserve a plaque or trophy or banner—anything like that . . . or at least something that celebrated your undefeated record?" I was pacing toward the couch when I turned back to the crammed bookshelf, my feet thumping the carpet with each step as I waited for Tricia to answer.

But the line went quiet, except for the noise of the newsroom. I took a step closer to my trophies and stared. Still silence.

"Hello? Tricia?"

"Yes, Sugar, I'm here."

"So what happened? I looked everywhere today when I got back from the funeral, after practice, I mean, and I couldn't find a thing."

"No, you wouldn't."

"But you won the biggest title in high school sports . . . and that makes a difference for players like mine." I stomped back to the couch, trying to understand.

"I guess it's complicated," Tricia said. "Tell you what. How about if I come out to the school so we can talk more? I need to make a visit there anyway for the Register to talk with that principal of yours. Maybe later this week?"

I dialed up my schedule of the week in my head and asked Tricia to come during my planning and lunch hour on Friday.

"Okie doke, Hon. Gotta go." This time the line did go dead.

My ice cream had melted so I slurped the strawberry cream and put away the dishes that had dried by now. I was tired and decided to ignore my novel tonight. It was hard to get comfortable in bed, harder still to turn off my thoughts. I listened to a few cars drive by as well as the nightly hum of our house. Blue, green and gold MVP cups blurred together in my mind before I finally fell asleep.

An hour after my mother had left for work—she punched in at 6 a.m.—I stumbled into the kitchen. The coffee pot had less than a cup in it and it was lukewarm anyway so I decided to pick up breakfast on my way to work. I'd need an extra jolt this morning, so by 7:45, I was standing in line at the bakery. Still sleepy, I didn't quite notice who took my order at the counter.

"Double espresso, please, and an apple muffin," I said, digging in my purse for a five dollar bill. "To go."

"You bet," the woman said. She was tall and lean, sandy brown hair tied back and twisted up in a black clip, giving her face a soft elegance. She moved quickly and easily from espresso machine to the trays of fresh muffins, still warm. She grabbed one with a napkin, dropped it into a gold bag with "Knudsen's Bakery" written on the side, and set it on the counter before me.

"$4.50, please," she said, looking to the customers behind me.

That's when it hit me: she was one of the women who spoke at yesterday's funeral.

"Hey, you were the goalkeeper, right?" I said as she dropped my change in my palm. The question stopped her motion, and she tilted her head at me, smiling at the same time.

"That was a long time ago—How'd you know?"

"The funeral. Yesterday," I whispered.

She breathed in deeply, then pulled back her shoulders and nodded her head. She seemed even taller as she did.

"Best thing that ever happened to me—Coach Crawford and that team," she said. "And you are . . .?"

"Sorry, Rey Wallace," I said, feeling the glare of two bulky and impatient construction workers standing behind me. "I'm the current coach of—"

"Rey Wallace. Ah, I mean, Reynalda, one of the Wallace Women, right?" she beamed. "Pleasure to meet you." She grinned again and took the order of the two guys in line. "Good luck this season, Coach," she said as she turned toward the muffins.

I thanked her and hurried away from the muscled hard hats as they clamored for their food. I wondered how Annie Knudsen, who had been a state champion goalkeeper, now felt about serving her family's homemade éclairs to a crowd of sleepy workers.

By 8:30 I was walking into Preston Hanks' office in the athletic office. He was seated behind his desk finishing a phone call when I tapped on the open door. He held up his hand like a traffic cop, signaling for me to wait outside, so I took a sip of my coffee.

When he hung up, he called my name in a tone that clearly communicated who was in charge. "What can I do for you?"

"Bailey Crawford's funeral yesterday, you know—" I said.

"Good girl. Appreciate your stepping up like that."

"Well, I'm a little confused about why no one told me I was going to the funeral of the man who not only started the program I currently coach, but who won the first ever state championship for girls."

Preston smoothed the sides of his hair with his index fingers and smirked as he glanced in my direction. "Oh, that's right. Bailey Crawford coached girls soccer a long time ago, fall of 1983, I think, and as I recall, they did have a fairly decent season."

I was still standing at his office door—he had not invited me in nor offered me a seat—and so I pulled back my shoulders to appear taller, like I'd watched Annie do at the bakery. "How come when I looked through the trophy case in the hall, I couldn't find a single clue that said they'd won, let alone ever existed?"

He picked up a pen and scribbled something on his clipboard tablet. "No? Okay, thanks, I've made a note of it. Anything else?"

I glanced at the shelf below the window filled with football trophies, framed certificates and glossy schedules of his upcoming season.

"Well, yes, sir. I think you could understand why I'd be interested in knowing more about this team—it'd help my girls if they knew their ancestors, so to speak, were winners. Besides, if it were my team capturing the state title—which I hope they will someday—I'd expect the school would honor us with a banner, a plaque or some—"

"Of course you would. And if you win a championship, we'll see what we can do."

I thought of my players, of Kate and Maggie, and rephrased my question: "Wait. Doesn't every winning team deserve the recognition of their efforts, especially if they—"

"You know how it is," my boss shrugged. "Budget cuts being what they are, and that being what it is, honestly, we're lucky to have all the programs we do, Rey."

"But we get a lot of support, I mean, some of their parents come, when they can and—"

"Football, basketball, those sports get support because they have a Booster Club that sees to it. Who do you think buys all the varsity jackets? Even baseball does well at the concession stand. Those are the teams most parents get behind." He rose from behind the desk, easily six inches taller than I was and twice as wide, and moved toward the door where I was still standing. His bald head reflected the florescent lights of the office as a tiny bead of sweat was forming across his forehead.

"Sorry, but I'm late for a meeting across town. Hang in there, Coach Rey," he said, grabbing his clipboard and hurrying out of his office. "Now go and have some fun."

He pulled the door tightly closed behind him, and my eyes followed his bulky frame pounding through the hall until he was out of sight. I turned and walked in the other direction, toward my classroom to put a few finishing touches on my walls before the school year started. I'd have to put Hanks behind me—for now.

I'd hung posters of authors such as Philiss Wheatley, Mark Twain, Langston Hughes and Harper Lee to get my class room ready for the new school year. Images like these, I believed, could inspire new ideas as well, which I suppose was MaeMa's influence stemming from our days at the library.

When I finished stacking books and dusting off computers, I turned to the first week's lesson plans, due at the mid-morning departmental meeting. I put a few more finishing touches on the room before heading out to practice with my team.

It was another cloudless August day when I ran out to the girls field. I grabbed several small orange plastic cones from our storage shed and began to set up rectangles for drills. A whistle blew about a hundred yards away and I saw dozens of boys' soccer players running sprints on their field. Behind them, the football team with at least 50 players in pads was out in full force with Coach Preston Hanks barking commands surrounded by six, maybe seven, assistant coaches. In the other direction, the baseball field sat empty next to the track where several local neighbors were jogging or walking. The sight of so many fields behind the school, representing a range of sports, had never before seemed unusual to me, until I remembered Tricia's comment about not having a field at all.

"Hey, Coach!" Kate yelled, her teammates following making their way from the locker room to the field, balls at their feet. I waved and counted 16 players running toward me, which meant five substitutes. Not enough to scrimmage full field with but not a terrible number to kick off the season. Some looked more like they should be gymnasts, while a few others were so gangly I hoped they wouldn't trip over their own feet. Thankfully, a good core looked like they were born with the ball at their feet, so I imagined we might have a decent season after all.

In matching blue shorts and T-shirts, the girls circled out to where I was and began to stretch their legs, leaning over toward their toes, laughing and talking about boyfriends and mall sales and vacations. I seized the moment.

"Did you girls know you're part of a championship program?" A few stopped talking and looked up, while others whispered like sisters sharing secrets. I spoke louder.

"Seriously, who knew the Lions girls soccer team was once a state championship team?"

The girls stood upright now, no longer stretching. A few tapped their balls with their cleats, but no one answered.

"It's true," I said, hoping the news would sink in. A few girls eyes widened. Others waited for more of the story.

"Was it the team you played on, Coach?" Kate asked.

"I wish. No, we had a good team my senior year but we weren't anywhere close to being district champs let alone state," I said. "I didn't know the story then. But I wish I had."

"You graduated a long time ago, didn't you?" Paula, a defender with bulky shoulders and an attitude to match, posed her question.

"Please. I was class of 2002, and, for those of you struggling with math, that was only six years ago. No, I'm talking about a team that played here twenty-five years ago this season," I stepped toward my players. "1983—the great year I also happened to be born—was the year our program started. They were the Class of '84. And what a season they had! Girls, we have state champs in our blood and that should matter every time we step onto the field."

Kate nodded, but Maggie shook her head.

"Are you sure, Coach Rey?" Maggie asked quietly.

Her question startled me. "Yes, I'm sure. Why?"

"Well, there's nothing in the gym or the Hall of Inspiration about a girls soccer team. So maybe you got them confused with . . . the boys? They've always been pretty good."

I blinked at her, challenged both by her suggestion and her perceptiveness, and continued: "No, I didn't get them confused with the boys. I saw a picture of the team in the 1984 yearbook and, well, remember the funeral I told you about yesterday?"

Maggie leaned in closer.

"Coach Crawford was the first girls coach here and took his team all the way to state." I waited for the impact. A few girls looked as if they were considering what exactly it would it mean to qualify for state.

But the inspiration was short lived.

"I have a question, Coach," Paula responded. I allowed it, breathing in the possibility of a teachable moment. "What time are we going to be done with practice today? Some of us are going to the movies."

I looked down at a ball, placed the laces of my right shoe under it and flicked it up at Paula who caught it with her hands before dropping it like a hot potato. That was the rule—no hands or everyone would do a lap. I pointed toward Paula and spoke as softly and patiently as I could: "The movies? Is that right? Glad you could fit in practice today. I guess we'll talk more about that championship later. Now, two laps, everyone. Games are won with conditioning."

The girls groaned but took off anyway. And for the rest of the practice, with too many missed passes, slow sprints and weak shots on goal, I struggled to believe any state championship team could have ever come from this school.

Two and a half hours later, I was stacking the cones and other equipment in the storage shed by the field as my players made their way toward the locker room. I looked beyond them to someone in jeans and a white un-tucked shirt running toward me from the main school building. He was waving one hand toward me but he was too far away to see who it was. As I clamped the lock on the shed, the man came closer and I saw his square glasses and brown hair bouncing off his shoulders. It was Will McCabe.

"Hey Coach. I've found something I think you'll be interested in," he said, catching his breath, his arms still waving in excitement. "Can you come to the library? You have got to see this!"

Will didn't wait for an answer but ran back toward the building. I was not far behind.

chapter
7

1983

July was hot. More so, Bailey thought, than in years past when he had organized afternoon scrimmages for the boys' junior varsity teams. While Cathy was typing newsletters or working in the garden, and the twins were at day camp, Bailey would be setting up obstacle courses on the football field. For eight straight summers he ran the preseason soccer sessions, applying to those workouts what Lars had taught him during the season.

Eventually, Bailey began to make the summer practices his own, tweaking drills, experimenting with new strategies, even going on occasional ice cream runs to make sure his players had some fun for all the hard work they did. He never doubted if those sophomore and junior boys would show up each afternoon, no matter the summer temperatures, because they knew if they didn't, they wouldn't have a shot at varsity. He and Lars had made it clear that playing varsity soccer was a privilege earned by developing their skills on the lower team. The more experience they had and the more invested they were, the more likely they'd move up to the third most prestigious team at the high school.

This summer was different. Harry Hanks had forbidden Bailey from using the football practice field, claiming it could only withstand so much wear and tear between football sessions, the marching band, and boys' soccer, and he was "not about to sacrifice it on some crazy experiment." Hanks had given him no equipment for the summer—no water bottles, drill cones, not even a first-aid kit—suggesting to Bailey that his new team wasn't likely to get much in the fall either, especially since Hanks had to buy new shoulder pads, practice uniforms, and helmets for each level of football. He also made known how the Booster Club had finally decided to spend its money: on an overhaul of the varsity weight room.

"We'll see what we can do later," Hanks had mumbled, hurrying out of his office on the last day of school. Bailey just nodded.

Now as he waited in the town's public park near the picnic tables, he thought Mandy and Tricia might be the only girls who came. They were already kicking back and forth near a large elm that shaded them from the afternoon sun but assured Bailey that a "bunch of girls were on their way."

By 3:07, two cars honked their horns and Bailey watched as they pulled into the parking lot behind the playground. Five girls about his daughter's age climbed out of each car, laughing and making their way past the swing sets to where Tricia and Mandy were. Bailey looked at his watch.

"You're late, Girls," he said, smiling but firm. "I'm glad you're here but that'll cost one lap around the park . . . for everyone. Stay on the grass." He looked toward his daughter, who smiled back and took the lead as the girls followed her. No one questioned the charge. And as they jogged the length of the green, past bushes and picnics in progress, Bailey counted and sized up his players, just as he'd done every summer. Most were lanky like Mandy, and a few were thick like Tricia, yet all twelve kept pace.

When they returned, he was surprised that no one was breathing hard. Then he called the girls into a circle and for the next half hour, he taught them how to stretch, which part of the foot to use when they passed, even how to watch the ball as they headed it. The girls nodded and did as they were told.

He didn't say anything when some slipped on the grass because they weren't wearing cleats. After one of the girls got kicked hard twice below the knee, she simply grimaced and played on. And Bailey noticed none of his players were wearing shin guards.

After another half hour of basic drills, he pulled them under a tree for a break and passed around cups of water from the jug Cathy had packed for them. He pulled out half a dozen faded yellow T-shirts from a bag and tossed them at specific girls. Then he tossed two old baseball gloves about six feet apart on the grass to represent the baseline of an imaginary goal, and two more about 40 yards opposite before jogging back to the girls.

"Who's never played a real game of soccer?" Bailey asked the question for what it was: the moment of reckoning. He expected most of the hands to shoot up but none did. Not one.

"You mean to tell me you've all played soccer before?" he said.

Tricia raised her hand. "Yes, Coach. Almost every week in Mr. Lambert's P.E. class, in the gym or out on the track, we get to play."

"You do?"

"We learned most of those things already," she said. Tricia's cheeks were pink, and sweat lined her forehead.

"What things?" Bailey asked.

"The things you just taught us," Tricia smiled as she spoke but seemed obliged to qualify her comment. "Except the heading. I'm afraid it'll knock my brains out so I just never tried."

The girls laughed at their friend as a slight breeze came through the park. Bailey heard a child cry on the swing set and watched a mother hurry over. He looked back at Mandy, than Tricia and their other friends.

"Guess what, Tricia? You just headed the ball and your brains are still there, right?"

"Last I checked, Coach," she said, massaging her skull with her hands. "Yup. Still there."

"That's because you were brave enough to try it." Bailey looked square into the clowning eyes of his daughter's friend and within seconds, she turned serious. "If you had the courage to come here today, then I know you'll be able to do just about anything. You know why?"

"Why?"

"Because you don't have to be the best to do your best. No matter what anyone else says. Folks aren't exactly convinced you can do this at all, you know, and they won't be afraid to tell you so. You ready for that, Tricia?"

A crease formed between Tricia's eyes, as if she'd just been asked to choose between life and death. "I think so." Then she jumped up from the ground, planted one foot in front of her and curled her hands into fists, her version of the ready position for heading the ball.

"Okay, Coach, let's try it again."

Bailey picked up a ball and tossed it at Tricia's head. She leaned forward, closed her eyes and hit it just at the spot where her hairline and forehead met. It ricocheted off of Mandy, who tossed it back to her dad.

"Eyes open, Tricia. Try again," he said, "and again." He tossed it over and over until finally his daughter's best friend modeled the exact way to head a soccer ball, her teammates watching back and forth as if they were spectators at Wimbledon. When she'd finally performed the move the right way, sweat dripping from her face, Bailey held the ball against his hip and looked at his team.

"See what you can accomplish with enough enthusiasm?" They sat wide-eyed. "That's cause for celebration, don't you think?" And with that he stepped toward Tricia and extended his hand. "Well done. That's only the beginning of great things from you!" She shook his hand with so much vigor Bailey thought it might fall off his arm. And within seconds, all of her teammates were on their feet, crowding around Tricia and slapping her back as if she'd just scored the winning goal.

And they hadn't even played their first game.

They finished that inaugural practice with so much excitement that Mandy could not stop talking about it when they got home. Over corn on the cob and hamburgers on the back patio, she described every aspect of their session to her family. Cathy nodded with each new anecdote, grinning and laughing like she'd been there herself. And as she listened, she glanced across the table at her husband and noticed a tiny twinkle in his eyes, as if the details were completely new to him.

B.J., however, was not impressed. Instead, he groaned every time his sister added one more detail about her new teammates, the scrimmage they played, even Tricia's heading skills. This last point was too much for B.J. who gulped a glass of Gatorade before finally mocking her passion.

"Oh, yeah, practicing in the park, by the playground with a bunch of kids. I'm sure you'll go real far."

"It's not our fault we can't use the field."

"That's because the field is only for real teams, idiot."

"We are a real team!"

"No, you're a girls team. There's a difference," he said reaching for a handful of potato chips and shoveling them into his mouth. "Besides, you don't even have enough players, do you?"

"We have 12. That means we have one sub," Mandy quipped, leaning over the last of her corncob.

B.J. laughed and looked at his father. "Well, we had 20 today, Dad, the biggest group ever. And that was just varsity. J.V. had 23. Bet you wish you were coaching us instead of a bunch of—"

"That's enough, Bailey Paul," Cathy scolded. She pushed her chair back from the table.

"It's okay, Hon." Bailey set down his hamburger, picked up a napkin and wiped his hands. Then he looked at Mandy's brother. "Listen, B.J., I'm glad a lot of kids are coming out for the team—that'll make all of you work harder for those spots. But let me ask you something."

B.J. pulled the bowl of potato chips closer to him and crunched.

"Did your sister ever miss one of your games? From the time you played little league to last year's J.V. regional tournament, did she? Ever? Answer me, Son."

"No." The word was more of a grunt than a response.

"Well, then, I think this is your opportunity to give back some of that same respect and support she gave you. I will be coaching her team and you don't have to like it, but you do have to respect your sister and her teammates. Period."

"But—"

"And that means your mother and I expect you to stand up for her in the way she has always stood up for you. It won't be easy, but that's how this family works. Understand?" Bailey waited for an answer. "Son?"

"Yes."

"This season will probably be tough for all of us, but together, we're going to make it through. Right?"

"Right, Dad!" Mandy cheered. Then she looked at her brother. "Don't worry, B.J., I'll still come to your games and scream for you."

"Just don't yell your head off," he whispered. "That's so embarrassing."

"Oh, you love it and you know it," she teased, punching his arm as she rose to clear the dishes. "Mom, is there ice cream?"

And with that, peace reigned again in the Crawford household, at least for this Monday night. Still, Bailey couldn't help but watch his son—who was now helping his sister devour a half gallon of chocolate ice cream near the garden Cathy was weeding—and thought about the challenges B.J. would no doubt face under his new coach.

Freddie Smith, Hanks' assistant coach, had taken Bailey to breakfast last week to break the news: Hanks had hired an old friend of one of his Booster Club parents. This new guy, Sean Flynn, came to Claymont Falls last year, had some experience with the game as both a player and a college coach, and was setting up a new law practice in town. Hanks put two and two together and saw the deal equal four.

"You, Crawford, will bring the girls what they need to look good for all of us, while Flynn will bring some money and clout to the boys," Freddie told him over pancakes. "He's networked with some decent colleges, too, so maybe B.J. will have a shot at a scholarship after all."

Bailey's memory of the conversation brought a tension that ached in his stomach the rest of the night. He realized he hadn't let go of the idea that he'd not gotten the boys' head position, but he couldn't deny the delight he'd witnessed in his daughter today either. Of course, he hadn't felt like he'd had a choice in the matter, that even after eight years, he had earned the promotion.

"But you've always had a soft spot for those kids who deserved a chance," Cathy told him as they talked it over before bed. "You just never imagined 'those kids' would include girls who wanted to play sports."

He sat on the edge of the bed considering her words as she turned up the fan.

"Yes, but—"

"No 'buts' about it, Bailey. You did earn that promotion, and guess what? You got it. You are officially a head coach," she said, letting the fact sink in. "And at least two members of your family are thrilled about it. B.J. will come around, trust me."

He stared at her, a little more certain of how to respond to this new title as well as its implications. As Cathy lay down beside him, he leaned back onto the pillow and he admitted to himself that she was right. All kids—boys and girls— deserved a chance. That's what had motivated him first to become a teacher, and then a coach. He couldn't help how things had developed with his son's new coach but he could do his part with his daughter's new team.

Whatever happened, he resolved, as sleep fell slowly over him, to give to his players what he always tried to give to his family, his students and his other teams: his best.

The next afternoon, he drove back to the park eagerly. Mandy had decided to ride with Tricia, and Bailey expected the girls would be sore today after being pushing for three hours the day before. And he worried that without cleats, shin guards or other equipment, he was inviting injuries or accidents, neither of which he could afford with so few girls already. Bailey wondered how to recruit more players to a team that didn't exist—before yesterday, that is—in a town that had few athletic options for girls except cheerleading and tennis. Again, Bailey decided he could only recruit in the way he always had—one invitation at a time—and hoped that would work.

By the time he arrived at the park, Lars was hobbling around the grass with orange plastic cones, making the area look more like a construction site than a soccer field. Bailey parked his car and walked past crowded benches, carrying a bag of yellow jerseys, baseball gloves and a water jug before he dumped them near a stack of orange cones.

"Sorry I didn't make it yesterday, Bailey," Lars said, his face already tanned from the summer sun. "Rotten knees—humidity makes them worse. How'd it go?"

"All things considered, pretty good, I think, thanks to you!"

"Me?"

"Really, Lars. Training future soccer players during your P.E. classes?"

The two laughed and Bailey realized how glad he was to see his mentor and friend, and to talk soccer again as they had so many times before, preparing together for summer practices, fall games and office meetings. And for the next few minutes, Bailey described the talent and fitness of his new team. He highlighted what he expected would happen in today's practice and what his goals were for the next few weeks. All the while he talked, Lars simply nodded, adding an occasional smile along with, "Good, good."

They were interrupted, though, by the honking horns of three cars pulling into the parking lot. Mothers on benches and children on jungle gyms stopped what they were doing to turn toward the noise. Lars looked over and lifted his hand. Bailey looked at his watch—2:55—and raised his baseball cap when he saw twelve girls emerge from the cars. Most of the girls had tied back their hair in ponytails, but each wore a royal blue T-shirt, dark shorts, white socks, and an array of brightly colored tennis shoes.

Near the edge of the lot, the girls formed a single line and slowly began to jog around to their coaches, chanting as they did, "Li-ons! Li-ons! Li-ons!"

Bailey raised his shoulders and drew in a deep full breath.

The team of blue jerseys circled the park, making their way past Frisbee throwers and picnic blankets before circling their coaches as well.

Still they chanted, "Li-ons! Li-ons!," and soon the girls and the coaches were clapping their hands in unison before Bailey directed them in one very loud and long, "Li-oooons!"

"Cool T-shirts, huh, Coach?" Tricia questioned the second the cheering died but too eager to wait for an answer. "We went to the Goodwill this morning and found them. A little worn out, but who cares? They're Claymont Falls blue! At .50 cents each, how about that?" She spun around as if she was modeling on a runway, and the others imitated her.

"Great!" Bailey said. "They match our colors and our budget!"

"You are now a team," Lars announced and then egged them on: "And who are you?"

"Li-ons! Li-ons!" the girls cheered.

He wasn't sure, but Bailey thought he noticed a few bystanders shake their heads when they heard the chant. Maybe he was reading too much into it, and so for the next three hours, he all but forgot about the rest of the park while his players passed and dribbled and scrimmaged as if their lives depended on it.

If anyone was unhappy when they finished that second practice, Bailey didn't notice. And when he returned the next day and the next, Bailey found himself paying more attention to the level of enthusiasm his players showed with each new drill and exercise than to anything—or anyone—else. In and out of cones the girls sprinted; up and down on the grass they fell and rose again. They worked on throw-ins, traps, and headers, jumping over balls or counting sit-ups and push-ups, mixing up partners until their coach called them in for a break.

"Great work. Great work, Lions," Bailey said. "You've been doing your best all week, and I'm seeing you push your teammates to do their best. When you do that, you can't possibly lose."

The words startled the girls at first, but only for a moment, as they listened to their coach passing around water cups and hand towels. They wiped the sweat from their faces and readjusted their ponytails. Mandy sat on the grass with her right knee behind her and leaned over her left leg extended out front. The other girls did the same, stretching their muscles while resting from the drills.

"Now it's time to think about shooting and scoring, but let's be clear—that's only one part of winning a game. The rest of winning relies on every trap and header and pass you make," Bailey said, pacing in front of them. "And it starts here." He put his thumb to his heart as Lars and the girls nodded.

"There's no question each of you has heart. You know how to work hard and you love what you're doing, don't you?"

"Yes, Coach!" they answered with one voice.

"So which one of you could be our goalkeeper?" Bailey took off his cap again and leaned on his back foot waiting for someone to extend her arm. No one did. He returned the cap and shifted forward. Still the players were quiet.

"Okay. Who's played basketball in Mr. Lambert's P.E. class?"

Twelve hands shot up.

"Great. Let's line up, please, hands out in front," Bailey said quickly. He wanted to measure the height of his players, to see who might be tall enough as well as agile for the job of preventing the ball from entering the goal, essential traits for the only player on the field who could actually use her hands without penalty. She needed to be tough as well as quick, a leader who was willing to throw her body at any offensive player speeding toward her and prevent the other team from scoring. She, after all, was a team's last chance to defend the goal. So of all the positions in a soccer match, the goalkeeper's was often the most grueling, where forceful contact was likely and often painful, and therefore, a position Bailey worried about for these girls.

How could a girl learn to defend the goal with her body? Was it asking too much?

As his players stood shoulder to shoulder, he saw that only his daughter had the height he'd hoped for in a goalkeeper, yet he knew her agility and passing skills were too strong on the field to lose her to the goal. He considered a few other players as they stood in front of him, even Tricia for a second, until he remembered their recent basketball game of P-I-G in their driveway. Tricia could learn to be a good defender on the field, but her eye/hand coordination were no match for some aggressive strikers they were likely to face.

"Hmmm. Coach Lambert, any ideas?"

Lars paced in front of the team, looking from face to face. Given how eager the girls had been all week, Bailey was surprised that no one stepped forward for the goalkeeping spot, but he didn't blame them, given the difficulty of the position. He wondered what Lars was thinking. Instead, his mentor shook his head.

"Each was respectable in basketball, yes, but one, one was tall and fast and strong," he said. He pointed across the lineup, and then glanced back at Bailey, his cheeks redder than usual from the July heat. Again, he shook his head. "Sorry, Coach Crawford, she's not here."

"What?"

"Our goalkeeper. She's not here," Lars said softly. "I think many of you could play there as winners, yes? But that's not the best spot for you. No, our goalkeeper is not here."

"Where, then?"

"I think I know, Dad, I mean, Coach," Mandy chimed in. "Are you talking about Annie, Coach Lambert? We tried to get her to come and she really, really wanted to. But she has to babysit her little brother so she can't play."

"Yes, Annie Knudsen. Solid player," he paused. "Too bad."

Bailey looked from Mandy to Lars. And instead of asking any more questions, he pointed to Hannah Brown, the next tallest girl to Mandy, and asked her to stand in front of his makeshift baseball-glove goal. Hannah looked unsure. She scratched her ponytail, re-tied her shoe and stepped toward the gloves anyway. Then Bailey showed her how to stand on the goal line and put her hands out in front to stop the shots that came toward her as the rest of the players tried to score.

It did not go well for Hannah. As hard as she tried, her hands just did not keep up with her feet, and the balls whizzed past her. But that did not stop the Lions from celebrating her efforts when Bailey moved her back out to the line of shooters. Bailey shook her hand as he had Tricia's, and the team congratulated her on giving them her best work.

Stepping into the goal himself, Bailey loomed large as the goalkeeper and most girls aimed the ball straight at him. Some hit the imaginary goal post above him, or shot far beyond him. But Hannah and Mandy both knocked the ball past their coach, scoring each time it was their turn to shoot. Theirs were quick feet, and they both anticipated the angles so that Bailey could not stop their shots. Between these two, Bailey thought their offense was off to a strong start, and after practice, Lars agreed.

By six o'clock, Bailey sent the blue jerseys home, told them to stretch and run over the weekend so they could keep their momentum going at Monday's practice. He packed up his makeshift equipment and helped Lars with his. Lars complained again about his knees but assured Bailey he would rest over the weekend.

"You're a fine coach, Bailey," Lars said. "Don't forget that."

"I learned from the best," Bailey answered, tipping his cap. He drove from the parking lot just as a pick-up truck was pulling in. A group of three, maybe four families with toddlers was gathering around the grills for a summer cookout as Bailey turned onto Main Street. He drove past the post office, Green's Grocers and the Claymont Falls Municipal Building, until he came to one of only three stoplights in town. He slowed to a stop behind a sedan, his eyes landing on a crooked blue sticker on the bumper that read, "CFHS Lions Football!" He sighed.

The light turned and within a few minutes Bailey was in the empty parking lot of Knudsen's Bakery. A "CLOSED" sign hung in the glass door but he approached it anyway and peered in. Walter Knudsen was wiping the counter.

"Coach Crawford," he said, pulling the door towards him. "We're closed, but I've got some day-old rolls if you need some."

"No, Walter, that's okay. Wait. You know what? Cathy would be very impressed if I brought some home," he said, reaching for his wallet. "I'll take a dozen."

Walter was slightly older than Bailey, probably in his mid-forties, but he was a much taller man with a belly and hands to match his frame. They knew each other because Walter's son and daughter had both been students in Bailey's history classes, and the Knudsens had once been active in the Parent/Teacher Association. But Bailey saw less of the baker these past two years. His wife Agnes had passed away suddenly of breast cancer. It'd been a blow to their small community, and folks started coming by the bakery more and more to check on Walter. Business picked up because of it, making Knudsen's Bakery a regular stop.

Walter wiped his thick hands on his apron and hurried to the back of his shop before emerging again with a clear bag of rolls. He placed them on the counter and punched $1.75 on the cash register.

"Half off," he said, smiling. "End of the day deal."

Bailey handed him three dollars and addressed the real reason he'd come. "Thanks. Hey, how's Annie?"

Walter's face filled with pride, pushing his eyes into tiny moon slivers that made his large frame seem small and gentle. "She's a trooper. Works for me every morning in the summer and then watches Wally in the afternoons. When they're in school, she takes him in and picks him up. I couldn't run this place without her, you know."

"I know, Walt. In fact, that's why I've come by."

Walter dropped two quarters in Bailey's palm and rested his hands on the counter as he listened to Bailey talk about the girls soccer program. Wasn't it great, Bailey said, that it fulfilled the league requirements for a new law called Title IX? Then he described each of the girls who came to practice that week—two or three of whom Walter knew by name because of his daughter—and how excited they were for this opportunity to play, even though they didn't even have a field or cleats.

"I'll be honest, Walt, I didn't know what to think when I first got the job. I wasn't sure girls could play. But I have to admit they're working really hard. We just need a goalkeeper, someone smart and strong, a good athlete who's a hard worker and a leader."

Bailey paused and put his coins in his pocket. Taped on the wall behind Walt, he saw a family photo with him, Agnes, and their three children, including a much younger Annie with her toddler brother sitting on her lap. It looked like one of those family photos taken for a church directory, with forced smiles and matching shirts, but Bailey could not mistake the sincerity in their eyes. Agnes's absence must have felt like a daily sting. He turned back to the big man in the apron.

"Listen, Walt, you probably know where I'm going with this. Annie's smart, I know it for a fact because I had her in class. And Lars Lambert told me today that she's also one fine athlete."

If Walter Knudsen had been wearing a shirt with buttons, one of them might have popped off and rolled out the front door. His shoulders lifted, his chin angled, and the pride that filled his face earlier expanded when Bailey mentioned Annie's academic abilities and athletic gifts. Even so, he scratched the back of his neck and shook his head.

"You know what? I always thought she was a natural," he beamed. "Problem is, Coach, I don't have anyone to watch Wally. He's almost 10 now, oldest one's off in the military, and I can't afford a sitter in the afternoons. So I just don't see how it could work."

He cleared his throat and met Bailey's honest gaze. "See, here's the thing, Walt. I could really use a ball boy as much as I could use a goalie."

The baker's grin grew larger still. And not more than half an hour later, Bailey arrived home with a bag of rolls that did indeed impress Cathy, who was grilling chicken on the back patio. He didn't mention his news to Mandy, since she was on her way to babysitting for a neighbor. B.J., too, was gone, still at the field with his soccer friends.

So it was Bailey who answered the door when he heard the doorbell ring. There he found a small African-American woman with wisps of gray in her hair standing calmly on his front porch.

chapter
8

2008

The library lights were dim by the time Will and I arrived from the practice field. He was breathing hard, having run through the halls and out to the field to find me, and then back again to his office amongst the books and reference materials. His hair was moist against his forehead.

"You won't believe this," Will said, collapsing in a gray swivel chair behind a desk. A wide computer monitor sat atop with a tower beside it. Will pulled the keyboard toward him and I grabbed a chair beside him. He picked up a thin black plastic box about six inches long and waved it in front of his face.

"Know what this is?" "I wasn't born yest—"

"A videocassette tape. Know where I got it?"

"No, but—"

"Never mind. It's top secret. And it's about to blow your mind." At that he pushed the videocassette into a VCR player that was built into the bottom of an old dual purpose television set, fiddled with some buttons and speakers, and, within a few seconds, we were watching grainy images of faces come across the TV screen. He glanced at me and chuckled.

"Get this."

Across the bottom of the screen scrolled words that were juxtaposed over a lion's face: "Claymont Falls High Lions! Fall Sports in Review, 1983."

Will punched the pause button on the VCR and leaned into the screen, tilting his head toward me as he did. His glasses slipped a bit down his nose so that I could see the blue of his eyes along with a glimmer of both satisfaction and excitement. His jaw was firm and smooth, except for the cool little goatee surrounding his lips. He smiled and, as he did, I suddenly felt compelled to study the frozen TV screen.

"This confirms it, Rey. You ready?"

I swallowed, still staring at the screen. The room felt hot and I felt weird.

"Do you have any water?"

Will shot out of his chair, filled a ceramic mug from the water cooler behind him and handed it to me as he returned to his desk. I downed it in one gulp.

"You okay?" Will asked, brushing his hair from his face and readjusting the glasses on his nose.

"Yes, fine. Great. Thanks," I said, staring back at the screen and pulling my shoulders up to appear composed. "Whatcha got?"

"Good stuff," he said. "No, amazing stuff. Just wait."

Will pushed the play button and a barrage of still images flashed across the screen as "Lions! 1983" stayed in place. First, there were photos of football players on the line of scrimmage, coaches on sidelines, and parents and students crowded in the bleachers, followed by close-ups of a quarterback getting ready to pass, a kicker focusing on a field goal, and cheerleaders jumping into splits mid-air. More photos of football players at a parade in town, and then at an assembly shot across the screen until merging into actual game footage.

"Okay, this is the boring part," Will interrupted, pushing the fast forward button for several long seconds, scrolling through more images of football games, until finally it came to a soccer field with boys spread out across it. A dozen or so posed pictures of players in blue jerseys jumped across the screen in a quick collage of soccer images, including a team photo with about 20 teenage boys and two coaches.

Next, Will pulled his finger from the fast forward so I could see a few seconds of actual footage of two shots on goal with great saves by the Lions goalkeeper. He pushed the rewind so that I could take in each shot and each save, the goalie flying sideways, arms extended to punch the ball out of bounds.

"Thought you'd appreciate that," he said. "Pretty good effort, eh?"

"Yeah, pretty good," I said, forcing myself to look in his direction yet not notice his face. "But, Will, what is this? I mean, where'd you get this?"

He leaned back in his chair and tapped his jeans like he was playing the djembe, which he probably did, given his current cool factor.

"The Booster Club apparently put highlights together of each sport during fall, winter and spring seasons in the 1980s. Not great quality, as you can see, and from what I'm told, probably the work of some parent who took his camera to the games and then pieced this together." He tapped some more. "Apparently the same parent did it the year before, which means he probably had a kid in school during those years and did his duty on the Booster Club, because there haven't been any videos like this since according to . . . my sources."

"What? I mean, how in the world did you find this?"

"I'm a librarian. I find resources for a living. It's part of the job."

"But—"

"Never mind. You haven't seen the best part."

Will reached forward and hit the fast forward button again, moving through a few more shots on goal and plays by the boys' team—though far fewer than the football montage—until he stopped at the image of the lion with small print below in blue type, "1983-Girls State Champions."

The same yearbook photo of the girls team we'd found yesterday appeared across the screen. There stood Annie and Mandy, Tricia and Nelli, and the others, with their coach on the end. I expected to see more still photos next, like we'd seen with the football team and the boys' soccer team. But that is not what I saw. Will turned up the volume as I heard cheers from what sounded like a small crowd. The screen went dark for a second as the cheers quieted.

Then, clear as sunlight, there was a shot of a scoreboard. "Lions 1—Eagles 1. Second Half. Clock: 63:41." Tied with about 17 minutes left in the game, the film jerked back to the field, Lions end. There was the young Tricia screaming her head off at her teammates from the middle of the defense, Annie behind her in the goal waving her arms like she was directing traffic, and walking back and forth directly on the goal line.

The Eagles were taking a penalty shot, so no other players were inside the goalkeeper's box, just the shooter and the goalie. Girls in blue jerseys elbowed girls in red as they crowded around the box or positioned themselves at different spots down the field. And then they waited.

Wearing a bright yellow jersey to distinguish her from the others, Annie, the goalkeeper, finally stopped in the middle of the goal line, stood completely still and crouched with her arms bent out in front of her, palms up. A referee blew his whistle and the girl in the red jersey threw all of her weight behind the ball as she kicked it as hard as a bullet toward Annie—right at her in fact. Annie caught it like she was a wide receiver and I heard Tricia scream again hysterically. Then Annie bounced the ball like it was a basketball before she booted it down to the middle of the field.

The film jumped back and forth trying to follow Annie's kick, before landing on a girl wearing the Lions blue jersey #10. She trapped the ball and began sprinting as fast as she could toward the other goal. All of her teammates, including Tricia, followed as she wove in and out of red jerseys. Just as #10 came to the edge of the goalkeeper's box, smack in the center and in perfect range for a shot on goal, she flicked it off to the right in between two defenders. Mandy burst through them both, tapped the ball and then nailed it toward the far post of the goal. The goalkeeper flew sideways to stop it, but just missed knocking it out of bounds, and the ball then bounced off the post and into the goal.

Tricia went crazy. She bolted up the field and jumped onto Mandy's back as the rest of the blue jerseys circled around her, forming one giant blue blob. The referee blew his whistle and the camera jerked to the sidelines of the Lions bench. There standing and clapping was Coach Bailey Crawford, wearing a baseball hat and blue jacket, surrounded by four girls in baggy jerseys who were jumping up and down and hugging each other. Bailey threw his fist in the air for a brief second before the camera shot back to the center circle where both teams were lining up for a kick-off. A quick blurry shot to the scoreboard again finally came into focus: "Lions 2—Eagles 1. Second Half. Clock: 66:32."

Then the screen went black. Will pushed pause again when I suddenly remembered we were watching a film. I'd been so absorbed in that beautiful goal that I forgot where I was.

"See what I mean?" he said. "Amazing. These girls were tough. They knew what they were doing."

"Is that it? I mean, is there any more?"

Will shook his head, punched the play button and the video faded from black to five skinny boys wearing blue jerseys standing at the starting line of a cross-country running race. Another series of photos moved quickly before the video ended the way it began: "Claymont Falls High Lions! Fall Sports in Review, 1983." And a single credit scrolled over the face of the school's mascot: "Sponsored by the CFHS Booster Club."

"That's it, I'm afraid," Will said. "But look what you got."

"Look what we got," I said, the words slipping out before I realized what I was saying. "I mean, this absolutely confirms that we—as in Claymont Falls High—had a team that both deserved to be champions and went on to prove it by winning the state title on one very pretty goal."

He grinned again while at the same time nodding his head toward me. "So?"

I rose from my chair and looked down at my feet to realize here I was wearing my stupid cleats in the library. Again. This guy was going to think I didn't own any other shoes.

"What do you mean?" I asked as Will also stood up. We were almost eye level.

"So don't you think you should do something about it?"

"Like?"

"I don't know. But something." He dropped the videocassette in a filing cabinet drawer and locked it. I watched as he gathered up some books and stuffed them into his bicycle bag before flinging it over his shoulder.

We walked out of the library together in silence. Then, as we passed through the Hall of Inspiration, where we had searched so frantically yesterday for some proof of a state championship team in the trophy cases, it was as if some divine vibe climbed up out of those shelves and took hold of us both.

"We should get them a trophy!"

"We should get them a trophy!"

Will and I were facing each other in front of a bunch of ribbons and plaques when we made our simultaneous declaration. And, from that point on, we knew what we had to do. I had no idea how we would pull it off, but the plan was set in motion.

And I didn't think I minded that some geeky librarian with a goatee and a cute tennis-player butt was helping me figure it out.

In front of endless honors and awards neatly positioned inside glass cases, we stood pointing and imagining a prominent spot for this championship trophy . . . for girls.

"Front and center," I said. "Why not? They deserve it. Not many other STATE champs, right?"

"Right!"

We stood a foot or so from one another, bobbing our heads, staring in excitement at each other. I felt like dancing, until he glanced at his watch and then back directly into my eyes, surprising me again: "Hey, want to dream about this over a cup of coffee?" He smiled as he said it, hope filling his face, his very fine but—it suddenly dawned on me—very white face.

My head worked up an instant lecture to my heart. I'd been prepared for a lot of situations as an African-American living in a mostly white town and competing in a mostly white sport—in the U.S., anyway—but not one like this, where a hip young white guy was asking this still-cleated black girl to get a cup of coffee. I shifted back toward the trophy case while looking every which way in case anyone should discover us.

"Coffee? Uh, good idea, but, you know what? I need to—"

"Rey, it's just coffee. For a good cause." He was still smiling, waiting, re-positioning his messenger bag over his shoulder. "Tell you what. I'll meet you at Knudsen's in 20 minutes, okay? I'm on my bike, so you'll probably beat me there." He turned toward the door. "Your treat!"

And with that, he was gone. I stared out behind him, then down the hall and back. My eyes landed again on the trophy cases. They reminded me of all the shelves of trophies and ribbons MaeMa and Mom had arranged at home. Displaying each symbol of my accomplishments was a seed, I now realized, that had been planted to remind me of what I could achieve. But those awards that gave me confidence also sparked pride in my mother and grandmother, a reflection that they, too, were a part of my success. Just as they encouraged me to victory, so, too, did my victories encourage them. One without the other was not possible.

"Why shouldn't the girl's soccer state champions get the same recognition? And why shouldn't I have coffee with a white guy? What's the big deal?" I asked out loud, as if the trophies would answer. It was for a good cause after all, I told my reflection in the glass, and sprinted back toward my office.

I changed my clothes, tossed some files and a notebook into my backpack and headed toward the parking lot. I dumped them in my car and turned on the radio, finding the station that sometimes played Motown oldies. Ah, there was Aretha Franklin singing "R-E-S-P-E-C-T," a theme song for the Wallace Women that I could never resist singing along to. I turned the corner and made my way to Knudsen's, belting backup for the Queen.

Will was waiting at a window table when I walked in, two cups in front of him. I didn't know how he got here before I did. Except for him and a few workers, the bakery was quiet and unhurried, a stark contrast from the morning rush.

"I guess I'm faster on my bike than I thought," he joked, pushing a mug across the table for me. "Didn't know how you liked it, but here's the cream and sugar."

I poured in both and stirred. Will pulled out a small pad of paper from his bag.

"I'll be the official note-taker. Go, Coach."

I sipped my coffee and closed my eyes to think. "Okay, trophies cost money. We don't have any but these women deserve to be honored. I guess we'll need to do a fundraiser."

"What about Hanks? Think he'd give any?"

"I'll ask. But I can't imagine he would. He's forever announcing how we've 'already spent our budget.'"

"On football maybe . . . don't get me started." Will picked up his pen and drew a dollar sign on the pad of paper. "Okay, I'll research costs. How many should we get?"

My mind flashed again to the displays in MaeMa's house of each individual award I'd won over the years. I felt a sudden sting at the thought of not having them.

"One for each player!" I blurted out. "And a team trophy as well. It's what other sports team would get . . . if they ever won, which they haven't. That seems only fair, don't you think?" I picked up another sugar packet on the table and slid it back and forth between my fingers, concentrating on our game plan while I tossed the white packet as if it were a ball.

Will scribbled and smiled. "Absolutely fair."

"And a sign. They need a sign or a banner or something like that—"

"Yeah! It should be just as you're coming into Claymont Falls, you know, one of those signs like the one I saw on a college road trip through Kentucky to Nashville that read, 'Welcome to Malaga, Home of the 1999 County Basketball Champions.'" Will drew an imaginary sign in the air, his arms waving wildly. "No joke. I think that'd be cool. Can't you see it? 'Claymont Falls—Home of the 1983 Girls State Soccer Champions!'"

"Great idea!" I said, imagining a green state sign on the highway before entering downtown Claymont Falls. "But how do we make that happen?"

Will scribbled something underneath the dollar sign. "Got it. I'll research that too—probably need some local politician to advocate for it."

As soon as he said it, I noticed the jet-black hair of a small woman pacing near the counter. She was talking on the phone at the same time she pointed from the cinnamon rolls and donuts to the fritters and turnovers before stopping at a peach pie. I watched as the same woman who'd served me coffee that morning, Annie Knudsen, followed the woman's signals like she'd done this a thousand times before, placing each pastry carefully on a tray and pulling the pie out of the case for its own box. Then the smaller woman, still talking on the phone, flashed an "OK" sign with her fingers, and reached into her purse for her wallet. Her quick motion and tiny frame against the shadow of Annie's was the hint I needed.

"Will," I whispered, leaning into my cup. "See those two over there? They spoke at the coach's funeral yesterday. They both played on that first team!"

Will glanced over at the friends as Nelli snapped her phone shut, dropped it in her purse and snickered at something Annie said while she tied string around the box. Then Nelli leaned into the counter, which sent Annie into a fit of laughter, her shoulders and head shaking in rhythm with Nelli's. No other customers now were in the bakery. I looked over Will's shoulder to the clock on the wall: 5:55.

"What time does this place close? I only come here in the morning."

Will ignored me, still watching the two women who by now were howling and snorting over their inside joke. "We should ask them what they think." And before I could stop him, Will had jumped out of his chair, pulled my arm toward him and marched us both across the café.

"Excuse me, ladies," he said politely, winding down their uproar as Annie resumed tying the string in a bow. He pointed to me. "This is Reynalda Wallace, you know, the new girls soccer coach at the high school, and I'm her friend, Will McCabe, devoted soccer fan and assistant librarian at the school."

Annie shuffled back, still listening but pulling a long piece of plastic wrap over the tray to protect the pastries. Nelli eyed us both, tilted her head and stepped away from the counter.

"Wallace, like the Wallace Women?" She said looking directly at me.

Annie answered. "Yup, she's a Wallace. We chatted this morning, didn't we?" I nodded. I was surprised she remembered me considering how busy she had been earlier when I came in. Then again, there weren't many other—make that no other—dark faces in the place, so I wasn't hard to forget.

"She was at Coach's funeral, Nell," Annie said gently. Nelli looked at her friend, her expression turning serious before looking back at me as Annie continued. "This is Gina Martinelli. What can we help you with?"

"Uh, well, I, hmm," I couldn't for the life of me figure out how to answer. Will, bless him, jumped in.

"We've been doing a little digging about your team, about your championship year and—"

"Honey, that was our only year since most of us were seniors, but I'll be damned if we didn't make it a good one, right, Annie?" Nelli said, pushing her fingers through her hair as if they formed a comb. Annie set the tray and box on the counter and handed back a five-dollar bill.

"We did our best." Then she folded her arms across the counter like she was resting from a long day. "We had a lot of fun, mostly because Coach made sure we did."

"And you really were state champions?" The question popped out of my mouth before I had a chance to think, as if the idea still had not registered as a fact in my head, though not more than an hour ago, I'd watched footage of their final game, with a much younger Annie saving a penalty shot. Nelli put a fist on her hip and shifted her weight forward.

"Never lost a game," she said, her face focused. "Not one. To this day I still think of it as the only miracle I've ever been a part of, but hey, it made me a believer."

Annie chuckled at her friend and the two almost rolled into another giggling spell.

Will joined their revelry before proclaiming our mission: "Well, we were wondering why we can't find anything but a yearbook page and a very brief video clip about your team? There's no trophy or plaque or anything in the Hall of Inspiration, you know, at the school, and so maybe we're—"

"Dear child," Nell interrupted. "You're not from around here, are you?"

This was a question I had not considered.

"No, ma'am. Chicago," he answered, adjusting his glasses and charming each of the three women standing around him.

"A city boy? Good Lord, how'd you end up in Claymont Falls?!" Nelli asked with a tone that betrayed her feelings.

"I came to college in Ohio—a proud Oberlin alum, as a matter of fact," he paused for effect. "One of my professors knew about this job, I applied and here I am, seven years later. Does that excuse me?"

"Almost," Nelli winked. "But why the interest in our team?"

Will almost looked offended but bounced back. "Like I said, I'm a soccer fan, but Rey was the one who first told me about your state championship. She got me curious."

Nelli and Annie looked at me, then each other, before Annie checked the clock and reached for her keys. "Well, we had a good team and a great coach. And that was enough for us. Now, sorry but I have to close up shop."

"Tricia Woodring told me it was complicated," I blurted out the name hoping it would buy a few more minutes. Neither woman moved.

"You talked with Tricia about our season?"

"Not yet. But we're meeting on Friday."

Nelli picked up her baked goods and began escorting us to the door, Annie close behind. "Tricia will be a wealth of information, and can speak for all of us."

Will didn't budge. "But we think you deserve recognition," he said, digging his hands into his back pockets and pushing his smile wide across his face. "Really. Why shouldn't you? You won a state championship. Besides, every team who won districts or county has some huge trophy or plaque or whatever in the school."

Nelli turned toward Will as Annie flipped around the OPEN/CLOSED sign on the front door. "You really are charming for thinking so. But that was a long time ago and we've moved on."

Annie nodded and reached for the doorknob, inviting us to make our exit. Instead, Will stood firm. "How about five minutes? I, for one, would just love to know how you remained undefeated in your first season ever, as I'm sure Rey would too, wouldn't you, Rey?"

"Of course I would." I raised my shoulders to look taller like I'd seen Annie do that morning. The two friends looked at each other and shrugged.

Nelli set down her box on a table and for the next few minutes, Will and I leaned near the door listening to stories about their one and only soccer season. Nelli described practicing in the school parking lot and dribbling in between and around cars and bikes before Coach would lead them in a jog to the park down the street where they'd run sprints or scrimmage two on two. At night, they'd go to each other's houses to do homework, watch soccer videos and bake enough chocolate chip cookies to sell in their classes so they could pay for gas to get to their games.

Annie filled in Nelli's points with a few quiet details: the ice she'd bring from the bakery in case someone sprained an ankle, the mothers who helped take in the jerseys so they'd fit and look more like a girl's cut than the old boys' uniforms they actually were. And the games where Coach would mix up the lineup based on whichever school they'd be playing. Everyone played different positions, except her—she was always in the goal.

"We didn't have much experience, but we had heart," she said.

"And we were tougher than nails," Nelli said. "No one was going to take away anything we didn't give them. Besides, Coach was always telling us that losing was not a possibility and for some reason, we believed him."

"It helped, too, that we had some good athletes, like Mandy and Kentucky," Annie added.

"And you!" Nelli slapped the taller woman on the back as if she'd just made another game winning save. "For heaven's sake, Woman, you stopped more shots than a Russian tank!"

"You weren't so bad yourself!".

"Me? I just ran around and got in everyone's way. It was very effective!" Nelli laughed at the memory. Annie did too, and the two started snorting again, recalling plays and goals and games where just about anything, it seemed, could, and did, happen.

"Wait, back up," I interrupted. "I know who Mandy is, Coach's daughter, right? But Kentucky?"

Will looked as puzzled as I did, but then took a stab at guessing the mystery player. "She wouldn't be #10, would she? In the video clip we found of your final game, she made an amazing attack down field after one of your punts."

Annie smiled and looked toward the window as she spoke. "Yup, that was Kentucky. I can't remember now who scored more, her or Mandy, but we could always count on one of them to put it in the net when we needed a goal."

Nelli looked at her watch and picked up her pie. "Those two were as amazing as the whole season," she paused, a far-off look filling her eyes before she returned to our conversation. "Shoot, this was fun, but I have got to get going. Nice meeting you kids. Good luck in your season, Coach."

She waved at her friend, darted out the front and into a black Mercedes that matched her hair and her style. I joined Will at the door as Annie thanked us for coming by and closed it behind us. We stood in front of the bakery awkwardly—

caught in that same kind of feeling you get when you've just seen a great movie and you leave the theatre still absorbed by its story, not quite sure how to return to reality. I glanced at Will's bike locked to a bench, but I was still "seeing" the images and anecdotes of that first team 25 years ago.

"Are you thinking what I'm thinking?" he said to me as he turned the combination of his lock.

"That we have to do something for them?"

He looked up, nodded and put on his helmet. "Exactly. But I'm running out of daylight here, so let's meet again tomorrow, okay? I'll do my homework and maybe you could talk with Hanks."

"Got it." I watched as he rode off, the sky stuck between afternoon twilight and evening darkness, making the shadows on the road bend and sway. The night breeze had settled as well, and downtown Claymont Falls was quiet and sleepy. A few businesses, like Knudsen's, had closed for the day when I pulled to a stop at one of the town's three stoplights. A pick-up truck idled beside me, and I heard a dog bark in the distance. Up ahead was an old station wagon with a bumper sticker on the back window that read, "CFHS Football—Go Lions!"

I sighed and began tapping to the beat on my radio.

By the time I turned into our driveway, the living room window revealed my mother on the couch, her television cooking show on. I planned to follow up on last night's conversation with her. And I would ask her to tell me about the man who somehow convinced a group of teenage girls they could never lose.

chapter
9
1983

"Mrs. Wallace!" Bailey exclaimed when he opened the door.

"You never could get used to calling me Reyola, could you, Bailey Crawford?"

She smiled as she stood gracefully on his front porch, her flower print dress hanging gently to her knees. Gray strands highlighted her hair, framing a face that defied aging. Her smooth brown skin revealed an enviable vibrancy, and apart from those grays and the bifocals dangling from her neck, few would have guessed she was a new grandmother. She reached for him with arms outstretched.

Bailey bent down to hug the elder woman, who then guided his arm over to the chairs on the porch. Bailey obediently sat, still wearing his T-shirt and shorts from practice, his head a bushy mess from the baseball cap he'd worn all day. Reyola just grinned, her lips and teeth wide with joy.

"Can't stay more than a second but, Lord, it's good to see you again," she said.

Bailey's face reddened and he was glad the sun had just set. He looked across at the tiny woman and saw the familiar warmth that Bailey received when he'd begun his career.

As a young father and teacher, Bailey took the first job he'd been offered after graduate school at the town's only public elementary school. For two years, he had filled in where needed, helping with P.E. classes, teaching history units, or shelving books in the library. Mrs. Wallace taught fourth grade there, and she considered herself his unofficial mentor. Bailey had been glad for the guidance. It had grounded him when he transferred to his dream job once a position in the high school history department become available.

"It's good to see you too, Ma'am," he said. "Can I get you some iced tea or something?"

She waved at him and adjusted her dress in the chair. "Thanks. No, like I said, I've only got a second. But I had to stop in and look you in the eye to say to you what I'm about to say."

Bailey smoothed his hair, suddenly feeling like he needed to get cleaned up. He sat upright and tried to look presentable. "Ma'am?"

"I've heard what's happened because, as if you didn't know it, not much goes on in this town without it landing in some grocery aisle or office building or backyard." Her index finger signaled up and down the street, hydrangeas and roses in bloom, cars driving slowly by joggers out for evening runs, neighbors spraying garden hoses on flower beds. Bailey nodded.

"What's happened, Mrs. Wallace?"

"What's happened? Girls are going to be playing soccer on an official high school team for the first time in history! That's what's happened." She folded her arms across her chest and shook her head.

"Oh, that. Well, I wasn't sure either if these girls could do it. It can be a rough contact sport and I know they could get hurt. But I didn't really have a—"

"Of course they can do it, Bailey Crawford. Don't you think for a minute they can't," she said, her arms still resting across her chest. "It's not them I'm worried about."

Bailey cleared his throat. "Ma'am?"

"Change comes slow, real slow, for some folks here. When I first settled in, I wasn't sure either how it'd go. In fact, I wasn't sure at all if I'd get a job at the school, especially with two children just starting school too. The district never had a 'colored' teacher before me, let alone two black kids for pupils, you know, and some folks just weren't sure what to make of it. But it was 1967, the district was short of teachers, and so I got the job. And you know what made the difference?"

"What?"

"The students. They wouldn't have cared if I'd been purple with green polka dots. Children just want somebody to love them and help them and, most of all, believe in them." She pulled a tissue from her handbag and dabbed her eye, then her nose. "But you already know that, Bailey. I saw that in you the first time I watched you helping those fourth graders during recess when we taught together. Organizing that kickball game, making sure every student of mine got to play, no one pushing out anybody else—that's when I said to myself, 'Well, he's a special one. He's going to be in this for the long haul. He's going to make a difference.'"

She paused, but never moved her eyes from Bailey's. "Being the first one at change is not easy. I've been around here awhile now, so folks are used to me.

But you haven't been in it as long, and having girls play at all is going to take some time for some of the knuckleheads to get used to it, especially if—"

"Chicken's ready, Bailey, come and—" Cathy pushed open the screen door and appeared on the front porch. But she stopped mid-sentence when she saw her husband sitting opposite the small black woman, and just as quickly, her face grew wide. "Reyola! What a great surprise!"

Cathy reached into Reyola, the two women's arms tight around the other. "It's been too long. Oh, it's so good to see you!" When she finally let go, Cathy leaned back and announced: "Just in time for dinner. We've got plenty."

Reyola chuckled, her frame swaying slowly with each sound. "Another time. Thank you. I've only got a couple of minutes—you know I've got a gorgeous grandbaby now, and I need to get home so her mama can get to work."

Cathy clapped her hands and nodded. "That's right! I saw the birth announcement in the paper. How is Jocelyn these days?" "Busy. Between the baby and her shifts at the diner, she's working pretty hard. But she's doing a real good job at both," Reyola said, rising to her feet. Bailey followed suit.

"I wouldn't expect anything less. She's a Wallace, after all," Cathy said, patting Reyola's shoulder. "What's the baby's name again?"

A mix of joy and pride swelled through the tiny body of the senior woman and she pushed out her hands to the sides as if she were commanding the entire world to stop and listen: "Reynalda Lynn Wallace. We call her Rey."

"Perfect!" Cathy declared as the three stood between the steps and the screen door. "How old is she now?"

"Born in February. She's a great baby girl," Reyola said. "And she's why I need to get going now, but she's also why I came by. Bailey, you're coaching those girls to be their best, right?"

Bailey towered over his elder in size, but not confidence. "I'm figuring it out as I go but, yes, I'm trying to coach as I always have."

She grinned again. "Exactly. But like I was saying, not everyone's going to be too happy about that. Some are already talking about this as if it's the worst thing to happen in the school since they integrated. So it's not going to be easy."

A neighbor's dog barked. Music from an ice cream truck jingled around the corner as the senior continued: "People can be mean. But you need to keep your eyes off of all the fools and just stick to giving your best and expecting the same from those girls, okay?"

Cathy turned toward her husband, who was taking in the wisdom. "He's already working hard, Reyola. And guess what? Mandy's on the team." Her maternal pride could not be concealed.

"About time she got to put that energy to good use." Then Reyola stared hard at Bailey. "Here's what I want you to know: no matter what happens, they got the right man for the job." She let the encouragement float into the air like a cool breeze on a hot day, and Bailey found himself unexpectedly refreshed. "That's why I've decided Jocelyn and I are going to try to come to every game, so I need your schedule." She held out her hand. "I don't know a thing about soccer, but if it's important to you and to those girls, it's never too late to learn something new, right?"

"Right. But here's the thing, Mrs. Wallace. We've only just finished our first week of practice at the park, and Harry hasn't put together the schedule," he said, remembering their last conversation. "Not yet. I suspect we'll have it in the next couple of weeks, though."

"As soon as you do, give me a call and I'll come by," Reyola said.

"I'll drop it off, Reyola," Cathy offered. "That'll give me an excuse to see you and get a peek at that new baby Wallace!"

Reyola Mae Wallace scooped her handbag on her wrist, waved over her shoulder to the Crawfords and marched to her car with the focused resolve Bailey had always admired. The moon was pushing its way brightly between a few slivers of cloud in the night sky making it seem as if several streetlights had just beamed brighter.

"Thanks for coming by!" Bailey shouted, arm raised in her direction. Had he previously felt even the slightest bit unsure about his new role as the girls soccer coach, he certainly didn't now. He had just been given an abundance of assurance, cloaked in the form of a small black woman who once took on the entire school district and was now a welcoming sanctuary in the eyes of those who mattered most to her: her family and her students. Bailey considered himself lucky to be included in both groups.

Cathy stood on the stairs next to Bailey, her hand on her husband's shoulder, and watched as the older woman drove down the street, past parked cars and trimmed shrubs, until the block was empty except for a teenage boy pedaling towards them on his bicycle. He waved at the Crawfords, who returned the gesture as they stepped inside.

"No question now, is there, Hon, about the season?" Cathy said, passing a plate of drumsticks to Bailey. Her face was soft and eager, contented, it seemed to Bailey, by both their recent visitor and the meal they shared. His wife was his daily support, and Bailey had marveled more than once in their 18 years of marriage at her steadfast ability to see the glass as more than half full.

"And I'll be sitting right there next to Reyola at your games, you know," she said, her elbows out as she leaned over her chicken, beaming like a child who looked forward to their next adventure together. "Can't wait, in fact."

Bailey reflected back her enthusiasm, and they spent the rest of the evening not talking about the upcoming season, but reminiscing on those first few years in the school district when the twins were little and money was even tighter on a new teacher's salary. Reyola Mae Wallace had been one of only a handful of friends who convinced them they could make it. Between her regular doses of encouragement and the deliveries of vegetables from her garden, coupled with Cathy's savvy shopping of the weekly specials at the FoodFair grocery a few blocks away, they learned to make the most of what they had.

The weekend meant yard work and long walks for Bailey and Cathy while B.J. and Mandy spent more time at summer jobs or with their friends than they did at home. Cathy saw it as a way to prepare for the time when their children would head to college in only a year and their house would be quiet again. Bailey, however, was too focused on the present to contemplate his children's departure for college. In fact, he couldn't stop thinking about the challenge he'd taken on for this summer: coaching an entirely new team. Who happened to be girls.

When he pulled into the parking lot for Monday's practice, Bailey told his passengers to duck down and hide. He purposely drove in a few minutes later than usual, sure that Lars would already be out setting up cones in the park, and that Mandy and Tricia would already be stretching and warming up with the girls in blue practice jerseys. He was right.

He honked his horn as he parked and motioned for the players to come over. They jogged quickly toward him, the late afternoon sky beyond them gray with clouds that threatened an early shower. Bailey was always glad when rain cooled off these summer days and made the July heat bearable. He didn't mind getting wet during practices, and his players never did either. He noticed the park's lush maples, the playground empty and parents already taking cover. But he didn't question how his new team would respond if the weather turned.

"Okay, Lions, I have good news and I have bad news for you. Which do you want first?" Bailey said, walking a few steps from his car as twelve 16- and 17-year-old girls gathered in a line across from him. He pulled his baseball cap off and readjusted it.

The team glanced at one another. Lars, too, had come up behind them, shrugging at their unspoken request for help on how to decide between the two options.

"The good news, Coach," Hannah said, sounding somehow more confident than she had been last Friday, Bailey noticed. The others agreed and echoed,

"Yeah, the good news first, Coach."

"Okay, then. The good news it is," he said. "I think we may have found ourselves a goalkeeper after all." Bailey reached behind him and pulled open the backdoor of his car.

A small boy in a blue baseball cap and orange shorts jumped out onto the parking lot like a jack-in-the-box, his ten-year old energy shooting through him, up and down, up and down, as he bounced on the pavement. Then, behind him, the long legs of his sister emerged from the back seat, her Converse sneakers dropping onto the blacktop until the rest of her body straightened, confirming that she stood a full four inches taller than anyone in the group. Every girl jumped beside the boy and hugged him. And cheered. And danced in circles on the parking lot.

"Annie! Wally!" The girls exclaimed to their friends.

"Lions, meet your new goalkeeper and our new ball boy," Bailey said.

The girls broke into a spontaneous chant of "Li-ons! Li-ons!" just as the rain began to fall. Not one of them seemed to notice as their ponytails got drenched; they were too busy chanting and dancing and slapping each other's hands. When the excitement finally subsided and the rain steadied to a consistent rhythm, it was Tricia who remembered the other half of their coach's opening question.

"What's the bad news, Coach?" she asked. The girls stopped suddenly. Wally drew near his big sister Annie, who plopped her elbow onto Mandy's shoulder for support. Their faces grew serious—and wet.

"The bad news? I think it's going to rain today for practice. Who's in?"

The girls cheered again and followed their coach as he jogged back across the park and started practice. Lars and Wally followed, with Lars rearranging the orange cones for each of Bailey's drills, while the newly-appointed ball boy happily chased after balls and returned them to their spots.

The longer the girls ran and kicked and passed, the wetter they became, slipping often across the soggy grass and sliding into one another. Just as quickly as one player would fall, another would help her back up, and so, the drills kept moving. Even as mud splattered across their legs and faces, and girls struggled to see through the steady shower, they pushed their hair out of their faces and kept at it. And when they took practice shots on their new goalkeeper, as she found the ball too slippery to grab with her bare hands, Annie instinctively punched it away with her fist. From tennis shoes and T-shirts, to socks and shorts, every player was soaked through to the skin. They were filthy and bruised, a few sporting skinned knees and knots.

But their enthusiasm, Bailey marveled, never wavered. Not once. And he didn't mind telling them, some two and a half hours later when practice came to an end, how impressed he was with their perseverance and hard work, before sending them on a final lap to cool down.

Still dripping and muddy, but with promises of a bluer sky peeking through the clouds, Bailey and Lars talked as Wally trailed the girls around the park. The need for cleats and shin guards was clear, the coaches agreed, as were goalie gloves for Annie. Lars offered to put in a call to the sporting goods store to request the same team discount the boys' teams received each year, though they didn't know how they'd pay for them no matter the price.

"I'm doubtful," he told Bailey. "They like selling equipment to other teams at a special rate but it can't hurt to call."

Bailey sent Tricia and Mandy to drop off Annie and Wally while he drove instead to the high school on the off chance that Harry Hanks would still be at the football field. He was. He was talking with a few players, quarterbacks probably, as Bailey watched a group of assistant coaches gather equipment and plod through the soggy field to pack it up for the day. Bailey parked in the empty lot near the classroom building and made his way across the field.

Hanks caught Bailey's eye as he approached.

"Looks like you got caught in the rain," Hanks quipped, noticing Bailey's wet and dirty outfit.

"Looks like you did too," Bailey retorted.

"Casualty of the job," he said, pointing to the field.

"Me too."

Hanks laughed. "No one melted, did they? It was raining pretty hard. These guys are used to it, but how'd your team hold up?"

"As I expected."

"Sorry to hear it, Crawford, but I told you it was a ridiculous—"

"I expected they'd do well. And they did. Even in the rain. At the park."

The football coach shrugged and sent off his players to their locker room. "Don't even think about asking for the practice field because it's not going to happen."

"Wouldn't want to impose," Bailey said, lightening the conversation just as the clouds broke and the sky returned to a summer blue.

Hanks was not amused. "What then?"

"We need some basics, cleats, shin guards, and gloves for our goalkeeper."

"And?"

"And?" Bailey puzzled. "Well, a first aid kit would be nice along with—"

"Spent. Sorry, Crawford. The budget's gone, as I told you in June, and not a penny more has dropped from the sky since then. I am sorry, though." The two coaches stood face to face for a chilly moment, though it was at least 85 degrees, and then turned toward the school. Slowly, they began to walk together.

"I understand, Harry. Lars is going to call the sporting store about a team discount."

"Good idea," he said. "I'll call my guy over there and put some pressure on them."

Bailey stopped. "You will?"

"Sure. They'd probably give your girls a discount when they go to buy their shoes."

"But the school's always bought all the equipment for each team and player in the past."

"That's the best I can do, Crawford," he said still walking toward the locker room. "See you next month. Good luck."

Change was not going to be easy, Reyola had told him.

The next morning when the phone rang, Bailey picked it up just as he'd poured his coffee. B.J. was still asleep and the phone ringing didn't seem to bother him. Cathy was already at work and Mandy was baby-sitting the neighbor's seven-year old. A typical summer morning for the Crawfords.

"Mornin' there, Coach. It's Bill Patterson over at the park," his voice was deep and slightly agitated as Bailey held the phone to his ear.

"Morning, Bill," Bailey said, stirring milk into the mug.

"Sorry to bother you this morning but you know the center of the park where your team was practicing yesterday?"

Bailey sipped. "Yes?"

"It's a mess today. Between the rain and all that running around, well, it is a public place, Coach, and we need to re-seed it now."

Bailey yawned. "Are you sure?"

"Course I'm sure. It'll take a while so I'm hoping you have another place lined up for your girls to play in the meantime."

"Another place?"

"How about the school's field?" There was silence on both ends. "Nah, I suppose the football team's already there, right?"

"Right." Bailey poured himself a bowl of cereal. "How about the corner by the playground at the park? Could we practice there?"

"Sorry, Coach. I really am. We just need to keep the park open and beautified for all the residents of Claymont Falls," Bill said. "Haven't let official groups in there for I don't know how long. Families, kids, that sort of thing is fine. But even the little leagues don't practice there in the summer. Except on the baseball field, cuz that's hard to mess up."

Bailey thanked him for the call, hung up and ate his breakfast mulling over the other spaces they could practice. His mind was not quite awake.

114

"Easy," Lars said, once he heard Bailey's explanation over the phone of the problem. "The school parking lot. It's empty in the summer on the side by the classrooms, and the surface will be fast so it'll help the girls learn quicker how to handle the ball."

"And it'll also hurt more if they fall."

"So you just teach them not to fall."

From that point on throughout July and into early August, Tricia, Annie, Mandy and the others drove back to their high school for daily sessions, and practiced dribbling soccer balls in the same place where they parked their cars. Each day, their reflexes got sharper and their reactions quicker, if for nothing else than to protect themselves from slipping on the blacktop and slashing open their knees or elbows. Hannah began bringing a bag of bandages, tape and gauze, and Wally hauled a small cooler of ice he filled each day at the bakery, just in case someone needed a bag for a swollen ankle or just to cool off from the heat.

The sun made the black surface seem hotter than the air temperature, so Bailey organized practices early in the morning or later at night, sometimes even under the street lights on the parking lot so the girls might learn to anticipate which way the ball would bounce with night shadows. The pace of the ball on the paved surface required concentration. Bailey once again was impressed with the discipline and desire his players showed, and he told them so. He was glad they wanted to learn as much as they could, gladder still, he said, each time they helped each other whenever someone got discouraged or sore.

By mid-August and the first week of the new school year, the Lions finally had their first game scheduled. September 4 at 4 p.m. at County Day Academy, a wealthy private school about 40 minutes away with its own girls field. Nine other games also were lined up around the county, though only four would be held at Claymont Falls High, when the boys soccer and football teams were traveling and the marching band wasn't practicing.

Bailey also had his class material and lesson plans lined up around his games as was his custom in years past. He purposely scheduled quizzes or guest speakers on game days so he wouldn't be worn out by the time the games started. Now with the first match of the season only weeks away, and his team still small, he marched down the hall to the gym at lunch hour. A talk with Lars about recruiting new players was in order. It'd be risky, he knew, trying to bring in players after the team had already spent the summer together.

"I don't think you can afford not to," Lars replied. "You need at least 15. Come to think of it, I do have one girl in P.E. I could talk to. She's fast, a real athlete, but very quiet. Keeps to herself. Hmm, Beaucamp's her name."

Bailey looked up at the ceiling, but the name was not familiar. "Don't know her, but sure, see if she'll come," Bailey said. "We could use some more speed."

Bailey nodded at Lars and noticed he seemed tired. Bailey wondered if he should have encouraged his mentor to retire altogether, since the summer sessions seemed to aggravate his health, but Lars had insisted on helping. "As long as these legs still work, I'll be there," he declared, and then added, "if you'll have me."

The older coach's presence had been invaluable, but now Bailey worried aloud both for him and the shortage of players. He was glad to be 13 players strong and blessed with an assistant coach and a ball boy, but he had to admit the team would be in trouble if someone got injured or penalized with a yellow card. True, they had come a long way so far, surprising Bailey each day in fitness and skill but he still wasn't sure they could handle two 40-minute halves with little or no time to rest. With only two substitutes, most of the players would have to play the entire game, a scenario he did not care to imagine.

The bell rang, and Bailey managed to convince Lars to take the afternoon off since they were just going to do fitness training on the track. Lars agreed. Then Bailey stopped by the main office to check his mailbox. As he sorted through district memos, announcements and flyers, he noticed a small dark-haired girl sitting opposite the faculty mailboxes, legs crossed, eyes closed.

He'd had her in class a couple years back, but she was a senior now and he was surprised at how grown up she looked. Maybe it was the thick eyeliner and mascara, or the low-cut top she wore, but Bailey was surprised at how she'd changed.

"Miss Martinelli?" He said, standing in front of her.

One eye popped open, but the tiny frame did not move.

"Hi, Mr. Crawford," she said, as if the greeting was a great effort.

"You okay?"

"Fine."

"Then why are you sitting in the office?"

"I'm in trouble." She closed her eye again. "Story of my life."

Bailey tucked away his mail and sat beside the young woman.

"Well, that's not the girl I knew in sophomore social studies."

She didn't flinch.

"No, that girl was smart, on her toes, always curious and always, I remember, moving." Bailey nudged the girl with his elbow. She shrugged.

"So why are you here?"

"I kind of got kicked out of math this morning. It was boring, and I said so."

Bailey grinned. "But today's only the second day of school. Not a good way to start."

"No kidding. Why do I need math anyway? My mom's gonna kill me." She sighed. "Again."

A chunky man twice Bailey's age suddenly appeared from behind the door and leaned across the office counter. "Gina? I certainly hope this is not how you're planning your senior year," said Principal Van Doren. "Please tell me you are not here already because you got in trouble in a class."

"It wasn't my—"

"We were just having a nice conversation, Paul, and I'm sure Miss Martinelli is planning a stellar senior year." Bailey chimed in, collected his mail and turned toward the hallway. "Come on, Miss Martinelli. Let's get that history assignment clarified. I'm sure she'd be glad to come back and chat later, if you'd like her to."

The principal shrugged and stared down the student.

The black line on Gina's eyelids jetted back and forth from principal to teacher so fast that it should have smudged. Within seconds, she was in the hall behind Bailey, clicking her heels on the tile floor to keep up, smoothing her skirt and primping her hair.

"Mr. Crawford, I'm not in your history class this semester," she said, pulling her blouse up a bit so the cleavage wasn't quite so obvious. "I couldn't fit it in."

Bailey turned the corner, but Gina kept up. "You're not? Too bad for you. I guess you better go back to talk with the principal . . . unless . . . "

"Unless what?"

"Unless, you agree to something that you might think is a little out of the ordinary," he said walking as he talked. "Show up on the track this afternoon for the girls soccer team practice and I'll talk to your math teacher and your mom. You're too smart not to be there, right?"

"Soccer?"

"I'm the coach. Wear your tennis shoes."

"But I don't know anything about soccer. I mean I played tennis a couple of times but I'm not much of a team-kind of girl. "

"Did you have gym class?"

"Yup, with Mr. Lambert."

"Then you know more than you think. Besides, we could really use you."

"Me?"

"You. Really. See you at 3:30 sharp."

"Uh, I'll see if . . . "

"Great. You won't regret it, Miss Martinelli. Now get to class."

Player #14 now accounted for, Bailey taught his American History class, typed up some worksheets on the New Deal, and wrote some key points on the chalkboard. The next classes came and went, and soon he was on his way to practice, hoping the track wasn't too crowded for them to share with the cross-country team. Annie would be late picking up Wally across town at the elementary school but the rest should be there.

On his way to the track, clipboard in hand, Bailey walked by the kids waiting for the school buses. Most came from what area locals referred to as the "country," near the Kentucky border where families who were too poor to rent an apartment in Claymont Falls lived. The parents struggled to find any jobs at all much less afford to drive their kids to school. With deep roots in the Appalachian Mountains, some families were still trapped in the cycle that made this region seem like a third-world country. Bailey mostly knew of it second-hand from his students and colleagues; he had never visited the area but always thought he and Cathy should.

Freddie Smith was on bus patrol that afternoon, directing students to line up for particular buses that were about to pull in at any minute, breaking up couples who were displaying too much public affection for his liking, or stopping teens on the verge of an argument about to turn ugly. But when Freddie saw Bailey, he stopped his directing and bumped his colleague on the arm, pretending it was an accident.

"Oh sorry, Coach Crawford," Freddie said loud enough for the students to hear. A group of longhaired boys wearing jeans and black T-shirts snickered at Bailey, amused by the football coach's antics. Bailey didn't mind the tease, and returned the favor, knocked Freddie with his shoulder.

"Sorry, Coach Smith." The two shook hands, asked about each other's summers and reviewed the prospects for the upcoming Bengals season. The conversation then turned to their respective teams, and Freddie's interest seemed genuine.

"Really, how is it going for the girls?"

"We've got some good players, Fred, and I'm amazed, to be honest. But we could sure use a few more."

Just then a bus pulled up and Bailey noticed a tall girl with stringy brown hair, who had been waiting alone, a beat-up backpack half off her shoulder. She was staring directly at him. He stared back and stepped toward her just as the bus pulled up. And she disappeared as quickly as that day they collided in the hall.

chapter
10

2008

"That man was always full of surprises," Mom said as she leaned back on the couch, her knees slightly bent and resting against the cushion. I'd settled into the old padded chair across from her. Though I was starving for some dinner, I didn't want to interrupt Mom's recollections of my predecessor.

"He was?"

"Absolutely. One minute he's cooking collard greens, the next he's telling a joke, and then he's talking about how to make homemade strawberry jam," she said.

"He made his own strawberry jam?"

"And blueberry. He loved him some blueberry jam, especially to top his homemade vanilla ice cream. He had a killer recipe for that, too, if you have one of those makers. Know his secret?"

"What?"

"Separating the eggs just so."

She pretended to have two eggs in her hands as she carefully poured the yolks back and forth before dumping them in an imaginary bowl on her lap.

"Eggs?"

"Eggs-actly," she said, laughing at her own joke as she "stirred" the ingredients.

This was not helping the hunger pains. I studied my mom, trying to figure out how she had access to so much information. She rambled for a few more moments about his "surprise recipes" until I realized what was happening.

"Wait, Mom. Are you talking about Chef What's-his-name on TV?"

"Who else would I be talking about?" She reached for a glass of water.

"I thought you were talking about Bailey Crawford!"

"I wondered why you were suddenly so interested in cooking!" She let go from her belly a chuckle that wound its way upward and shook her arms and shoulders. Whenever my mother started laughing, she could not stop until it ran its course. All sorts of sounds and snorts would erupt from her nose and mouth until her eyes watered and her breath faltered. I couldn't help but get sucked into the moment until the joy subsided and I was holding my stomach.

When we both finally managed to stop shaking, she plopped her feet on the floor and turned toward me. "Ha, I needed that," she squeaked. "Always good medicine." She gulped the rest of her water as I dashed into the kitchen for some leftovers and back again. "Now, about Coach Crawford . . . "

With a tone in her voice she used only for people she admired—her mother, the minister, Aretha Franklin—my mom shared with me what she knew about Coach Crawford: "His first job in the district was at the school where MaeMa taught, which is how they met. Then the high school history job opened up, along with the coaching position, and MaeMa was sad to see him move on, but real glad for him. She always said he was 'one of the good ones.'"

"Did you meet him?"

"Saw him a lot, but only talked with him a couple of times, that I can remember. There was one time I'll never forget."

"How come?"

"He was walking MaeMa out to our car. I'd barely graduated from high school and had just gotten off of work at the diner. We only had the one car. Anyway, MaeMa introduced him to me, and he smiled real big before he reached out to shake my hand. So proper-like. Know what he said?"

"What?"

"'It's an honor to meet you, Miss, to know another member of the Wallace family.' Shoot, I was all of 20 and a mess, wearing a hair net and a dirty uniform, and he was probably, I don't know, maybe 30, in a tie and jacket, tall with neat, dark hair. And he said it was his honor to meet me. How about that?"

Mom's eyes closed as if she were reliving the scene. I shifted in my chair, suddenly feeling the pull of fatigue from a busy and chaotic week. I took another bite of dinner and rubbed my neck.

"Saved you some pie too, Hon. Help yourself," Mom said. "School starts tomorrow so I think I'm gonna head to bed." She rose from the couch. "You look tired. Everything okay?"

"I think so. It's just there's a lot to learn."

"Nothing you can't handle, Rey. Maybe a good night's sleep will help."

"Maybe it will."

Mom shuffled toward her room, passing the bookshelf filled with plaques and trophies I'd won. She stopped, though, when a question blurted from of my mouth: "Why do you suppose Coach Crawford and his team never got any recognition?"

Slowly, my mother turned back toward me, her face a mix of concern and pride. "Same reason lots of bad things happen and some good things don't."

I listened, waiting. Instead, she just shook her head like there was simply no understanding the existential messiness of human beings.

"But really, Mom. MaeMa never said anything about it?"

She lifted her shoulders and then relaxed, exhaling as she did. "That was the same year you were born, and I had a lot to figure out. Your grandmother was always real supportive of us, as much as she was of them, but I was too busy taking care of you to pay much attention." She paused but her eyes held my gaze.

"Besides, it was a whole new thing. Girls in sports, I mean." She rubbed her eyes. "I'm done for the day, Sugar. 'Night, Baby Girl." She moved again toward her room. "A piece of pie might help."

She was right about the pie. I devoured the first sliver, then a second, while thinking over the events of the last couple days: class introductions, small improvements from my players, the video Will discovered, even the conversation between him, Nelli and Annie at Knudsen's. Now, I added this detail of Bailey Crawford from my own mother's past and I felt like a detective trying to piece together clues for a crime. Because that's what it was beginning to feel like: a crime. Or at least a wrong that needed to be made right.

Not tonight, though. I was too tired. So I dropped into bed and skipped my nightly reading, the novel for the next day's lesson. Tomorrow was the start of another school year, and I was prepared—enough—for two sections of brand-new high school freshmen, about 65 total, plus my other three classes. I was asleep as soon as I turned out the light.

Mom was gone by the time I tied my shoes for my morning run. She'd chopped up some fresh strawberries and bananas and put them in a covered bowl by the toaster with her scribbling on a napkin: "For you—Have a good first day."

Even as I swallowed the last of the fruit, I felt the same bundle of nerves that visited me last year on my first professional day of teaching. It was a familiar combination of emotions that used to motivate me as a player before big games. I knew what I had to do.

I jogged off through the neighborhood, down the street and around by the river before heading back down Main. Parents were waiting with their children at bus stops, and delivery trucks were rumbling by. I ducked down a side street, past the Daily Register building that occupied a corner near the municipal center. Joe's Diner, where Mom had worked when I was little, now sat boarded up across from the gas station.

I'd worked out my route to be about a three-and-a-half-mile run, just enough to push off the jitters and get the focus I needed. I liked that about exercise—whether it was a run through the neighborhood, a workout in the weight room, sprints, a pick-up game or whatever, pushing my body—the sweating, breathing, aching—always seemed to turn my fear or disappointment into something better. No matter what kind of day I was having, a good workout could steer me back in the right direction.

By the time I'd showered and put on a new skirt, top and matching pumps, I was a force no student should mess with. I was armed with Harper Lee and Langston Hughes, ready to tackle metaphors and punctuation with first-day pre-tests, and guide introductory paragraphs with great moments of inspiration. The classroom was my castle and I was ready to rule. Even sleuthing a mysterious coach and championship team was simply another rival to confront, and conquer.

But after a day of being elbowed in and out of conversations in the crowded halls, having my lesson plans cut short, and surviving technology malfunctions, I was more of a rookie than a warrior. And when the final bell of the day rang, I was running in my sweats to the girls soccer field, tired, hungry and only mildly prepared for practice.

Kate and Maggie were already leading their teammates in stretches, which surprised me since I was usually the first one at the field, setting up cones or mini-goals. I looked at my watch to confirm that I wasn't late. As I ran nearer, I could hear them directing the girls to follow them, moving through sit-ups and toe-touches and one-legged stretches by the time I arrived. I blinked. Maybe some ghosts from our school's first winning season had roamed the halls and possessed my players.

I could only hope. Yet somehow, today's traps seemed more consistent, their sprints quicker and their shots on goal slightly more accurate. Maybe it helped, too, that three more new girls had come out for practice—one, a transfer student from a school in our conference who seemed eager to do whatever she could to earn a spot on the team. Tammy told me she hadn't known about pre-season practices; if she had, she'd have been at every session.

Between her enthusiasm and the team's baby steps, I felt the warrior return, a sign that good still existed in the universe. At least today.

"I like the progress you've made today," I told my team while they formed a circle around me on the grass, stretching and guzzling water bottles. "We've got a tough first game coming up but nothing you can't handle, right, Lions?"

"Right, Coach!" Kate and Maggie answered at the same time and seemed to like the sound of their combined voice. They turned to the other girls and began to chant, "Li-ons! Li-ons!" Soon the entire team was on board, clapping and stomping their feet in the center of our field. They did a final lap to cool down, past the football field and boys' soccer players who were also winding down for the day. Around the complex, I watched as teams dispersed and athletic trainers dispensed ice to players with sore muscles, creating packs from the coolers and kits they carried on the back of their golf carts.

It seemed crazy now to think Annie Knudsen had once brought ice from the bakery if someone sprained an ankle. Even during my days as a student here, athletics had employed its own trainers and fitness experts to handle injuries when they happened and to try to prevent them in the future. The times I'd been hurt as a player flashed in my mind. Whether I had a pulled muscle during practice or a bruised shoulder from a collision during a game, the trainers at our school stopped everything to take care of me.

I'd never thought twice about it—until now.

I picked up some chicken and shrimp stir fry and egg rolls for dinner and walked into the living room just after six o'clock. Mom was sweeping the kitchen floor and never looked so happy to see me as she did when she smelled the paper bag I dangled in front of her. The first day of school, as far back as I could remember, for her, MaeMa, and now me as an English teacher, always meant someone else cooked dinner. Tonight it was China Palace.

We moved to our spots in the living room and ate our entire dinner out of the white boxes in front of the nightly news. Mom muted the television sound when the broadcast ended. Then she tossed me a fortune cookie from the couch and unwrapped hers.

"Anything interesting happen today?" she asked while breaking open the cookie to retrieve the little white slip of paper.

"You first."

My mother pushed on her glasses and read her fortune: "'Success will keep you very busy.' Ain't that the truth? I get the manager job and I can hardly keep up." She popped one half of the cookie into her mouth, then the other, and crunched. She pointed to me.

I snapped the cookie apart and pulled the thin white slip: "'Take each opportunity that comes your way.'"

"Good advice all the way around." She began dumping empty boxes back in the China Palace bag. "Speaking of opportunities, how's your team lookin' anyway?"

"So far, so good. Pretty decent practice today—even had a few new players come out, so that'll help."

"Good ones?"

"Not bad. At least they're eager," I said.

Mom headed for the kitchen to put on a pot of decaf. I followed, trash in hand.

"I keep waiting for the day when a young Reynalda walks onto your team," she said. "There's nothing as fun as watching a good goalkeeper . . . like my daughter. That's what makes a game exciting." She was putting away silverware and pulling out the sugar bowl along with two blue "Lions" mugs. I poured cream into one and decided tonight I'd join my mother on the couch as she watched her cooking shows. I could tune them out while I graded quizzes.

Halfway through the second show, she punched the remote and turned off the television. "Reynalda?"

I looked up from my papers.

"Take the opportunity. With your team, yes. But be careful with this Coach Crawford curiosity." Her voice hit a notch of seriousness.

I'd spent almost the whole day thinking more about classroom management than the school's first coach, yet now my mother wanted to talk about him. Her comment took me back to Will, whom, I'd just realized, I'd forgotten to visit today and wondered what he'd discovered about—

"Rey?"

"Huh?"

"Just be careful. I know you—when you get some big question in your head, you don't stop till you find the answer. If you snoop around enough with this, well, I don't want you gettin' hurt or disappointed."

She caught me off guard. "What are you saying?"

"Just that not everyone saw Coach like MaeMa did." She finished her cup of coffee and returned it to the kitchen. She paused as she grabbed her glasses and headed toward her room. "Promise me?"

I had no idea what she was talking about but we'd just celebrated the first day of a new school year and I didn't want to wreck it with an argument. "Promise, whatever that means."

She warned me with a glare before she took her 45 years of hard work, laughter and a couple of regrets, and shuffled slowly down the hall. "Night, baby girl."

"Night."

The pile of quizzes I needed to grade didn't leave me much time to consider my mother's strange request. I decided to sleep on it.

Her words surfaced again the next day as I waited to meet Tricia Woodring

Johnson during my lunch hour. I wasn't sure how I was supposed to be careful; I was merely fascinated by a coach who could take a brand-new sport and produce a team with a 14-0 record and a state championship. I wanted to know if—or how—Will and I could award them the credit and trophies they deserved.

"As I said, it's complicated," Tricia explained, her personality filling the room the same way it had the memorial service. A green silk blouse hung breezily over the top of her slacks and a soft leather briefcase hung from her shoulder like a purse. "Holy cow, this place sure has sure been spruced up since I was here."

"When you were a student?" I asked, pointing her to a chair across from my desk.

"Goodness, no. That building's been converted to a storage unit, last I checked. When I was here three, maybe four, years ago, the mayor was using the gym for his campaign night, and I was covering it. Even since then, they've added onto this building so many times it feels like a maze. Except for the "media center"— that remains the spittin' image of the library back when I was a student. Probably even houses the same books, which is ridiculous, if you ask me."

So Will was not alone in his dismal assessment of the library, I laughed to myself.

"Well then," she said, pulling from her briefcase a reporter's notebook and a ballpoint pen she clicked with her thumb. I must have looked surprised by both since she commented, "Force of habit. Just in case. Now how long have you been here again?"

"I'm starting my second year as part of the English department and as girls soccer coach."

She scribbled a two. "Straight out of college, eh? And you're a graduate, right, of Claymont Falls High?"

"Class of 2002," I responded. She kept scribbling.

"What, you're about 23, 24?"

"25. Born in 1983 at the county hospital."

"Ah, our year. And a local girl. Hmm," she said. She leaned over her notebook, her hair falling forward as she did. I fidgeted in my chair. I hadn't been expecting this kind of an interview, so I tried to redirect the conversation.

"I'm curious as to how Coach Crawford did it that first—"

"Hold on. Something just occurred to me. Your last name is Wallace, right? You're not one of the Wallace Women, are you?"

"Yes, Ma'am, I am."

"Well, why didn't you say so? That makes a big difference," she said, resting her notebook on her lap and shaking her head like she'd just uncovered a great scoop, before her face turned somber. "I'm so sorry about your grandmother's passing. She was a strong and wonderful woman."

The comment came at me like a shot on goal I'd not seen coming. I froze, then bristled, before a sudden sting filled my eyes. Tricia Johnson set down her pen and patted my arm. Then she rose from her chair, whirled across to my desk, grabbed a tissue from the box and returned with equal speed. I took it and nodded.

"Okay, let's move on. Coach Crawford was the best coach we could have gotten, you know, to start the program—and let me just say I'm thrilled to bits that you're coaching here now to help these girls. The last few years haven't been so hot. Any-who, Coach spent eight years with the boys so he knew his stuff. And you know what? He coached us exactly the same way."

I turned my emotions back to the reason for Tricia's visit and pulled myself together, scrunching the tissue in my fist.

"But 14-0 in your first season? What was his secret?"

"Plain and simple, Doll. He cared. He respected us as human beings first, then as athletes. That's it." She paused to let it sink in, in case I thought super strategies or extraordinary talent defined a winning season rather than this simple factor. "He taught me how to play—which now I think was an act of God—and I wasn't terrible. Then Mandy, well, she was always a natural. In fact, all the girls were pretty good, Nelli, Hannah, Annie and the others, but we hit our stride when he brought Kentucky."

"Kentucky?"

"Leading scorer, #10. Between Kentucky and Mandy, nothing could go wrong. Even if we were behind in a game, which happened every now and then, that pair always managed to turn things around. Those two and Annie in the goal," she said, brushing her hair from her face. "Yup, we were a pretty good underdog team, if I do say so myself. It was a lot of fun."

"State champs isn't just pretty good," I exclaimed. "That's the ultimate."

"Things were different then. True, other parts of the state had had a few girls teams for a couple of years, but it wasn't the same game as it is now," Tricia said. I was surprised to hear she still followed the sport.

"But without all of you, the game wouldn't have become what it is now, right?"

And for the first time, Tricia looked as if she really did not know what to say next. Her cheeks reddened slightly and she flicked her pen on and off again. I sat up straight and continued.

"You were the best soccer team this school's ever had, yet there's no trophy anywhere to tell people. Not a single thing in the Hall of Inspiration—or anywhere else for that matter—to celebrate what you did."

"That's the complicated part," she said, pulling a bottle of water from her bag. "See, that was the same year the football team qualified for state finals as well. The whole town had a parade for them the day of the game, and the Booster Club bought them jackets and sponsored an assembly that brought everybody and their uncle to the field. Problem was, their championship game was the night before ours. They played Friday night at the Cincinnati stadium and we played Saturday at noon in Columbus."

I leaned forward. "So?"

"So? God bless that mama and grandmama of yours, Honey!" A sudden spurt of laughter escaped the sides of her mouth. "Between them and the Crawfords, they made us believe the entire universe backed us the minute we walked onto the field. We felt extra lucky when our own moms came to the championship game. Usually they were about the only ones who showed up anyway."

"But—"

"That's how it was. The Booster Club was not about to let some silly girls soccer team steal the thunder of their boys. Champions or not, we just weren't important enough."

I looked around the room, at the posters and desks of my classroom, then out the window until Will's talk of trophies dropped back into my head and an idea popped out of my mouth: "What if my team got your team trophies? We could do some fundraisers to pay for them and present them to your whole team at halftime during one of our games this season."

"Like a little reunion? That'd be fun," she said. "I mean, you saw us at Coach's service. Most of us are still in town or at least close by—you know the feeling. You form a bond with those players, and the friendships don't end just because the season does."

I stared at her blankly. It was another unexpected shot. Goalkeepers were generally their own best company and though I never would have admitted it to her—or anyone else—I hadn't scored much in the socializing category. Friends and boyfriends were what other women had. I deflected again.

"You deserve to be recognized. We were thinking that each of you should get your own trophy and then, one big team trophy in the display case for the whole school to see, maybe even a sign as you come into town that says, 'Home of the 1983 Girls State Soccer Champions.' That'd be cool," I clapped.

"That'd be nothing short of an act of God," Tricia said. "But, hell. Why not? You're right. Why shouldn't all of us get together and show your girls what they can do with enough enthusiasm and heart? That they've got championships in their blood?!"

She was on her feet now, her notebook and pen balanced in her left hand, her right hand plopped on her hip. I rose, too, looking a few inches down into her face.

"But listen, Honey," she said, dropping her tools into her briefcase. "No offense, but what in the world am I—or any of us girls—going to do with a trophy? Those things just collect dust and then you put them in a box in the garage. The team trophy might be nice, I suppose, for the school." She paused. "Besides, isn't all the rage these days to get championship rings? That's what I want, a ring!"

She spread out the fingers of her right hand and admired the imaginary ring. "Yes, indeed a ring will be much more interesting. Tell you what. I'll see what I can do about that sign and about rounding up the girls, though I already know it'll be tricky tracking down Kentucky. She moved away after graduation, and I've hardly heard from her since."

"Does 'Kentucky' have a real name?"

"Of course she does. Adeline Beaucamp. But we called her 'Kentucky' because that's where she was from, or near enough. But we'll figure it out. I'll even write up something for the paper. Now you see about those rings and scheduling our ceremony at one of your games. Be sure to pick the most exciting game because I know we'll all want to come and scream and holler for your team. Make the most of it, you know? Deal?"

"Deal!"

Tricia pulled out her business card, handed it to me and looked at her watch. "Now, I have to swing by to see that pathetic athletic director of yours—you did not just hear me say that—and ask him about the new stadium bond his Boosters are trying to get on the ballot for the spring. Wish me luck!"

"Good luck," I shouted as Tricia disappeared out the door, hollering over her shoulder, "Great to meet you, Coach Wallace. Call you soon!"

I had only five minutes left before my next class, not enough time to hurry to the library to tell Will what had just happened. So news of Tricia's visit and our plans for an awards ceremony—minus the individual trophies—would have to wait until the small window of time between the end of my last class and the start of practice.

It seemed a legitimate reason to look forward to seeing Will.

chapter
11

1983

Mandy pulled another cookie sheet from the oven with what could have doubled as a baseball mitt, twirled around her mother like a dancer and tossed the tray onto the kitchen table with the finesse of a quarterback. Every inch of her 5'10" frame was pure muscle, and her every move reminded Bailey of a cross between strong and solid, yet graceful and agile. If they'd been able to find—and then afford—tennis or figure skating lessons for their daughter, Bailey and Cathy Crawford had no doubt Mandy could have made her own name in either sport.

For now, Bailey had to admit he was happy simply watching her hover over her chocolate chip concoctions, pointing at each and counting silently, because to her, they were not just cookies. She hadn't stopped baking since they got home from practice passing and dribbling on the dirt track.

"That makes 108, Dad. If I sell them one quarter apiece, I'll almost have enough money for my cleats," she said, slapping Bailey's hand as he reached for one.

"What if they're terrible? Your brother's not here to taste-test them," he said, reaching for a sample. "And someone should."

"Don't you dare!" Spatula in hand, Cathy stood guard over nine dozen cooling cookies. "This girl's worked hard on these and she's going to need all the help she can get at the bake sale tomorrow."

"If her cookies are as good as her game, she won't have any problem."

Bailey paid her the compliment as he leaned back in his chair, sounding and looking like the coach he was, still dressed, in fact, in white tube socks, blue polyester-knit shorts and a white Lions golf shirt.

"Thanks, Dad." His daughter bounced from stove to sink and back to the table. "I guess it wouldn't hurt to share a little."

Mandy set down a bowl once filled with cookie dough beneath Bailey. Together, they ran their fingers across the bottom again and again, licking what was left of the batter until only the shiny silver of the bowl remained.

"So between babysitting and the cookie sale, I should have enough for a new pair, right?"

"Think so. Let's hope the other girls bake like this!"

He poured himself a cup of coffee and thought back to the rainy afternoon practices held at the park—and the recreation department's concern with the wear and tear there. Now, with just two weeks before the program's inaugural game, he knew that, whether on the grassy football field at Claymont Falls or the turf at County Day Academy, his players would need the stability of cleats. Plain and simple. He wasn't sure if they'd get used to them in time for that first kick-off. Shin guards would be nice, too, but if they didn't get them, the girls could just pull up their socks to their knees, maybe even tuck a piece of foam inside, and play so they didn't get kicked.

Some had already mastered the skill of sidestepping incoming whacks, so Bailey was hoping for only a few bruises and knots this season. They actually were beginning to look like a team. Their hand-me-down jerseys and shorts still needed to be taken in but Cathy and a few other mothers had agreed to help. So far, Bailey believed the newest team at the school was making the most progress.

The front door slammed just after Mandy's last batch of cookies came out of the oven. Bailey heard a thump against the wall—like a duffle bag being slung— and another door slam. Cathy pointed Bailey in the direction of their son's room. This was his turn.

"B.J.?" Bailey leaned against the door, knocking softly near the knob.

"What?"

"Can I come in?"

Slowly, the door opened and father and son faced one another. Both were wearing soccer clothes, their hair curly and wild, though B.J.'s was thicker, and their eyes met inches from the other. They were the same height, but Bailey had added to his lanky frame thanks to the passing of years and Cathy's cooking.

"What's up?"

"What's up? You should know!" The younger sulked back onto his bed and stared at the ceiling. Bailey sighed, pulled a chair around from B.J.'s desk and closed the door.

"Okay. But help me. I don't want to assume."

The silence grew heavy. B.J. folded his arms across his head and Bailey waited. He'd learned long ago to give his son time to think through what he wanted to say. Unlike his sister the extrovert, B.J. couldn't always find language for his emotions. He was either all-in, bouncing through the moment with confidence, or withdrawn and unsure whether his words could deliver the same message as a slammed door or flung bag. Bailey never stopped marveling how children from the same parents—twins, at that—could be so different.

A slight whistle escaped B.J.'s nose. He ran his hand back and forth across his head, a sign, his father intuited, that a sentence was forming. Bailey leaned in, noticing the stubble on his son's face. He stared, and waited.

"It's just so different from last year, Dad. Coach is making us watch videos on weird stuff like visualization and simulation, not even soccer games, and the guys aren't listening or working like they did when you and Mr. Lambert coached us. Some are even skipping practice, figuring Coach will play them anyway. And some of them keep on . . ." B.J.'s throat tightened.

Bailey sighed.

"Some of the guys, you know, never let up about you coaching girls. Every single day, during sprints or Coach's 'visualizing sessions' or laps, they make some crack. I try to ignore them, but today in the parking lot after practice they just kept at it, calling you . . . all sorts of stuff and I wanted to punch them."

"But you didn't?"

"Dan pushed me into his car and told me to forget them."

Bailey pulled back his shoulders and glanced around the bedroom. A few of B.J.'s ribbons and trophies from little league still filled the top of his bookshelf, just above his most recent collections of science fiction novels and French philosophers. A framed photo of last year's soccer team—a gift from Bailey and Lars to each player—sat prominently on his desk beside Webster's, a sketch pad and a calculus text. Though he'd be in college a year from now, Bailey's son was a teenager, full of contrasts and questions.

"Dan got it right. It's not going to be easy, we all know that," Bailey said. "But, son, there's a lot more to all of this than just soccer. In fact, that's only one part of it."

"What do you mean?"

"Your sister and her teammates are getting a chance to do something that you and the guys have been able to do your whole lives." Bailey cleared his throat and looked square at his son. "And I'll tell you, man to man, I've had to admit to myself that that matters far more than what people say about us. B.J., if you could have seen Mandy's face at practice when she dribbled in and out of her teammates, you'd know how important this is for her and for her friends."

"Yeah but—"

"And they might even have a shot at winning a game or two. No kidding.

They're pretty good," Bailey spoke softly. "But don't tell your sister I said that. It'll go to her head, you know, and—"

"And that would not be good!" B.J. sat up suddenly, slyly smirking. "Did Mom save me any dinner? I'm starving."

"We could probably do something about that."

"It's training season. Gotta fill up."

Bailey marveled at the power hunger could have at rearranging a teen's emotions in an instant, and watched his son pounce toward the kitchen.

"But keep away from the cookies. They're for the bake sale tomorrow!" He yelled to B.J., who was quickly browsing through the refrigerator and mumbling something to his mother. Bailey laughed when he overheard his wife, "Where they always are. In the cheese drawer!" Life in the Crawford household was back to normal.

Whatever "normal" was.

Gina Martinelli was waiting in Bailey's classroom when he arrived at school the next morning. He'd set down his coffee and briefcase, pulled some papers out and stacked them on his desk before he noticed the small black-haired girl alone in the back row. The first class of the day wouldn't begin for another 35 minutes, so Bailey was surprised to find any student at school so early. Especially Gina. She sat up straight, her face serious, crossed legs swinging to a nervous rhythm. At least she was wearing slacks today, Bailey noted, and a baggy button-up blouse, rather than a tight-fitting low-cut top.

"Miss Martinelli, good morning. You're in early today."

Her legs' rhythm increased. "My pop dropped me off on his way to the warehouse, so I figured, why not stop by and—"

"Give me an explanation?" Bailey sipped his coffee while he grabbed some chalk and began writing "Today in History" on the board.

"Yeah, so here's the thing, Mr. Crawford. I won't lie. I thought about coming to practice yesterday, but everybody knows those girls don't like me. I'm not really one of, you know, one of . . . "

Bailey turned around. "One of what?"

"Them. I'm not like those girls. Everyone knows that."

"They do?"

"Probably. So I wouldn't fit in. That's all. So I guess I'll take my chances with Mr. Van Doren." She rose from her desk, adjusting her hair and cracking her gum.

"I suppose that's your decision, Miss Martinelli. But how will you ever know if you fit in somewhere if you don't at least try?" Bailey set down his chalk. "The way I see it you can keep doing what you're doing and get a permanent seat in the principal's office—which wouldn't make anyone very happy—or you can come to practice today and see what happens."

The smacking stopped.

"Besides, I could really use a player like you."

She looked at Bailey and, for the first time since he met her in her freshman year, he saw the honest face of a young girl, rather than the wannabe adult underneath the caked-on layers of eyeliner, blush and lipstick.

"Like me?"

"Yes. We could use you."

"Why?"

"You've got spunk."

"I do?"

"You do. Of course, you might have to work harder than you ever have before, but as far as I know, no one's ever died from hard work."

A tiny flicker of hope spread across Gina's face, but just as quickly the gum cracking returned.

"What would I need to do?"

"Run. Sprint. Kick, that sort of thing."

"Well, I am pretty fast. At least I used to be in gym class. And I work out all the time at the gym with my boyfriend."

"That's a start. There will be a lot of hard exercises and drills, and your legs and arms probably will be sore—initially."

She shrugged. Sore muscles were the least of her worries.

"So, Miss Martinelli?"

"So, I guess I could try. Beats Van Doren's office."

"It certainly does. Three o'clock sharp. On the track." Bailey turned back to "Today in History" and heard the door shut. He wasn't sure but he thought he might have heard a gentle whistle as she left.

Three classes later, Bailey wandered toward the teacher's lounge to refill his coffee. On his way, he'd hoped to find Lars in his office but instead discovered a substitute filling in for him. Surprisingly, Lars had called in sick. Since the two met, Bailey could count on one hand the number of times Lars was not at work: whether a grandchild's birth or his anniversary, a day off was usually family-related time away for the Coach.

But Bailey decided to call just in case. When he picked up the phone in the teacher's lounge, he noticed one of the science teachers looking his way. The balding teacher whispered something to a basketball coach sitting at the table with him—the guy whose name never seemed to stay in Bailey's memory—and the two broke out in laughter. One flicked his elbow, then his fingers and struck a mockingly feminine pose, as if he were a girl worried about her nails.

Bailey yawned and dialed the number. Lars answered.

"These knees are just tired today," he told Bailey. "Thought I'd give them a little rest. Not sure I'll make it today but I'll try. I'll be there for sure tomorrow."

"Take it easy, Lars," Bailey said. "Wanted you to know, though, I think we have another player coming."

"Ah. Good." Lars gave him some history on Gina's athleticism according to past gym classes and seemed satisfied with the new recruit.

By the time Bailey hung up, the teacher's lounge was empty. He poured his coffee and almost collided with Donna Sanchez, who, though she'd been at the high school five years, was the newest teacher in his department.

"There you are. Got a minute?" she asked.

"Need to prep a bit for the afternoon, but sure. Want to walk with me?"

The two history teachers turned toward the hall and Donna began to talk about a few of her students from the country, the area near the Kentucky border. One girl in particular was struggling, not with the material—she was smarter than most of her classmates—but she couldn't seem to get to class on a regular basis.

"I know you're starting this new girls team, Bailey, so maybe that could help."

"How is being part of the soccer team going to ensure this student comes to class?"

"Well, there's no guarantee, but it might give her something more to look forward to. She's here today."

Before Bailey knew it, he was standing opposite a girl with stringy, shoulder-length hair whose worn green pants and faded striped T-shirt looked like they had once belonged to someone else. Her eyes were wide and stark like her bangs, and her nose long and thin like the rest of her body. She was as tall as Bailey, but he did not mind one bit.

"Adeline Beaucamp, isn't it? I ran into you once in the hall, right?" He looked at Donna. "Just about knocked this young lady down, but she caught herself and sprang back up. I wasn't so lucky, clumsy oaf." He turned toward the student. "You ran like lightning down the hall. Then I saw you at the bus stop a few days ago and poof, you were gone again. That was you, wasn't it?"

"Yes, sir." Adeline tucked her hands into her pockets like she didn't know what else to do with them and fixed her eyes on Bailey.

"So, Miss Beaucamp, I could really use another player on the new girls soccer team and Mrs. Sanchez thinks you might be interested."

Her eyes stayed focused.

"Have you ever played before?" Bailey asked. It seemed a question she could answer.

"Yes, sir. A little. In Mr. Lambert's P.E. class and at home with some of my brothers and cousins."

"Do you enjoy playing?"

She looked harder at Bailey and he saw something he instantly recognized. She nodded.

"Well, then, how could I persuade you to join us?"

"Can't."

"Why not?"

"Gotta catch the bus."

"What if you didn't have to catch the bus?"

"Sir?"

Bailey and Donna exchanged glances. "What if we arranged another way for you to get home after school? Think your parents would give you permission to play?"

"It's only my mama and she probably won't like it."

"How about we ask her together?"

She shrugged. "I guess."

He drew his last sip of coffee from his cup to emphasize his point. "I'll be honest. I need another player who is fast. And smart. Miss Beaucamp, think you could join us today at practice if I took you home after?"

"Really? I suppose that'd be okay."

Bailey stepped toward his classroom. "Don't worry. We'll make sure your mother knows. Right, Mrs. Sanchez?"

"Right. I'll call her now." She turned toward the teacher's lounge leaving Bailey and Adeline in the hall.

"We start at 3 sharp—on the track."

The girl's eyes still locked with Bailey's. "Something else, Miss Beaucamp?"

"I don't have the right shoes."

"Don't worry. No one else does either. See you later."

He waved over his head as he passed the hall lockers to his classroom. Bailey had about fifteen minutes left to review his lecture on the context surrounding FDR's New Deal, and another on the abolitionist movement. He pulled last year's notes and worksheets from his file when he got back. He felt as ready as he could be when the bell rang and his juniors strolled into class.

The lectures and discussions were lively, scattered and quick. So much so that

Bailey was surprised to see Lars hobbling toward him at 2:50, a bag over his shoulder, just as the last bus was pulling out of the parking lot under a warm autumn sky. Bailey couldn't miss his bright red cap and wobbly gait in the midst of the students and teachers coming and going.

"Lars, you should be home."

"I know. I should be. But I didn't want to miss the new girl," Lars spoke quietly, a weariness in his voice that he did not try to hide. "You okay?"

"Me? Well, I made it through the New Deal, and a few political crises. Oh, and we found another new player," Bailey said. He took the bag from Lars' shoulder, tossed it over his own, and slowed his pace.

"Besides Gina?"

Bailey nodded. "Adeline Beaucamp is coming."

Lars stopped walking. "Kentucky? Good, good."

"Hope so. I mean I hope they both come. If they do, we'll be in better shape, I think."

Bailey looked back at Lars. He had watched his friend's health deteriorate since he'd known him; once able to lead sprints and passing drills himself as well as long distance runs, Lars had been the model of a coach. Fit and smart. Kind, but demanding. Now the years and practices had taken their toll. Bailey understood why Lars had wanted to step down.

By the time they were almost at the track, they saw Mandy, Tricia, Annie, Wally and the others stretching and joking together near the broad jump pit. A short girl with jet-black hair was sitting on a bench opposite the pit, examining her fingers and smacking her gum. Her legs were crossed and her bright red sneaker bounced up and down. Another girl towered over her a few feet away, swaying slightly as she stared at the team. She wore green sweat pants, a faded striped T-shirt and high tops. Both girls forced a half smile when they saw the two coaches approach them.

"Miss Martinelli, Miss Beaucamp, glad to have you both here." Bailey meant it. "You know Coach Lambert, from P.E.?"

He pointed to Lars. Gina rose from the bench—her T-shirt as tight as her shorts—the top of her head only reaching Adeline's shoulder, a chimp beside a giraffe. She nodded and smacked. Lars grinned.

"Welcome, yes. Kentucky, very good you are here. You, too, Gina. Come, join the others," Lars said, reaching his arm behind them and guiding them to the team who expanded the circle to give them a spot. Bailey looked around the track—it was busy with cross country runners, football players, and junior varsity soccer boys all crammed in various corners of the field. He noticed Hanks

136

with half a dozen coaches gathered in front of offensive linemen and defensive backs. They were learning to block.

"Sorry, Coach Crawford, but we need the entire track today." Bailey looked toward the voice of the boys' cross-country coach, a young man with a blonde crew cut whose skinny arms and legs were constantly moving.

"You don't think we can share again?" Bailey looked at the track where fewer than 10 boys, smaller versions of their coach, were jogging and stretching.

"Afraid not." He turned toward the boys, ignoring Bailey and the girls. Lars had heard the conversation and quickly pointed to an empty portion of the parking lot.

"Okay, Lions, change of plans," Bailey said, hands on hips and feet apart. "We've got a new spot to practice today."

"We do?"

"Goes with the game. It's always moving so we will too," he smiled. "And by the way, how'd the bake sale go?"

"Think we're almost there, Coach," Mandy beamed. The girls congratulated each other, elbowing and shaking each other's hands on their accomplishment.

"Good work," Bailey said, calling them back together. "Oh, and let's hear it for our newest players: Gina and Adeline."

"Nelli."

"Kentucky."

"Like I said, let's hear it for Nelli and Kentucky!"

He and Lars clapped, and the other girls joined the applause. Then Bailey directed his players to gather the few balls they had as well as their school backpacks. Wally picked up his cooler of ice and Hannah grabbed her shoebox of tissues, tape and bandages. Dodging in and out of runners and coaches, hurrying past a few whistles and taunts, the team scrambled off of the football field and track to the far end of the school parking lot, near a grassy island of streetlights and shrubs, far from the few parked cars still in the teachers' spots.

They started with 50-yard sprints between parking spaces. Two by two the girls raced, from Lars to Bailey, as he captured their times on his watch before they jogged back to Lars. His two new players were faster than he—or they themselves—had expected.

Bailey knew since he first saw her that Kentucky was born fast. She had the lean physique of a sprinter and the reflexes to match. Each corner of her arms and legs was naturally sculpted as if she'd been lifting weights all her life. And Bailey wondered if perhaps, in some ways, she had.

Nelli was equally quick, but in a scrappy way. Her elbows flung to the sides as she ran, her head bobbed back and forth as if she couldn't quite find the right rhythm. There was a toughness to her running style, not as natural as Kentucky's, but every bit as determined. Bailey smiled at the instant impact the contributions of his new recruits brought. Without even knowing what they were doing, both girls were already pushing the others merely to keep up.

The team worked next on one-touch passes where each girl was allowed only one tap of the ball in the direction of the next player before moving to the back of the line. The ball zipped across the blacktop, making the passes tougher to maneuver. Each time, though, Nelli and Kentucky concentrated harder, it seemed to Bailey, forcing the others to move faster to their next spot.

They jumped sideways for agility drills, leapt back and forth over balls for speed and height skills and hurled throw-ins to one another before Bailey brought them in for a drink and a huddle.

"Wally, could you get each girl a piece of ice to chew on?" The young boy hopped from one player to the next with his cooler. "You're making good progress, Lions, each of you. How does it feel?"

"Hot." Sweat smeared Nelli's mascara and eyeliner so she had black smudges beneath her eyes. Bailey laughed and tossed her a towel. She dabbed it against her face and continued: "Seriously, do you guys work like this everyday? Cuz I'm gonna lose a ton of weight if you do, not to mention get muscles bigger than my boyfriend's. I mean, I work out at the gym and stuff, but wow. This is for real."

Silence fell over the girls like a raincloud on an otherwise sunny day. They turned toward their new team member and tried to make sense of her ramble. Hannah rearranged her ponytail. Someone coughed. Bailey waited, shifting to his other leg. And then Tricia nodded at Nelli, shrugged and slapped the new girl on the back so hard she jumped forward.

"Welcome to our world, Nelli! I'm already down three pounds. Cool, huh? And at least you have a boyfriend!" The girls fell out laughing, snorted and just about howled in the parking lot. One tossed a ball at Nelli, another put ice down the back of her shirt, sending her into dance moves that egged the others on. Each gesture became an unofficial part of Nelli's inauguration to the team.

Even Kentucky laughed, Bailey saw. At least, her shoulders shook a little and her eyes widened just so. She pushed the hair out of her face and reached for another piece of ice, the corners of her mouth curling slightly.

When the fun died down, the coach stepped in. "Okay! Now, let's keep up this enthusiasm and hard work, Lions. We've only got a few weeks before we meet County Day Academy and—"

"County Day?! They're rich. And aren't they about the best in everything? Are we really playing them?" Nelli yelped, wiping her nose, cracking her gum and looking hard at the coach.

Bailey thought for a second. He took off his cap, brushed through his hair and replaced the cap, yanking the bill. He smiled at Nelli, then the others, one by one.

"No matter what anyone else says, or does, we'll be ready. Besides, you don't have to be the best to do your best."

He paused for the words to sink in before delivering the line again, this time almost whispering: "No matter what anyone else says, or does, we'll be ready. You don't have to be the best to do your best."

They leaned in to hear him. Mandy hung her arms around Tricia and Annie's shoulders.

Lars nodded. "Coach is right. You'll be ready. Your best will be enough."
Nelli stood up as tall as she could and raised her voice to match. "Well, okay, then. What's next?"

They spent the rest of practice that day in the parking lot shooting on Annie in a makeshift goal by the light post. Nelli scrambled her way through each drill, Tricia and Mandy and the others hustled and pushed with each new task. Wally chased balls, Lars clapped with each effort, and Kentucky hammered the ball so hard that Annie struggled to punch it away from the goal.

The sun was setting now and, with only a few scraped knees, Bailey sent the girls home. As the players wandered toward their cars, Kentucky stood back, re-tying her high tops.

"Maybe we can have that talk with your mom when I drop you off?" Bailey said, tying his shoe alongside his newest player.

"Nah, that's okay."

"I don't mind. She should know you're going to make a big difference on our team this season, Miss Beaucamp," Bailey rose. He spoke gently, his voice deep and gracious, so that when she finished with her laces, Kentucky looked surprised.

"No."

"Yes, you are. You're fast and strong and you know what to do with the ball instinctively, so I'm sure you'll—"

"I mean, no, she doesn't need you to talk with her."

Bailey waved to Lars, who had offered to drop off Annie and Wally on his way home. All the other players by now had crammed into Tricia's station wagon and Hannah's car. By the time Kentucky climbed into the front seat of Bailey's car, their practice area looked again like an empty parking lot.

As Bailey drove toward the country, down Main and just outside of Claymont

Falls city limits, neither coach nor player said much of anything. He tossed out a question about her classes and another about her family, but Kentucky didn't offer more than one-word answers. Only when they came to an intersection of three country roads with a truck stop and a tiny motel beside it did she speak up.

"You can pull in up ahead at the truck stop," Kentucky said softly. "I can walk from there."

"You sure?"

"Yes, sir."

"I don't mind taking you home all the way, you know." "No, sir. I can walk. It's not far . . . here."

Bailey stopped the car down between the State Line Truck Stop and the Star Wind Motel. Kentucky picked up her backpack, unlocked the door and reached for the handle. She stared at the gas pump and mumbled, "Okay. Uh, see ya tomorrow."

"Yes, Miss Beaucamp, see you tomorrow. And really good job today."

The girl her teammates called Kentucky stood motionless near a dirt road behind the truck stop until Bailey drove off. He kept sight of her in his rear view mirror as he turned back toward town, worried about whatever it was she was going home to, but aware that teachers could only do so much for a student. There had been other students or players like Kentucky he'd worried about, but they'd rarely seemed as . . . tough.

At least, that's how he described her to Cathy that night as they got ready for bed.

"She's got more natural talent than any kid I've ever coached," Bailey said, pulling back the sheets, "and more strikes against her as well. She's from the country, struggling just to get to and from school every day, probably from a poor family, and—"

"And a girl!" Cathy couldn't help herself. "Let's not forget that fact."

"Meaning?"

She pulled the covers up and turned off the lamp. "Meaning, if she'd been on your boys team, you'd already be looking for a scholarship, something that would give her an opportunity to get away, to start over, to develop her skills and get an education, which would help change things for her. That's what you'd be doing if she were a he. That's how you've always helped your boys teams."

The truth had been exposed in the darkness of the bedroom, and, although he didn't answer, Bailey realized his wife's challenge was a prod he could not ignore. If this girl was going to be as good as he expected, and if she were as tough as he suspected, he'd need to get started soon. Cathy's breathing quickened, but that wasn't what kept Bailey awake that night.

He made a list in his head of the calls he could make.

After two more weeks of parking-lot practices, the team gathered up their hand-me-down jerseys, packed their brand-new cleats purchased with the proceeds from three more bake sales, and piled into a half dozen personal cars. Since Hanks hadn't reserved a bus for them because there were too many "scheduling conflicts" with the other teams, it took them 40 minutes to drive to County Day Academy for their first game. They parked outside the stadium and wandered in looking like a group of tourists who'd never been outside of their town before.

Bailey was nervous, but he tried not to show it when he shook hands with the Academy's three coaches, ignoring their smirks as he agreed to pay half of the referee fees. Hanks hadn't told him about that either. He directed the girls to warm up on the turf, and tried not to worry when he saw them gawking at the size of their opponents in their stylish, new, and freshly-laundered uniforms.

He'd talked over his lineup with Lars on the way to the game: Kentucky would start as the striker on the front line, with Mandy on the wing, Annie in the goal, Nelli and Tricia the leaders in the midfield, and Hannah as the center back, with other players on the outsides. That left the Lions with three substitutes. Lars thought it would work, but Bailey was anxious, especially when he looked across the field and saw two-dozen girls on County Day's squad. He paced the sideline, called in the girls as the clock wound down, and simply reminded them to "give your best and have as much fun as you had in practice."

Then he sent them onto the field, a father sending his offspring out into the big, wide world.

The whistle blew, and Kentucky quickly intercepted the ball. She pushed it out to Mandy who had a breakaway down the sideline before a defender kicked it out of bounds. The pace continued back and forth, but the County Day Eagles were caught off guard. With 13 minutes remaining before halftime, Tricia booted the ball up from the middle of the field. Kentucky tracked it down like a hunter stalking her prey and pounded it off toward the goal.

The goalkeeper never saw it coming.

Halftime found the Lions up 1-0. Bailey gathered his team on the sideline while Wally handed out cups of water. They talked about pressure and open space, offense and defense and making sure they remembered the corner kicks they'd practiced. With a collective "Li-ons!" the girls were back on the field before the Eagles.

Bailey glanced in the stands and spotted Cathy, who returned his wave. He also saw her sitting beside two small African-American women. The younger held a bundle in her arms as the older joined Cathy in several cheers: "Go Lions!" "Come on, Girls!" "You can do it!"

If Bailey had been nervous about this historic game, he wasn't now. Though there were no other spectators on the Lions side of the stadium, the presence of these three women was just enough. He exhaled and turned back toward the center of the field for the second half kick-off.

The Eagles attacked straight away but Annie dove, caught their shot, and punted it out toward the other end, which is where the ball stayed for the rest of the game. Though they couldn't connect again, Kentucky's first half goal was enough to take home the Lions first win of the Claymont Falls High girls soccer debut season.

At dinner that night, B.J. fidgeted in perpetual motion, boosted by confidence following the varsity boys first win, the complete opposite of his sister's mood. Mandy sat sulking, staring at her meat loaf and pushing around her green beans with her fork like there was something wrong with them. Cathy noticed. Halfway through his mashed potatoes, so did B.J.

"What's up with you?" he asked between bites.

Mandy's eyes filled. She dropped her fork on the plate, pushed her chair from the table and ran to her room. Cathy's eyes widened and she pointed the direction of their daughter's room. Bailey sighed and followed.

He knocked on her door.

"Mandy?"

"What?"

"Can I come in?"

She pulled open the door and they stood eye to eye. A tear slipped down her cheek and she brushed it away as she retreated to her bed. Bailey pulled around a chair from her desk and faced his daughter.

"What's the matter?"

"You should know!"

"Help me. I don't want to assume."

Mandy looked toward the window then back at her father, her lower lip trembling. She wanted to say something, but the words were not cooperating.

"Come on, Hon, what is it?"

"I wanted to be the best one on the team, Dad. I wanted to score the first goal. I wanted to make us win." She hesitated. "But Kentucky had to come in and— why'd you get her on our team anyway?"

Bailey had not expected this, but he tried not to show his surprise.

"You did help us win. You kept the pressure on."

"It's not the same." She reached for a tissue.

Assuming his role as coach, he suppressed his emotions as her father, which allowed him to see the moment for what it was. "Listen, Mandy, there's no room for selfishness on a team. That might sound tough, but that's how it is. We won today because everybody played hard. Practiced hard. And worked hard—together. It wasn't because of one single person."

She sniffed. "But I wanted to score."

"And I have no doubt you will. In fact, I'm expecting you to," he nodded. "You're hungry. That's one of the best qualities a player could have. You want it. And guess what?"

"What?"

"You'll get it. But not on your own. Together. With Kentucky and Tricia and the rest of the team." He rubbed his daughter's hand. "Just wait. You'll see."

Mandy blew her nose, leaned forward, and shook her head.

"But I want to be the best."

"So be the best you can. Your best, okay?" He tapped her elbow. "Now let's finish our dinner, what do you say?"

She didn't say anything. But four days later against the Smithtown Tigers, her father was right: Mandy did score. And so did Kentucky, giving the Lions a 2-0 victory. They won again the following week, and then against the next four district opponents. If it wasn't Mandy putting the ball into the net, Kentucky would follow through with a goal or an assist. Annie kept every team from scoring on her in the goal, and every time Bailey looked into the bleachers or off to the sideline, he'd see his wife sitting in a lawn chair beside Reyola Wallace, sometimes accompanied by her daughter.

At every game they shouted, "Come on, Girls! You can do it!" Though Bailey knew full well his mentor had no idea what "it" was.

The night before their sixth game, as Mandy and B.J. worked on homework, and Bailey read the Register, the phone rang at the Crawford household. Cathy looked up from her book. Bailey set down the paper and picked up the receiver.

"Bailey, this is Reyola. I'm at the hospital."

"What's the matter?"

"It's Lars. He's had a heart attack."

chapter
12

2008

Will was not in the library when I stopped by between my last class and practice. I peered over the desk where we'd watched the video together and saw his bicycle bag and helmet leaning against the chair. Maybe he had a meeting with one of the academic departments. I didn't have time to wait, so I fished out a piece of old copy paper from the trash and scribbled a note: "Will, Had a good talk with Tricia (W) Johnson re: first team. You? Rey."

I debated about whether I should include my phone number but just as I finished writing the last digit, another librarian walked in cradling a stack of books like it was firewood. She was about 300 years old and wore a cotton-white bun tacked on the back of her head. Her floral print dress might have been in style when my grandmother first started in the district. In fact, she probably was the librarian back then, just as she had been during my days as a student.

"May I help you?" she squeaked.

"Oh, Miss Wolfe," I spoke loudly at the woman who terrified teens without even realizing it, and whom even now I tried to avoid.

"No, thank you. I was just looking for Will."

She did not budge.

"McCabe. Will McCabe, your assistant here, in the library."

Miss Wolfe softened at his full name and title and set down her books. But she did not smile. "I believe Mr. McCabe is occupied elsewhere."

She offered no specific information and I didn't ask. I thanked her—though I wasn't sure for what—left the note on Will's desk and hurried toward the coaches' locker room.

By the time I arrived at the soccer field, the sky was turning ominous, so I ran through an indoor practice in my head, just in case. But I hoped we'd get another typical Ohio fall day where the rain fell long enough to water the grass and the blue sky returned within minutes.

As I was lining up tiny orange cones, the girls trickled out to the circle, soccer balls at their feet and matching team bags hanging from their shoulders. Crammed with shin guards, rain jackets, water bottles and who knows what else, they plopped the bags on the sideline as the sky opened. But the captains led their teammates anyway, first through warm ups, then through a series of sprints in and out of the cones as the field grew wet. Their cleats gave them the traction they needed to stop and start without slipping or colliding.

When the drizzle stopped ten minutes later, they wiped off their faces and worked their way through trapping drills, shots on goal and 2 v 2 mini-scrimmages. Nearly two dry hours later, I gathered my players in to stretch and tossed out a question.

"How would you feel if you won a championship and never got a trophy?" My eyes jumped from Kate, then Maggie, Paula and the other girls. A few studied the grass as they stretched or looked toward the football players, but their faces contemplated my question. Someone grunted, which I took as an answer.

"I wouldn't like it either. You work really hard and you get that first win. Then you keep winning until you've gone all the way to be the best in the state. Undefeated. You deserve to be recognized, don't you think?" A few blonde heads bobbed, ponytails swishing back and forth. "Remember how I told you Claymont Falls once had a state championship girls soccer team? Well, that team in 1983 never got a trophy or a plaque or anything."

"That's not fair," one girl mumbled into her knee as she stretched.

"Lame," another said. "But nothing to do about it, I guess."

"Why not?" I asked.

"Cuz it's a long time ago. Who's gonna care now?"

"For real," said Monica, a dark-haired junior whose attitude matched her style of play—aggressive. I liked her. "Besides, only the guys get that kind of stuff here. Girls never get anything. Even when the girls won that volleyball tournament last year, remember? Mr. Hanks didn't even mention it at the assembly."

"That's how it is," Maggie shrugged.

"Why does it have to stay that way?"

"What do you mean, Coach?" Kate asked.

"What if things changed? I mean, we didn't always have a girls soccer team, and then girls just like you thought maybe they could make a difference and gave it a shot."

They pondered this.

"They'd never had a team before?" Kate's eyes widened.

"Not even little league for girls."

Paula shook her head. "See? Girls never get anything."

"But we do! I mean I got a chance to play here and then get a scholarship because of what they started. See? And because of what that first team did twenty-five years ago, we get to be a team now. I'm even expecting a few of you go on to play college ball."

Kate stood taller. Monica crossed her arms. Maggie tilted her head. The others stepped closer together, as if a big light bulb had turned on above them.

"So, what if we decided to get them something?" I asked quietly.

"They deserve it," Kate responded. "Well, yeah," Monica rolled her eyes. "But it should be more than just a trophy."

"Maybe some sort of ceremony—"

"Like the Olympics or something!"

"Yeah, that'd be cool! I know—we could have it at one of our games!"

"Invite a bunch of people and—"

"Or we could hold an assembly for them and invite the whole school—"

"Or a town parade, like the football team does, with the marching band—"

"And get our picture taken with them for the paper so everyone sees them—"

"No, we should get them championship rings, you know, like the Super Bowl!"

The girls tossed ideas back and forth at rocket speed, combining creative details with sheer excitement as if they were planning their own celebration. And, in some ways, they were.

I let the brainstorm continue for a few more minutes, amazed at their sudden shift in idealism, before I joined the conversation.

"So, who thinks this is a good idea?"

Every girl raised her hand. As they did, I saw them inch closer to one another, a few elbows resting on shoulders and eyes focused ahead. Not only did they look like serious athletes for the first time—eager, excited, deliberate—they reminded me of, well, my own team. I cleared my throat.

"That's great. I'm proud of you," I said, not thinking before the affirmation popped out of my mouth. They exchanged glances and grins.

"Coach, how about if we invite them to our first game and, before kick-off, they come out onto the field and we put medals around their necks?"

The girls cheered. When I told them we'd probably have to raise the money ourselves to buy these rings, medals or whatever it was we were going to get to honor these former champions, their excitement rose, along with my surprise. They talked about car washes, bake sales, even a dance, until finally they settled on a raffle ticket sale with an array of prizes, including yard work and housecleaning for which they'd gladly volunteer, and five free pizzas from one girl's family restaurant. Everyone could buy a ticket for a dollar, they decided, and some might even buy more, so that would be the best fundraiser.

"How much will we need to raise, Coach Rey?" Kate asked, her arm now around Maggie's shoulder.

"Good question. I'll get back to you on that," I said. "For now let's decide who's going to do what, and we'll take it from there. Good?"

"Good!"

We spent the last 10 minutes of practice under a crystal sky, sweaty, still a little soggy from the rain, but mostly invigorated by both the chance to restore a forgotten team to its rightful glory. The girls collected their bags and raffle responsibilities, high-fived each other and passed the balls back and forth as they jogged toward the locker room. Even Monica, Tammy and the other newest members of the team were fitting in as they made their way across the complex.

Once I returned the equipment to its storage shed, I unlocked the door to my office to gather my briefcase and gym bag, and check my phone messages, just in case. Two messages had come since practice began. I punched in my password and listened as Tricia Johnson's voice rang, a rhythm of steady but obvious warmth:

"Hi, Darlin'. Tricia here. Glad we got a chance to chat today. Listen, I've already talked with a couple of the girls. Apparently, you met Nelli and Annie the other day at the bakery—they told me they had a real nice visit with you and some soccer fan named Will. Sounds interesting. Anyway, they like the idea of coming to a couple of your games. So we're going to meet at Nelli's on Sunday night around 5:00—she's got one of those gorgeous historic houses that's to die for: 16 Chestnut Avenue. How about you two come by then and meet some of the team, okay? Call me back. You've got my card."

I reached for a pen to write down Nelli's address, and took a long sip from my bottle of water as the next voice message came on:

"Sorry I missed you today, Rey. Oh, this is Will. Ginny told me you came by the library, just when I was dropping off some films for the history department. I got your note—obviously I got your note because I'm calling you. Here's what I found out. If we got a team and individual trophies, we'd need just about two thousand bucks. Not impossible, but a good challenge. I found out some other things as well. So I'll call you later. I want to hear what Tricia said. Hope you had a good couple of days."

I pushed the replay option. I liked the sound of Will's voice and imagined him sitting at his computer, tapping his jeans every now and then while he spoke into his phone and fiddled with his glasses. He said he was sorry he missed me. I listened again.

The drive home must have happened because I found myself walking into the living room some twenty minutes later. But I didn't remember much about it. My head was full of conversations and ideas and faces. One pale face framed by straight brown hair kept popping into my mind in particular. And in my head I heard him say over and over how he'd hoped my last few days had been good.

Mom was not home, though the house smelled like something had just come out of the oven. I walked into the kitchen and found a "Please Don't Touch" note in front of two loaves of banana bread cooling on the counter. My mother could spend the entire week in a school cafeteria cooking and baking for children, yet she still come home and pull out recipes and ingredients for new experiments. Usually she baked for friends she'd visit on the weekends, but lately she'd been stopping by the hospice where MaeMa had stayed, delivering baked parcels of gratitude to the nurses who'd taken care of her mother during the last days of her time on earth.

I didn't want to think about that now. I glanced instead at the calendar on the refrigerator and saw my mom's "Friday Night Ladies' Club" scribbled in the box. Sometimes they'd play Bingo at the Catholic Charities hall or go to the movies, but usually she'd just meet for coffee in someone's living room, babbling about their jobs or children or neighbors. At least that's how she described it. And given how hard she worked and what the past years had been like for us with MaeMa's passing, I was glad when she started going back to the ladies' club. At least one of the Wallace women had somewhere to go on a Friday night.

I boiled some pasta, added tomato sauce, dumped it into a bowl and wandered into the living room. The Daily Register lay on the table, still folded with a rubber band around it. I shook out the front page. There was a story on the new stadium bond that voters were going to have to decide in the upcoming election and, as I read, I came across my boss's name: "According to Preston Hanks, CFHS athletic director and head football coach, the new stadium is long overdue and would provide his team with more opportunities to pursue professional experiences: 'Our kids deserve a new stadium and it's my job to give them the best.'" His bravado was all over the rest of the article, which only made me roll my eyes and swear out loud at his arrogance.

I flipped the pages, reading the headlines, advertisements and photo captions of the small paper that was as local as it got. But I stopped on the opinion page, when I saw a brief editorial from the Register calling on voters not to approve the tax increase bond just to fund a new stadium. The public parks, housing complexes and school libraries needed funding far more than a new sporting facility, it said, especially since the high school complex already included multiple fields, a new all-weather track, and tennis courts with lights.

Tricia Johnson's name was not on the column but I couldn't miss her voice. I raised my fist in solidarity, licked my pasta spoon and flipped on the movie channel to see what was playing. Yes, Rocky III would certainly fit the bill. Apollo Creed re-training the underdog seemed fitting.

I spent most of Saturday reviewing chapters in Mockingbird, polishing lesson plans for next week's classes and helping Mom in the back garden. Just as I was yanking an entire section of tall prickly weeds, the phone rang. My mother was on her knees in the corner of the garden, clad in hat and gloves and so focused on her plants that she didn't seem to hear the phone.

The kitchen table was not clean for long. I jumped over the chair, a mix of dust, sweat and weeds spilling as I picked up the phone on the fourth ring. A blade of grass stuck to my lips as I answered. Then I sneezed. Between the pollen and the dirt, I was a mess. I sneezed again.

"Sorry. Hello?"

"Gesundheit," the voice said. And if ever there was I time I was glad my phone only broadcast my voice, this was it.

"Will. Hi."

"Bad time?"

"No, um, just—" I stared at the black grit beneath my fingernails and the stains across my shirt. Thankfully, my mother was busy climbing up from her hole in the yard and rearranging some tools. "Just doing some gardening."

"Good for you. Well, I won't keep you. Just wanted to hear what Tricia said."

I explained to Will the details of Tricia's lunchtime visit, her agreement to round up her teammates, and even how my own players had come up with several possibilities on how to honor the team. They'd surprised me with their excitement and were already working on what they could do for the event.

"I'm sure they'll be bugging you to buy a raffle ticket, or ten!" I held the phone between my ear and shoulder and bent into the kitchen sink to wash my hands.

"Happily," he said. "That's great, Rey. And it's a great thing for your team to do at the beginning of the season. It'll give them a chance to connect more."

This guy was good.

"So what did you find out?" I asked, reaching for a dishtowel to dry my hands.

"Only that the 1983 Girls Team didn't just win the first state title," he said, the volume of his voice intensifying. I heard clinking in the background as if he were tinkering with his bike. "They are the school's ONLY state champions, Rey!"

"What do you mean?"

"The Lions of Claymont Falls High have exactly one—count 'em—ONE state championship on the record books in the entire history of the school, boys or girls. 1983. Girls Soccer. That's it!"

"But what about all the trophies and ribbons in the Hall of Inspiration? Football or baseball or basketball had to have won state at some point, right?"

"Wrong. Oh, they all qualified for state or regional or district playoffs plenty of times. But they never won one state title. Period. And you know what?" he added, "I think it's simple justice that the football team has never won a championship, whereas girls soccer has! I love it!" He laughed so hard that he snorted slightly, and I couldn't help but join him.

"Do you know how great that sign will look now as you're entering Claymont Falls, 'Home to the 1983 Girls Soccer State Champions, the High School's Only State Winner?!'" Will was revved up now. "Really, can you imagine it in a town of football maniacs? It's justice, pure poetic justice, Rey!"

For another twenty minutes, we laughed and talked and envisioned the absurdity of our plan coming to life. I was on the front porch now, out of my mother's earshot, and our conversation turned in a more personal direction. He asked about my family, and I deflected by asking about his. He'd grown up in Chicago with parents who were inner city teachers and he chose Oberlin College in Ohio because of its heritage. He liked the idea of attending one of the first colleges in the country to admit African-Americans and women, and that it had once been a stop on the Underground Railroad.

"My grandmother went there too," I whispered, sharing the name with someone other than my mother for the first time since she'd died. And even those moments had been rare, though it'd been more than a year since her funeral.

"No kidding? I'd love to meet her," Will said. And when I breathed only silence into the phone, he interpreted it correctly. "I'm so sorry for your loss, Rey. I didn't know."

I changed topics again. "So, how'd you get to be a soccer fan?"

He sighed, then laughed softly. "Manny, Garcia, Enrique, all these guys from Mexico lived in my neighborhood and I grew up playing with them. They loved soccer and it was contagious. God, what a great game! We'd watch World Cups at my house, and I've been hooked ever since. Never missed a World Cup yet, including the women's since they started. Impressed?"

"Very," I looked up as my mother poked her head out the front door to ask if I wanted a glass of iced tea. I cupped the phone with my hand and whispered, "No, thanks." Mom nodded and went back inside.

"Better get going, Will," I said. "But listen, Tricia is meeting with her old teammates tomorrow night and she's invited us."

"Us?"

"Annie and Nelli told her about our conversation at Knudsen's and said we should both come."

I gave him the address and we agreed to meet there at 5. When we hung up, I was so thirsty that I drank almost the entire pitcher of Mom's iced tea. I could tell she wanted to know who I'd been talking to, her face lined with hope that I might actually have found a friend, but she respected my privacy too much to ask. She simply made another pitcher of tea, whistling as she did. And throughout the rest of the day and into the evening, I didn't think about much besides the news Will had managed to dig up: that Tricia's team had somehow pulled off the never-repeated title as Claymont Falls only state champions.

The Sunday morning breeze matched the pace of the day: slow and easy one moment, and impatient and hasty the next. The trees swayed occasionally as if they couldn't decide which direction to go, and the leaves rose and fell without much force. Thankfully, it wasn't so hot that we needed the reprieve, but the calmness was an odd contrast to the anticipation stirring in my gut.

Mom went to church. I read the Sunday newspaper, glanced through the shoe sales, and finished some eggs and bacon by noon when I decided to take a run through the neighborhood. Lined across the floor of my closet were four pairs of running shoes sitting next to my practice and game cleats, basketball shoes and tennis court shoes, neatly arranged across from my stand-by black, white and brown pumps.

Shoes made an outfit, as much as they defined a player, and I'd always loved the feel of mine, the confidence they gave me as I brought them home from the store and wore them in until they were comfortable. Each pair was a regular feature on my list of necessities, and as I stood in my closet, I decided that once I got paid next week, I'd hit the mall for some new game-day shoes.

I reached for my favorite Nikes, threw on an old Lions T-shirt and running shorts and took off. The sky was cloudless, a pale blue against the green of the trees that lined the street. I headed toward the small cluster that made up the historic district of downtown Claymont Falls—some two and a half miles from our house—and as I drew near, the image of that 1983 yearbook photo dropped in my mind. I remembered the young Annie in her goalkeeper uniform as I passed Knudsen's Bakery, the parking lot full of Sunday customers. I remembered the teen-aged Tricia as I passed the three-story brick office building of the Daily Register, and the little Nelli as I rounded the corner where Martinelli Real Estate sat.

These women had gotten their start on the soccer field twenty-five years ago and emerged champions the same year. I wondered how they felt now, their athletic days behind them, still working hard but in new fields and careers. What difference had playing on that team made for them? Had it prepared them for the challenges they now faced?

The questions popped around in my mind, so that by the time I turned onto our street, I was both sweaty and curious. Mom's car was back in the driveway and I found her kneading a flour mix on the kitchen counter.

"Got some fresh blueberries on the way home from church," she said pointing to a small green cardboard box brimming with fruit. "How about a pie tonight?"

I wiped my forehead with a dishtowel and gulped some Gatorade. "Save me some. I'm meeting a friend."

She stopped kneading. "Is that right?"

The gleam of hope in her eyes made me nervous. I'd seen that look before every time she thought I might actually have a social life or a possible date. So I knew I'd better kill the dream—again—and fast: "No biggie. Just a little research about Bailey Crawford's team."

Her eyes dropped to her knuckles and she began kneading again. I swallowed and continued.

"Going to Gina Martinelli's house where Tricia Johnson is bringing over some of the old players."

"Are you?" A slight ticking sound escaped from my mother's mouth as she punched the dough.

"Yeah, something the matter with that, Mom?"

"No, no. Please tell them I said hello."

I about dropped my glass. "You know these women?"

"Sort of. Just a little, through MaeMa and Coach Crawford." She picked up the future crust and flipped it over. "When we went to their games."

"You went to their games?"

"Not all of them. MaeMa went more than I did. I was busy taking care of you and working at the diner, but we managed to see a few games. Course, I didn't know one thing about soccer then, but that didn't really matter."

"It didn't?" I was leaning against the refrigerator, gripping the dishtowel like it was a ball, my eyes narrowing in on my mother like she was a stranger in our kitchen.

"Rey, don't do that to the towel," she said, still working her crust.

I let go. "How come I'm only now hearing about this?"

She shrugged. "Guess it never came up. We were always so busy with your games that we never thought about it, I guess."

"So you not only knew this Coach Crawford, you went to his games and knew some of his players?" I loosened my hair as if that would help my brain better process what I was hearing.

"It was just something MaeMa wanted to do, to support him. And I wasn't much older than those girls so I guess it was our little way of, you know, helping out some folks when others didn't really think they had much of a chance." She looked up from the crust, smiled and grabbed her pie pan. "We knew what that was like."

"But they became champions."

"So did you, Baby Girl. So did you. Like I told you that day you came home from his funeral, Bailey Crawford did a lot for the girls of this town." Her tone turned serious, as if the mention of his name reminded her of something more dramatic. "But not everyone was happy about that, so you need to watch yourself. What time's your meeting?"

My mother had actually watched some of those early games! I could barely process the image as I watched her lean over the crust, fold it into the pan with her thumbs, her apron dropping from her neck, her thick frame jiggling with each motion.

"Rey," she said concentrating on her art. "What time are you going tonight? Maybe I can get this done and you can take it along with you. That'd be nice, wouldn't it?"

"Yeah, but . . ."

She waited for more, but I was too stunned to ask anything else, so she whisked me out of the kitchen, telling me to "go clean up" so she could concentrate on her pie. I struggled to move my feet. She pointed again and soon I was in the shower, replaying each question or thought that tumbled around in my head. By the time I slipped my clean body into pressed jeans, a black tank top and matching pumps, put on some mascara and earrings, I hoped my mother would have answers, stories and details.

Instead, Mom was leaning over the couch, clipping coupons from the newspaper and glancing at the television: it was halftime and the Bengals were tied at 10 in a pre-season home game against Detroit. The smell of blueberry pie in the oven floated hypnotically into the living room. The television trumped conversation so I made a sandwich and waited for an explanation that never came.

By the fourth quarter, I was ready to leave. Detroit had come back to score 17 points in the fourth quarter, taking the lead to 27 - 10, and I'd had enough of the losing and the silence. Mom delivered a typical "tsk, tsk" to the television screen, and I followed her to the kitchen, where she handed me the pie, reminded me to bring back the pan, and returned to the couch, "Just in case these Bengals do something."

I still couldn't believe it: My own mother had gone to those first games . . . with her mother. This was getting weird.

Will, however, was anything but. He was leaning against his bike on Chestnut Street when I drove up, looking cool and hip in his jeans, striped T-shirt and high tops. His hair was tied back in a tiny ponytail, and his glasses sat snug against his eyes. I drew in a breath of fresh Ohio air and walked toward him, pie in hand, pumps in place.

"Yoo-hoo!" Tricia Johnson was hollering from the porch of Nelli's house, a mansion really, that looked like it should grace the cover of Better Homes and Gardens. I glanced from Will to the woman with the thin bobbed hair and orange pantsuit now walking down the steps toward us. Will wheeled his bike beside him and joined me as we passed perfectly arranged flowerpots and manicured shrubs up a curved pathway to a white brick house that stood three stories high. The charm of the rounded bay window above the veranda was inviting.

"Let me guess, that's one of Jocelyn's homemade pies, isn't it,?" The fact that Tricia knew both my mother's name and her reputation for baking was as surreal to me as the fact that I was now walking into a beautiful historic home next to a handsome white man.

"How'd you—"

"Reporter's instincts, Hon." Her grin spread so far across her face I thought it might mess up her hair. "Please give my happiest thanks and appreciation to your—" She was taking the pie out of my hands when she was interrupted.

"You mean our deepest thanks, Tricia Woodring Johnson. You have to share that gorgeous treat with the rest of us, you know!" Nelli held open the screen door as the two old friends laughed like it was a regular part of their everyday. Will parked his bike against the steps and followed me inside the foyer where we stood on hardwood floors that merged into meticulous wood panels and stained glass flowers that nearly matched the real ones we'd just passed. I'd never seen anything like it.

"Built in 1898 for an old transportation tycoon who made a boatload in buggies before he bellied up when Ford came out with this thing called a car . ."

Nelli was delivering the speech as if she'd given a thousand house tours.

155

Dressed in black capris, a sleeveless silk blouse and white sandals, she continued: " . . . this house is on the national historic registry. It's just under 5,000 square feet, including the attic, and came with its own orchestra pit and linen room for those of us who still need both!"

"Wait 'til you use the marble toilet!" someone yelled.

"And watch out for the heated bench on the back porch. It about singed the skin on my butt last time I—"

"Now, girls, don't you give away my secrets," Nelli tossed back. She guided us into the living room where she, Tricia, Will and I joined six others, most of whom I remembered seeing at Bailey Crawford's funeral. Though the room was huge with towering ceilings and a gleaming chandelier, the women chose seats near each other, shrinking our meeting area to a warm and intimate space. Annie was squished on the couch between a plump blonde woman and a youthful man in a baseball cap, and the other women brought their chairs so close their knees nearly touched. Each held a wine glass. Tricia passed me a glass and a bottle of Sam Adams to Will. A long platter of fresh veggies, crackers and cheese sat on a coffee table.

"Ladies, meet Reynalda Wallace, third generation of the Wallace Women, English teacher and current coach of the girls soccer team at our alma mater," Tricia extended an open palm in my direction, and I offered mine in my most regal wave to the guests before nervously returning it to my front pocket. Annie then jumped to her feet, set down her glass and began to clap and cheer with all her heart. All present followed suit until the applause neared a thundering crescendo.

One of the ladies guided me to a chair near the couch. I crumpled into it, guzzled my drink and tried to take in all that was happening. I found it difficult to follow simultaneous conversations intended for me:

"Haven't seen you since you were a baby!"

"We were so proud when you won that scholarship—saw it in the paper."

"I'll bet you're a natural coach—Bengals could have used a real coach today!"

"No kidding. They might be about the most pathetic thing since—"

"Tricia tells us you want a little help for your team this season and—"

"How's the season looking?"

"God, look at those—I love your shoes!"

"No, Hannah, I told you that Rey thinks it'd be important for her girls to meet us."

"Isn't that the same thing as helping them? I mean, for heaven's sake, if they met this sorry bunch of girls, they'd know anything is possible!"

Snorts and cackles filled the room. Someone howled, another snapped her fingers and one woman quipped, "Speak for yourself, Hannah!" When the raucous squabbles died down and the women returned to their seats, Tricia again took the lead.

"Now, hush, all of you. Seriously, Coach Rey and her friend here, Mr. Will McCabe, right? They have come across the mildly remarkable fact of our 1983 Lions state championship." She raised her shoulders as she talked, her voice as commanding as if she were directing her reporters in the newsroom. "And they have also discovered that there is absolutely nothing at the school, or anywhere in town for that matter, that recognizes our accomplishment. So they thought perhaps it could be helpful for future athletes to know."

"Actually, if I may," Will spoke softly, one of only two men in the room. From the approving nods, no one seemed to mind. "First, thank you for letting me come today. I'm a huge soccer fan and I have a ton of respect for all of you as members of that first team."

Nelli raised her eyebrows and elbowed the woman beside her. Hannah reached for crackers as Will continued: "In my research, I found out that you were not only the first girls state champions at Claymont Falls, you're the only state champions to date. In other words, no other team has ever garnered a state championship—not baseball, not basketball, and not, I'm happy to report, football."

When he paused to let the truth settle in, the only noise in the room was a grinding crunch coming from Hannah. "So Rey and I thought it was only fitting that you should receive some sort of formal recognition, right, Rey?"

I nodded. "Absolutely."

The women exchanged looks, shrugs and talking points. Finally, one slender woman sitting opposite me cleared her throat and all eyes in the room turned toward her. The woman's dark, curly hair was stylish; her face serious, but stunning. She sat straight in her chair, crossed her long legs, and looked directly at me.

"Rey, I'm Mandy Crawford. And my dad was our coach." Her eyes clouded and no one moved.

I held her gaze and as I did, my eyes filled as well. It was a familiar and raw grief. "I'm sorry for your loss," I whispered.

She nodded and then waved her hand like a magician to regain her composure. It seemed to work. "I know everyone in this room feels as sad about losing Dad as I do. He brought us together and made us believe we really could do anything. And you know what? If he were here now, with you sitting here with all of us, well, he'd be really proud." She reached for a tissue and did another magic trick. "I drove down from Cincinnati to be here, but I don't need a special reason to be with the girls in this room again. We would all make the trip, right?"

"Right!"

"So what can we do for you and your girls?"

Her voice, combined with the collective enthusiasm of her teammates, sent a shiver of confidence through me and, for the first time since walking into the house, I felt comfortable, at home even. I presented my own team's plan: "First, I'd like to invite you to our games whenever you can make it. We'd be honored to have your support. At our final match, we'd like to invite you onto the field, you know, hold an official ceremony where we'd give you the trophies you should have received a long time ago."

"Rings, Doll, rings," Tricia reminded me. "And I'm going to push for a sign outside of town."

Will jumped in. "I'll help with that!"

Dear Will. I went on to explain the specifics of our intentions: "I talked with my players about it, and we know it'll be tight, but they've decided to raise money for the, uh, rings, and—"

"It wouldn't be the first fundraiser for the girls soccer team!"

"All those kazillion cookies, remember?"

"How do you think I became so good at sales?" Nelli infused the group with her humor before the laughter faded again.

"I can ask the district to help as well," the other man spoke swiftly. He lifted his hat and introduced himself. "Sorry to interrupt, but I'm Wally Knudsen. Annie's younger brother. I was the team ball boy, a position that launched my career, I'm proud to say, thanks to Coach Crawford and Coach Lambert."

There was a solemn pause at the mention of these names. I glanced at Will, who shrugged. The first team had two coaches? But there was only one in the yearbook.

"Wally's now in charge of the elementary PE teachers throughout the district," big sister Annie chimed in. An old leader guiding her teammates back on course, she brought the focus back onto the topic at hand. No wonder she was a goalie.

Annie patted Wally on the back and, as she did, I remembered the photo in the yearbook with the little boy opposite Coach Crawford. Wally's face filled.

"Well done," Will said, clinking his bottle with Wally's. Taking their cue from the men, the women all sipped their wine.

"So, do you think we could get your whole team there for the ceremony?" I asked, looking from Wally to Annie, then around the room at Tricia, Nelli and Mandy.

"Probably," Tricia said.

"Even Kentucky?" Hannah asked, nibbling some cheese. Tricia first glanced at Mandy, then back at Hannah, and lastly at me.

158

"We'll do our best. Heck, we don't have to be the best to do our best, right, Lions?" Tricia raised her glass and the others toasted in solidarity.

Nelli suddenly disappeared and returned with pieces of Mom's blueberry pie on white china plates and, for the next two hours, the women talked more about recipes and sales, jobs and babies, than they did about soccer or championships or coaches. Someone filled my glass with more white wine, and another passed around hors d'oeuvres and fruit trays. Will lobbed out questions, and I took it in, listening to stories about law schools, husbands, partners, health clubs, road trips, city council members and teenagers. I laughed at their stories and relaxed at their teasing.

With a pillow curled beside me, I rested under that chandelier, watching the prisms of light illuminate the faces in the room. Listening to the voices of friendship, I had become so captivated by the song of shared memories, that it was only upon pulling into the driveway, that I realized I'd forgotten my mother's pie pan. Somehow, though, I didn't think she'd mind.

chapter 13

1983

Rain clouds in the distance were the least of Bailey Crawford's concerns as he pulled out of the driveway. With his wife beside him, son and daughter in the back seat, he drove to the church parking lot across town and pulled into a space near the front steps, just yards away from the long, black hearse. As he got out of the car, Bailey felt uncomfortable in the suit he reserved for occasions like this, not because it stretched tightly across his shoulders, but because he had to wear it at all.

Sunlight weaving in and out of the stained-glass windows, the Crawfords entered the small Lutheran church silently and occupied the second row. The casket lay open near the pulpit. No matter what his mind told him, Bailey could not accept that the body inside was that of the man who had stood next to him only four days ago as they coached their sixth game of the season.

He gripped Cathy's hand; she clutched a tissue in her other. Mandy pressed softly against her mother just as B.J. did his father. Each looked to draw strength and composure from the others, but emotions weighed heavily on their shoulders. So as the church filled with dozens of other families and friends, and the pastor stepped forward, the Crawfords no longer fought to restrain the raw release of shock and grief.

The organ music swelled and eulogies were offered, but Bailey felt trapped in a fog, a far-away confusion where this moment did not seem real. He stared at the casket, but could not focus. He listened to the prayers, yet could not believe. The darkness of the hour stunned him, and this gathering made no sense to him.

A small African-American woman with gray wisps in her hair rose from her seat on the stage and spoke softly into the microphone: "'The Lord is my

Shepherd, I shall not want. He makes me lie down in green pastures. He restores my soul.'" The words swept through the room like a breeze, and she let their soothing balm sink in before she continued: "Lars Lambert loved this psalm. He once told me he was convinced those green pastures were soccer fields and, because the good Lord had included them in the Good Book, it must have meant that his coaching was a holy deed."

Sniffles mixed with soft laughter and nods as the woman lifted her shoulders and her voice. "I don't have to tell you all that Lars was a man who knew what was important, what really mattered. How many times would he stop and listen to you any time of the day, just because? Or give away anything he owned if it helped someone else? He knew just how to make anyone—and I mean anyone—feel welcome."

Reyola Mae Wallace stood firm, her cream-colored dress hanging neatly on her frame, her folded hands resting on the podium. "I know that to be true. Lars was the first person I met when I moved to Claymont Falls. Maybe I should say he was the first friend I had, too, when I started teaching fourth grade. He was the one person who introduced himself during our fall faculty meeting, shook my hand and welcomed me to the community. I never forgot that. Lars told me if I needed anything, I could find him in the gym. And during those first couple of months, I stopped by the gym so many times for advice or encouragement that he almost recruited me to play basketball and help with the fitness classes. Almost."

Her lips pushed up her cheeks into a smile that could have captivated or comforted any human heart. No one moved.

"Lars helped me, just like I know he helped all of us. That's who he was. And his impact on everyone in this room is something that words can't come close to defining."

The elderly woman's eyes made contact with every single face in the sanctuary, finally resting on Bailey and his family. "But the most remarkable thing about Lars? He passed on his greatness to others." Her deep brown eyes held Bailey's and for the first time that morning, he felt some glimmer of light slice through the fog. "I'm not sure how he did it, but Lars Lambert helped each of us become better people than we ever thought we could be." Her gaze then passed from the row of high school girls sitting behind the Crawfords to the Lambert family in the front row.

"Priscilla, thank you for the great honor of letting me speak today on your behalf. We will miss your husband terribly, and there's no question he has left us too soon. But we are—all of us—so grateful to have known him, for his example, for his inspiration and most importantly, for his friendship. I have no doubt he's resting on a very green patch in heaven, near, of course, a goal post, a soccer ball underfoot, just waiting for the whistle to blow." She drifted down to the row of Lambert family members and hugged each one, embracing Priscilla long and tight. When she finally let go, the pastor reminded the congregation of the burial and reception and dismissed them with the benediction. Vibrant organ chords guided them up the aisle, in strange contrast to the weary sorrow that filled each face.

Cathy tugged at Bailey's arm, steering him gently into the crowd. Mandy and Tricia and the other girls on the team cried softly, holding one another as they followed the lines of visitors. B.J. and a group of boys gathered beside coaches and teachers and soon the crowd had spilled into the parking lot, waiting and whispering about the shock of losing a beloved teacher and coach to something as unbelievable as a heart attack. It was a terrible irony.

Bailey mustered a tiny portion of strength as he spoke with students or players, looking to offer some consolation he himself did not have. He held teenagers, shook hands with colleagues, or simply listened to the sound of broken human voices as the school and community honored a man who had influenced every one of them for the better. Reyola was right about that.

By the time they got home that night, the Crawfords were all tired, though not very hungry. Cathy and B.J. scrounged around and found enough ingredients for a few sandwiches, while Mandy and Bailey attempted to get ready for the next day with homework or lectures. Soon the family simply turned out the lights for the evening.

But sleep did not come for Bailey. With his friend and mentor taken so suddenly from this life, his mind was filled anxieties. Simply put, he wasn't sure how to keep going. So much of what he knew about coaching and leading and serving young people he had learned from Lars, and Bailey didn't feel up to the task alone.

"Those young women deserve a coach like you. You are ready."

Lars' words on the telephone last spring emerged from the recesses in Bailey's mind, while a wild mix of emotions collided in his gut. He opened his eyes and stared into the night darkness, as Cathy breathed rhythmically beside him. Bailey began to cry, for the loss and the indignity and the challenge. He rolled onto his side away from his wife so as not to disturb her, brought his knees to his chest and put his face in his hands. All he could see was Lars, hobbling out onto the field, quietly guiding and caring for each player.

Without even realizing how, Lars had shown him what it meant to become a good man.

Reyola had been right about that too.

By the time the girls gathered for practice the next day, Bailey felt a physical weariness in his body. But he also found a deep sense of gratitude that both surprised and energized him. Though he had no idea how to prepare for today's practice, the rich and sustaining memory of his colleague gave Bailey a strength that grief could not steal.

The girls, however, stood limp around him, their bloodshot eyes and emotions still evident from the funeral. This day, they were meeting on the grassy edge of the baseball field—an area Bailey had managed to convince Freddie to let them use—and when he saw the girls faces, he instructed them to sit. Slowly, they dropped to the ground, some sitting cross-legged, others with their feet out in front. Their ponytails swept the top of their shoulders as their heads hung forward. Nelli picked blades of grass and flicked them into the air, smacking her gum nervously. Mandy tapped a ball with her fingers like it was a keyboard, and Tricia rummaged through her backpack for a tissue. But Annie, Kentucky and the others just sat, staring at their feet, at the grass, or at nothing in particular. The joy that defined this team every other day of their season had evaporated at the funeral and Bailey realized he was facing the hardest coaching challenge of his career.

How was he to talk with a group of 17-year-old girls about the death of the man who had helped bring them together?

With the autumn blue of the sky above them and the sounds of whistles across the field, Bailey searched for something—anything—to say. Nothing seemed right, and for several minutes the team sat in silence, but together. Bailey dropped to one knee and rested his elbows on the other. He took off his baseball cap, rubbed the back of his neck and picked up a soccer ball, spinning it in his hands before letting it fall to the ground.

"We've finished more than half of our season, Girls, and I have a really big question for you: do you think we should go on?"

Mandy's eyes locked with his, fear and confusion reflected in her glare. Nelli hurled an entire wad of grass, frustrated by the question. Annie simply shook her head.

"What do you mean, Coach?" Nelli, as usual, broke the silence before wiping a smudge of mascara from her eyes and reached for another piece of grass.

"Well, we've just lost a significant member of our team, and I think everyone would understand if we needed to take some time from—"

"But isn't that what people will expect?" Tricia had given up on the search through her bag and threw out the question with her usual passion.

"Yeah, but without Coach Lambert, well, maybe we should think about what Coach is saying," Hannah said, wiping her nose with the back of her hand. "After all, he got us playing in the first place. I just can't believe he's . . . "
Bailey considered this remark and remembered another phone call with Lars.

"You're exactly right, Hannah. Because of Coach Lambert, we have this team at all. When I first got this job, he told me that he'd pressed Coach Hanks and the district for years to let girls play. He saw what you were doing in his P.E. classes and he knew that the law meant the school had to give you a team."
"The law?" Nelli clung to her grass. "There's a law that says we have to play soccer?"

"Not exactly, Nelli," Bailey smiled. "There's a law—it's called Title IX—that says if there's a boys soccer team and enough girls who want to play, the school has to provide them with an equal chance. Coach Lambert kept pushing them to give you that chance."

"Then we should play!" The response was immediate, and it did not come from Mandy or Tricia or any of the other girls who sat in front of Bailey. It came instead from a ten-year-old ball boy. Wally jumped up and held his arms out to his side.

"If Coach Lambert did that, doesn't that mean we should play? I mean, you should play?" He giggled at himself and the girls joined him. When they stopped, Wally scratched his arm and turned serious: "Annie's always telling me that even though our Mom died last year, we should keep working hard for her every single day, doing the stuff she'd want us to do. Right, Annie?"

Annie's big eyes filled and in a tone barely audible, she said, "That's right, little brother."

Then Tricia jumped up beside Wally and put her hand on his shoulder. "So we keep playing. Harder than ever. For Coach." The entire team sat frozen at her declaration, unsure of the challenge. They stared at the boy, at their teammate, at Bailey and back again. Then a tall, stringy-haired girl rose quietly and stood beside Tricia and Wally. She dropped her arms to her sides and swallowed.

"I agree," Kentucky announced. "We keep playin'."

That's when Mandy joined Tricia, Hannah following, and soon the entire team was crowding around Wally. They broke into a spontaneous cheer for the "Lions!" and a unified applause for their ball boy, who was now balanced between the tall shoulder of his sister and Nelli's much-lower shoulder, a lopsided star whose knees poked upward.

They paraded him all the way to the infield, a steady jog around home plate, his arms thrown into a V above him and his face aglow with the joy of achievement.

When they returned to where Bailey stood, they set Wally down from their shoulders and rubbed his head like he was a lucky charm. His cheeks red from pride, Wally pointed to Bailey.

"What you want me to do, Coach?"

"I think you just did it, Wally."

Bailey had never watched soccer players, girls or boys, work as hard as these players during the next two hours. They chased down balls, beat out teammates, raced the clock and pushed each other so much that their shorts, socks and T-shirts were stained with sweat and grass by the time they finally stopped for water. As they sat stretching and gulping, Bailey congratulated them on their "incredible effort" and talked about the next game, focusing on their teamwork and attitude to carry them, one game at a time.

"I don't need to remind you that you have been through a lot. And you've responded to each challenge as champions, which makes me really proud of you all." He paused. "And I know Coach Lambert was really proud of you, too. You know why?"

"Why?"

"You never quit. Every single day you give your best. Not anyone else's. Yours. And you keep at it. That makes you part of the great soccer tradition he established at Claymont Falls High. You are included in that now. You are his winners and because of that you can never lose. You are . . . Lions."

The girls listened intently to his words, passing around cups of water and orange slices Cathy had sent with Mandy. As Bailey looked at his clipboard and was about to review the new lineup for the next game, the goalkeeper raised her hand as if she were a student in his history class.

"Annie?"

"We're your winners, too, Coach," she said softly. She brushed the hair out of her eyes and repeated her comment to make sure Bailey heard her. "We're your winners, too. It's also because of you that we're here, that we're a team at all." Nelli and Kentucky and Tricia nodded emphatically to punctuate the point, and Bailey felt a sudden sensation in his throat. His eyes watered, and Mandy put her arm around her dad.

"Yes, we are a team," he whispered. "Now, I think we're done for the day. Three o'clock sharp tomorrow in the parking lot to go to Watertown. Who can drive again?"

They organized the carpool for tomorrow's game, collected their backpacks and drove home that night a stronger group of friends, resolved to honor the memory of one coach and the presence of another with the best they had to give.

The drive to the country after practice included Bailey's usual attempt at conversation: he would ask Kentucky a question to which she would reply with a word or two. This time, however, when he pulled into the usual truck stop drop-off, Kentucky did not get out of the car right away. Instead, she stared straight ahead like she was searching for something. Bailey waited.

"I'm real sorry about Coach Lambert," she spoke quietly. "I lost my dad when I was little, and it was hardest thing I ever went through. 'Til now." She stared at the truck stop sign, her fingers on the handle of the door. "Daddy loved games and sports. He was real good at everything, and Mama thinks that's where I got it."

"Wherever you got it, Miss Beaucamp, you are one of the finest athletes I've ever had the privilege of coaching."

Kentucky looked at Bailey like she wasn't sure she could believe him but she couldn't afford not to. She pushed her hair back, her eyes gentle, and her mouth slightly open. She gripped the door. Bailey continued.

"Really. In fact, I called a couple of college coaches, and found some good programs for women's soccer that have started to offer scholarships. Colorado, North Carolina, California, all of them seem like good schools, and if you're interested, I could—"

"Leave home? Not sure Mama could handle that."

"Maybe not forever but it'd be a good opportunity to get a good education and then decide what you want to do. I checked and your grades are good, your speed and talent are just what they're looking for. I could talk with your mother if you like."

Her eyes softened again. And for the first time since he'd run into her in the halls last spring, he saw Adeline Beaucamp smile. She relaxed her hand, nodded at his offer and sighed.

"I'd like that. My little sister and brother keep her plenty busy and I try to help, but she knows how much I like playin'. And I think, if I got to go to college because of it, well, that'd be amazing . . ." The dream grabbed the girl's imagination and filled her face. Bailey saw in her eyes that hope he spotted each time a student or athlete captured a vision of what they could become. Gladness thrilled his heart at that moment, as it did every time a young person considered a good possibility.

"I'll bet your dad would be really proud, and I'm sure your mother is too, Kentucky, right?" Bailey rested his hand on the back of her seat. She nodded. "Coach Lambert and I are too. I'll set up a meeting with the guidance counselor this week so we can get those applications started, okay?"

"Okay." "Okay! I'll see you tomorrow."

Kentucky looked again at the neon sign, but now it was if she was looking far beyond it, someplace that lit up more than the highway. She pushed open the car door, still smiling, and jogged toward the dirt road behind the truck stop. Bailey watched her run—as he had watched her on the field—and for the second time that day, his eyes got misty.

Game after game for six games straight, Kentucky and Mandy found more opportunities to score—and the Lions celebrated every play that led to every goal. If the other teams did manage to dribble around Tricia, pass the ball beyond Hannah, or outrun Nelli, Annie would usually fly sideways across the goal to keep any wayward shots out, her long body reducing the angle for any opponent. And if the ball did manage to sneak into the net, one of the Lions offensive players—Mandy or Kentucky in particular—would simply return the favor a few minutes later with a goal for Claymont Falls. Bailey's team came away from most games ahead by at least two. Sometimes three. But they were always out in front, and always brought home a win. Losing didn't seem to occur to them, maybe because they were playing for more than the score.

Lars taught them that. Bailey tried to build on it.

Soon, in fact, their combined efforts meant the girls soccer team had somehow compiled a record equal only to the school's football team so far that season: undefeated. Of course, stories of football success dominated the Daily Register— profiles of linebackers or game-day strategies from Coach Harry Hanks. Bailey had not read a single story of his team's record in the newspaper. Even his son's soccer team received a small mention now and then, though their record was an even five and five.

B.J. didn't care so much about press, but having what he considered an "unsuccessful" season didn't sit well with him. With Lars gone and his father coaching girls, B.J.'s expectation for his senior year had dwindled into discouragement, despite the fact that he started every game as a midfielder and was also the third leading scorer. It just wasn't the same. He also knew that, since his team had lost their last game, their chances of qualifying for the state tournament had been virtually eliminated. With only one league game left in his high-school career, he didn't suppress his frustration at the Crawford dinner table.

"So why don't you come watch some of our games," Mandy asked as she passed her brother the mashed potatoes. "You only came that once when we played before your game and you had to be there. But we've gotten pretty good, right, Dad?"

"So far, so good," Bailey answered. "Your sister's got a point, B.J. We could use a few more voices on the sidelines."

His son shrugged and pushed around the food on his plate.

"You could sit with your mother," Cathy said with a wink. "It probably won't do much for your reputation, but it'd be nice for me. And for your sister."

He drew in a deep breath.

"I suppose, since there's not much else to do." The slightest tremor of a shrug emerged from B.J.'s shoulder and his family took that as a "yes." From that night on, Bailey could count on at least a handful of fans at the games: his wife, the Wallace Women, and his son. An occasional parent stopped by as well. That made a handful cheering for the Lions girls soccer team. If anyone else came, that was a crowd.

By late October, the Claymont Falls high school varsity football team had qualified for the final game of the state tournament, while its boys soccer and cross country seasons had long ended with respectable records. The first ever girls soccer team, on the other hand, had also earned its way to the state finals, yet few at the high school knew anything about it. Bailey's team might as well have been invisible, given the lack of acknowledgement. Except for an occasional congratulation from teachers like Donna Sanchez or Delores Winston, Bailey wondered if his colleagues even knew about their impressive rookie record. Hanks was so busy organizing the football assembly, studying his opponent and preparing final plays, that he also hadn't noticed another team from Claymont Falls was contending for a state championship.

Bailey knocked three times on Hanks' half-opened door before he looked up. "What?"

"Got a minute?" Bailey held his clipboard under his arm, the statistics and results of the season firmly attached.

"What does it look like?" Hanks twisted his chair around to grab a pile of papers from a table and swiveled back to his desk.

Bailey sighed and walked in anyway. "Since you hired me, I thought you should know." He slipped the top document from his clipboard and laid it on the desk. Hanks reached not for it, but for his coffee mug.

"Aren't you going to read it?"

"Does it have anything to do with the state title? Because if it doesn't, I'm not interested right now." Hanks emptied the cup in one gulp.

"As a matter of fact, it does."

The athletic director reached for the paper and brought it close to his face. He pushed his glasses closer as if he were having trouble reading what it said. Or believing it. He studied it from top to bottom, re-read it and then yanked it away from his face.

"You've got to be kidding." He stared at Bailey. Then he shook his head and tossed it back to the soccer coach. "Well, congratulations, Crawford. I didn't think they had it in them."

"Congratulations to you, too, Harry."

The brief moment of satisfaction that stirred through Bailey's lungs was quickly extinguished when Hanks said, "Yeah, it's about time we made it to the state finals. Anyway, how are you going to pay for your refs?"

Bailey exhaled. "I thought that'd be the least the school could do. We are representing them in the state tournament, after all."

Hanks pushed out his jaw like he was chewing on the idea. "Good point. I'll see what I can do. When is it anyway?"

"Next Saturday, November 5, at noon, up in Columbus."

"Ah, the day after ours," he raised his eyebrows as if the timing were anti-climactic. "Sorry, but we'll have spent all our travel money on the buses for the varsity team, marching band and cheerleaders that Friday night, so how are you going to get—"

"The same way we have all season, Harry. We'll carpool." Bailey slid the paper back onto his clipboard, the faces of each of his players suddenly filling his mind. He planted his feet and spoke clearly. "One more thing: I know you're planning a school assembly Friday, and the Booster Club is doing something in town for the boys."

"A parade down Main Street. Marching band and everything." Hanks leaned forward in his chair and reached for his pen. He looked at the paper beneath him and was not expecting what Bailey Crawford said next:

"It'd be only right to honor our girls soccer team as well at the assembly—and the parade—since they will also be playing for the state championship."

Hanks tapped the pen against the desk and looked up. A silent tension hung between the two men. Neither moved. The buzz of the heating unit kicked in at the same time Hanks's assistant knocked on his door.

"The superintendent is on the phone, Mr. Hanks," she said. "Line 2."

Hanks straightened his shoulders and reached for the phone. But he did not pick it up. "Fair enough. I'll talk to the Booster Club president—it's Stan Gullen this year—and see what he says about the parade. I'm planning Friday's assembly, so why don't you and the girls come out first, then we'll introduce the varsity team. Okay?"

He did not wait for an answer, but instead grabbed the phone.

"Thanks, Harry, that'll mean a lot to them—and the school," he said. His boss signaled for Bailey to leave. And for the first time since Lars had died, Bailey felt a steadiness and a certainty that had before seemed only like faraway solace. Now the emotions were real, here, deep within him.

"You are ready for this," Lars had told him.

"They've got the right man for the job," Reyola Mae had said.

"They couldn't get anyone better than you," Cathy had whispered.

Each word of confidence wrapped its way around Bailey's heart as he walked down the school hall, past the classrooms and lockers and onto the track where his team was warming up. He watched them for a few moments before calling them into a huddle. And when he told them they'd be recognized at the Friday morning school assembly and probably the parade, he was surprised at their response.

No one said a thing.

"What's the matter? Isn't this good news?"

Mandy tossed a glance to Tricia, who did the same to Nelli and Annie. The track was quiet. All the other teams had finished for the season. The football team had already practiced that day, and except for a few joggers from the neighborhood, the track was as silent as the fall air. For a team on its way to a state championship game, there was no sense of wonder or excitement or even curiosity. It was as if they had already played.

"What's going on?" Bailey tried, but he couldn't keep anyone's eye contact.

Mandy looked down. Tricia wiped her nose. Kentucky cleared her throat before bringing the emotion into a barely-audible sentence: "Coach Lambert won't be there."

Bailey removed his baseball cap, a natural reflex for the hard reality Kentucky had just put into words.

"No, he won't. But you know who will be?"

They shifted, their faces somber but earnest. "Who, Coach?"

"You. You're a team. You won these games . . . together." Nelli rested her elbow on Annie's shoulder. Tricia hung her arm around Mandy's. "Coach Lambert, who would be as proud of you right now as I am, he and I both taught you what we could. But you know what? We never walked onto the field with you. We never scored a goal—or stopped one. We never jumped over a defender in the middle of a game or helped up a player when she was down. And we never scraped our knees on the parking lot pavement during practice or baked cookies to raise money just for the chance to play a game. You did. On the field you became your best because off the field you came together. And you can't lose when that happens."

Hannah leaned into Kentucky and soon the girls formed a circle, arms draped over shoulders, heads leaning toward the center. One body of athletic friendship, one team, one symbol of hope.

"You deserve to be recognized, Girls, because you've worked harder than any team I've ever seen. And because . . . you . . . are . . . Lions!"

Their loud and enthusiastic chant swelled as the girls clapped and hopped around the goal posts and back down the track. When they finally stopped, they waited for instructions from their coach regarding the final practice of the season.

"Coach, you know what?" Nelli asked as they warmed up. "With all due respect, maybe it was a good thing you never baked cookies. I'm not sure we could have sold many, if you know what I mean."

Bailey tossed his hat at the girl, who tossed it back, laughed and joined her teammates in drills. Eventually, they packed up and drove home. They completed math assignments and research projects, washed their family dinner dishes, stayed on the phone with one another too long into the evening. The pattern repeated the next day and the next, until finally, Friday morning came.

Bailey's team dressed in their uniforms and walked into the packed gym, sitting side by side on a bench diagonal to the basketball rim. A few boys pointed at the girls and snickered until Bailey walked in front and glared. The band started up with trumpets and drums as the cheerleaders took to the center of the gym, jumping and chopping the air with their routines. Dressed in a suit with a wide green and blue tie, athletic director and football coach Harry Hanks walked to the edge of the court, pulled a microphone close, and tapped it.

"Is this thing on?" The students and teachers in the stands went wild. They jumped to their feet and hollered, "State! State! State!" Bailey and his girls joined them. Hanks waved his arms, beaming at the praise, before asking the crowd to sit.

"We are proud to have our varsity football team in the state finals tonight, and we hope we'll see you all at the game." The energetic enthusiasm soared again until Hanks once more waved for the students to be seated. "But we also have another team representing us at the state level. This year's first-ever girls soccer team."

He pointed to Bailey and his team, who stood up and walked across the gym floor. Mandy, Tricia and Kentucky led the way, with Annie and the others right behind them. They waved their hands in the air, and the crowd offered them polite applause. The cheerleaders clapped, the band rearranged their instruments.

"Congratulations to Coach Bailey Crawford and his girls soccer team." Hanks spoke an inch from the microphone, himself applauding the girls until they stood against the wall under the basketball rim and the attention faded. "Now let's hear it for this year's varsity football team, led by quarterback Preston Hanks, and your state champions after tonight's game!"

The team burst from the locker room, wearing jerseys and jeans, slapping each other's hands while they jogged around the gym. They filled the entire basketball court along with their coaches and trainers. The band played louder than before and the cheerleaders led the crowd in another fight song. Hanks introduced the Booster Club president, Stan Gullen, who invited the entire school and their families to Main Street that afternoon to celebrate with "the parade that would lead the Lions to a historic championship!"

Bailey listened and clapped, and as he did, he noticed a smaller, brown-haired man with a video camera filming Gullen, Hanks and the team. He stood with his tripod on the back bleacher to get a better camera angle. Bailey recognized him as a father who'd attended parent-teacher night, although he couldn't recall the man's name. Bailey was glad the assembly was being captured on film, because for him, chronicling history was crucial in any form, even if it was just an amateur video camera at a high school assembly.

When the assembly was over and the crowd spilled onto the floor around quarterback Preston Hanks, his father the coach, and the rest of the football players, Bailey gathered his team and gave them instructions for the parade: They were to meet at the corner of Chestnut and Main at 3 o'clock sharp. They'd lead the march at the front of the parade, with the band right behind them, followed by the cheerleaders and then the football players, the offensive and defensive lines walking first, with the seniors riding in convertibles.

The girls had fought hard all season, endured a program that offered no equipment or support, not even a field, but in no way had they expected what they received at the start of the Claymont Falls parade. As they passed families and children lined on the sidewalks, they heard taunts and jeers: "Stay in the kitchen!" "Girls can't play sports!" A few small boys tossed apple cores and laughed with contempt as they did.

But the girls kept their heads up, pretending they didn't hear anything but cheers, and instead of wanting to punch the guys, Bailey followed the lead of his players. Even that night at the football game, as his team gathered in the stands together to cheer on the Lions at kick-off, Bailey was on the receiving end of jabs he'd hoped he wouldn't have to hear, mostly along the lines of "girls shouldn't compete." One shout even chastised him for "letting females doing something they weren't born for!" That's when he stood up, looking for the culprits.

"Just ignore them, Hon," Cathy said, pulling him back to the bleachers. "Believe me, the girls are a lot tougher than you think, and certainly stronger than those jerks yelling." She laughed and clapped. The whole town, it seemed, had come to the football game, just as they had shown up at the parade. Football was indeed King in Claymont Falls and, as a referee blew his whistle, the game began with the subjects bowing to His Sovereignty.

But not for long. By the end of the second quarter, Claymont Falls was down 21-7 and the fans were not happy. Quarterback Preston Hanks had fumbled twice, thrown an interception and, as is often the case with quarterbacks, received the most jeers, as if trailing the state championship were entirely his fault. Bailey didn't dare head to the concession stand at this point. He knew that the Booster Club parents who manned it would be as sour as the sausages and kraut. He wasn't even sure they'd make much money for the team this night, but his mind wasn't entirely on this game anyway.

Harry Hanks must have given one heck of a halftime talk, because within minutes of the third quarter, the Lions were back. The band, it seemed, turned up their volume, the cheerleaders were losing their voices from yelling so loudly, and by the middle of the fourth quarter the town remembered why they had crowned the game and these players with royal status: it was tied at 27.

The Lions receivers were catching everything Preston threw. Then with one minute left in the game, it was third down and two yards to go for a first down. They were on their opponent's eleven-yard line. Preston got the snap, shot back into the quarterback's pocket, and instead of passing the ball to his wide receiver—who was jetting back and forth in the end zone—he decided to keep it. He ran straight ahead, the ball in his gut, and just as he was close to the ten-yard line, a defensive back collided with him so hard the ball popped out of the quarterback's hands and into the air. Another defender snatched it and ran like there was fire in his cleats all the way to the other end zone.

Touchdown.

The undefeated Claymont Falls high school football team had lost. They would not bring home anything but a busload of disappointment and heartache.

Bailey and Cathy threaded their way through the glum crowd and toward the parking lot. Mandy was heading home with Tricia and their friends, and B.J. was doing the same, by way of the Pizza Palace. But just as Bailey closed the car door for his wife, he saw Stan Gullen charging toward him.

"Crawford, got a second?" Gullen's face was red, and a spot of mustard stained the middle of his blue Booster Club T-shirt.

"Hi, Stan. Tough loss," Bailey said, walking around the car toward the driver's seat.

"Tougher than you know. We should have had a state title by now, and it's all Hanks fault for not bringing it home."

Bailey looked at the pavement, his hands in his jacket and his mouth closed. He knew better than to talk to a football parent whose son's team had just lost.

"So I'll get to the point. We've never had a state title." "There's always next year," Bailey said as groups of sullen fans moped past.

"Damn right, there's next year. That's exactly what I mean. Next year will be the year to bring it home." He shifted sideways then moved in so close to him that Bailey could smell his breath.

"Not sure how I can help you, Stan." Bailey stood his ground.

"The last thing this town needs is for a bunch of girls to be the first to win a state championship. So you just do what you have to make sure that doesn't happen."

Bailey blinked. "You're kidding, right?"

Gullen's eyes shrunk. "Hell no. We will not have a bunch of tomboys break the curse, and then think they can do God only knows what else. I'll only tell you once, Crawford: Lions football will win the town's first championship. Football is what people care about, what they spend their money on and what gives these kids a chance to go to college."

If the man's tone hadn't been so ridiculous, his eyes so beady, Bailey might have laughed out right. "Are you asking me to throw the game?"

"I don't care what happens, just as long as those girls don't win."

"And if we do?"

Stan shifted to his right, smirked and whispered: "If you do, no one will ever—and I mean ever—hear about this ridiculous little program. Girls playing soccer, what's next? We'll make sure it never gets funded. That's all."

Bailey smiled and exhaled a mighty breath of impatience. "Well, Stan, thanks for the support. Sorry about tonight." He turned away from the sputtering ego, got into the vehicle and drove slowly out of the parking lot. As Bailey looked into his rearview mirror, he watched a Gullen still as a statue, glaring at the car as it pulled out.

"What was all that about, Hon?" Cathy asked.

"Just wishing us good luck for the game tomorrow."

When they turned into the driveway, Bailey saw a string of clouds float across the moon and then disappear. The stars were bright and clear, and that night, Bailey slept more soundly than he had in a long time.

But by 11 a.m. the next morning, he felt anything but rested. Had he done enough to prepare his team, or were they walking into their first embarrassment of the season? Had he made the right decisions for the lineup? Would they have enough to bring home a victory, in spite of everything? And what about Gullen's threat?

He fought the barrage of thoughts as he pulled into the parking lot of the stadium. Cars and vans filled the lot, but Bailey found several spots reserved for Claymont Falls near the entrance. He put his car in park and turned to Cathy. He sighed. She brushed his hand and nodded. B.J. and two of his soccer buddies sat in the back seat as quietly as if they were going to their own final game. When they all climbed out of the car, the rest of the caravan pulled in behind them. Bailey's stomach flipped. He swallowed a twinge of nervousness, dismissed the doubt, and shouted, "Lions!"

The girls echoed their coach: "Lions!"

They walked slowly through the gate, ponytails tied back with blue and green ribbons to match their uniforms which still hung too wide for their frames. When they came to the grass, they dropped their shabby bags and saw the Eagles side of the stadium packed with families, teenagers, even a band. Cheerleaders in red skirts and white tops were rousing the fans and showing off their moves. An army of athletic trainers and coaches scurried around the sidelines as some twenty tall girls in slick red uniforms stretched and jogged on the field. The Lions had met this team at the start of the season on their home turf, and their opponents would want revenge, especially with so much on the line.

"Try to ignore all of this," Bailey said softly as they crowded around him at the bench, "Just remember you don't have to be the best to do your best. That's what you'll think about the rest of your life when you think about this game." He nodded at each of them as they ran out on the field to warm up, although the sound of the Eagles marching band challenged their focus.

Bailey turned to see who was in the Lions stands behind him. It didn't take long to identify each fan—there weren't many. But there were more than usual. Cathy sat, as usual, by Reyola, who had brought her daughter and baby granddaughter. They were talking and sipping coffee from thermoses. B.J. and his friends sat beside them, waving their baseball caps and pointing at players on the other team. Behind them were Tricia and Hannah's mothers, along with a few other parents who'd brought their younger daughters. Bailey also saw baseball coach Freddie Smith talking with a few teachers. The short man he'd seen at the assembly with the video camera was there as well, setting up his tripod. Bailey even spotted Walter Knudsen who happily hollered, "Closed the bakery for this, Coach! Go, Lions!"

Bailey waved back. And though he counted about twenty-five Lions fans compared with the 150 or so on the Eagles side, somehow Bailey felt the number was just right.

The whistle blew and the game began. The Eagles, as expected, came out in force, dominating the ball and pushing the play downfield until, fifteen minutes into the game, one of their shots snuck by Hannah and angled just out of Annie's reach and into the net.

Eagles 1. Lions 0.

Kentucky took the kick-off and belted it out to the wing, challenging her teammates to stay the course. Each Lion ran to open space, supported one another and talked constantly about where they were. Back and forth the ball zoomed, while the band played and the crowds yelled. Annie flew through the air to block more shots, while Mandy, even Nelli, kept the Eagles on the defense. It was a tight, evenly-matched game.

Bailey had no reason to worry.

With two minutes left before halftime, Kentucky intercepted a pass and sprinted with all her might downfield, around defenders, until she was one on one with the goalkeeper. She faked right, drawing out the keeper, and then cut back inside, pushing the ball past her opponent and into the near corner of the goal. Tricia screamed. Nelli jumped on Kentucky's back. And Bailey heard 25 Lions fans shouting with all their might.

Eagles 1. Lions 1.

When the halftime whistle blew, the girls hurried to the sideline, grabbing water and oranges before sitting in a huddle at Bailey's feet. He talked about movement, positioning, even making sure they were having fun. And when the second half was about to start, they all stood up, faced their fans and applauded them, thanking them for coming. Their voices grew louder, as if 25 more had joined them.

"You can do it!" Bailey heard Reyola shout.

"Come on, Mandy! Score!" B.J. yelled.

"Go, Girls!"

"Li-ons! Li-ons! Li-ons!"

Sunlight shown on the scoreboard as the Lions took the field and the whistle signaled the second half. Both teams played harder than they had in the first, and Bailey simply marched up and down the sideline, shouting occasional instructions and gulping water from small paper cups. With the score still tied and 17 minutes remaining, a whistle stopped the chaos created by a cluster of players in front of the Lions goal. Someone—Bailey wasn't sure who—had touched the ball with her hand in the goal box, and the referee was calling for a penalty kick. Arms folded across his chest, Bailey took a deep breath and stood completely silent.

But Tricia began screaming at her teammates to get into position. Annie was directly behind her on the goal line waving her arms like a traffic cop, pacing back and forth. The Eagles striker was taking the penalty shot, which meant all the other players had to be standing outside the box. Girls in blue jerseys elbowed girls in red as they crowded the line or positioned themselves at different spots down the field. And the entire stadium held its breath.

Wearing a bright yellow jersey to distinguish her as goalie, Annie finally settled on a mid-goal stance, stood completely still and crouched with her arms out in front of her, palms up. The referee blew the whistle and the striker threw all of her weight behind the ball, firing it like a bullet toward Annie. Right at her in fact. Annie caught it with the flair fitting a wide receiver, and Tricia again screamed hysterically. Annie gave the ball a bounce before booting it down to midfield.

It landed on a girl wearing #10. Kentucky trapped the ball and began sprinting as fast as she could toward the other goal. All of her teammates followed as she wove in and out of red jerseys. Just as she came to the edge of the goalkeeper's box, smack in the center and in perfect range for a shot on goal, a defender came at her. She flicked the ball off to the right, just out of reach of a second defender. Mandy burst through both defenders, tapped the ball a yard in front of her and then nailed it toward the far post of the goal. The goalkeeper flew sideways to stop it, but just missed knocking it out of bounds. The ball bounced off the post and into the goal.

Tricia raced up the field and jumped onto Mandy's back as the rest of the blue jerseys circled around her forming one giant blue blob. The referee blew his whistle and Bailey threw his hands in the air while his team cheered and jumped and hugged. Fans behind him began the victory shout, "Li-ons! Li-ons!" And when the referee reigned in the excitement, and the teams lined up for a Eagle kick-off, Bailey had to look at the scoreboard:

Eagles 1. Lions 2. Clock: 66:32.

Twelve minutes later, after two or three more shots and saves, the referee blew his whistle. The game was over. The Claymont Falls girls soccer team had won the state championship, the first in school history. And fifteen teenage girls, along with a small crowd of friends, smothered Bailey Crawford so that you could hardly see his hat.

chapter
14

2008

My phone was ringing. I reached for my bag across the driver's seat just as I was getting back into my car at Knudsen's, coffee and muffin in hand. Too late. Missed call.

I sat in my car, enjoying the crunchy dome of the muffin. I turned up the volume on the radio—jazz today—and thought about the week ahead. We were playing our first two games against teams twice our size, and I had only five real subs. But that wasn't what worried me. It might have last year, when I had higher, less realistic hopes for what a young team with a young coach could accomplish. My players now would be fine. They might not be an equal to their opponents but they'd battle to the end. That much was sure.

What I couldn't stop thinking about instead were those women at Nelli's house, sitting together, eating and drinking as if they'd simply gathered for a family reunion, as if an undefeated season twenty-five years ago was just another memorable occasion like vacations or funerals. Their conversations and jokes, their enviable familiarity and gentle jests, all were teasers to an underlying story I'd not heard before, but one that left me wanting more. What happened to them in 1983 seemed to have created some magic formula, one with its powers still in tact, even if others had long since forgotten what they'd achieved.

And now I felt like I should do something about it. I would make sure they were not ignored, that they were given the prize they'd never received as champions. They deserved that, no matter what it took.

MaeMa would have done that.

I drove into the school and parked, grabbed my bag and books and marched to Hanks' office. Classes didn't start for another 35 minutes, so the halls were empty except for teachers, aides and specialists trickling in. If anyone should be helping in the effort, my athletic director should.

Will jumped out of nowhere. I dodged, fumbled for my books and regained my balance.

"Morning!" He beamed, adjusting his glasses.

"Sheesh, where'd you come from?" I jumped back and stared. He wore black jeans, loafers and an un-tucked striped shirt, his bicycle bag slung over his shoulder. This guy was getting really good at surprising me—and looking better each time he did. I sighed.

"The library, of course. Hey, I just tried calling you."

"That was you? I was getting breakfast."

"Ah."

We stood silently among the sounds of a school just waking up around us. Doors opening and shutting, voices rising, security guards barking formal orders.

"You look great." Will said suddenly. I looked down to remember what I was wearing: one of my new skirts, a sleeveless cotton blouse and heels, the kind of outfit I turned to on days when I wanted to distinguish myself as older than my students.

"Thanks. I'm trying to look professional. Is it working?"

"Definitely."

"Good because I'm about to pitch Hanks our idea."

"You'll do great. After meeting that first team, how could you lose?"

"No kidding, right?" I set down my bag and readjusted my books. "They deserve this." The proclamation increased my urgency to see Hanks, and I moved toward his office until curiosity got the best of me.

"Hey, why'd you call? Did you find out something else?"

Will nodded. He took off his glasses and wiped them with the tail of his shirt. "Listen, Rey, I know you have a game Friday afternoon—"

"You had to remind me." I glanced at my watch. "Two this week. Hope we survive."

"You will."

A cluster of social studies teachers walked past us, and nodded. We returned the greeting.

"So," Will turned back toward me. "After the game, I was wondering, if, well, you'd like to go with . . . me to get . . ."

I blinked. "You're asking me . . . out, aren't you? Like, on a date?"

His looked straight at me, his kind blue eyes most serious. "Is that okay?"

"You can't answer a question with a question."

"Fair enough. So, Rey, I'd like to buy you dinner after your game on Friday."

"You what?"

"I would like to buy you dinner after your game on Friday."

I swallowed the morsel of muffin that'd gotten lodged in my teeth—self-conscious that Will had noticed—before staring down the hall. This was a white man—who also happened to be a librarian—doing the asking. Yes, we'd been brought together by the history of our institution, joining forces in our challenge to organize an honorary ceremony for the school's only championship team. Yes, we'd already had some great conversations in the process and, truth be told, I hadn't minded one minute of it. But take me out to dinner? I needed to confront this head on.

"You are aware of the fact I'm African-American, right?"

He didn't miss a beat: "And this is 2008, right?"

"Okay, just so you know."

Will tilted his head. The smile widened. "Is this how you turn down all the guys?"

I burst out laughing. The idea that "all the guys"—white, black or purple, for that matter—would ask me out at all was one of the funniest things I'd heard in a long time. The closest I'd come to any kind of long-term relationship was the four years I'd spent in college with my 56-year-old, wife-and-three-kids-at-home goalkeeping coach as I blocked the soccer balls he'd throw at me every afternoon. I'd always been too busy with school and sports and work for clubs or friends, much less dates or romance or anything others might call "a social life."

So I kept laughing. Will did, too, not because his question sounded absurd, but because he was determined not to back down. When I finally caught my breath, there stood Will, waiting, hopeful.

"You're serious?"

"It's just dinner."

"In public?"

"That's where the best restaurants are. In public places."

I tried to visualize the moment, like I had when I was on the goal line defending a penalty shot. I always had a fifty/fifty chance with the shooter. Either she'd go left or she'd shoot right, and I'd have to guess.

"I have to warn you. I won't be very good company if we lose."

"I'll take my chances." He scratched his neck but held his gaze. "Besides, you've got to eat." He paused. "So, is that a 'yes'?"

I studied his face, in all its whiteness. He was not joking.

"I guess I do have to eat."

"Yes, you do. Great. I'll meet you in the parking lot after the game and we'll go from there. How about Thai?" I nodded. He pushed his glasses back up his nose. "Hey, let me know how it goes with Hanks."

"Yeah, wish me luck." "Good luck!" Will's smile was full and wide, a slight dimple I'd not noticed before formed at his cheek. He placed his hand on my shoulder and tapped it lightly before pulling it back. "You'll do great."

I was glad I'd had my coffee and muffin already because my knees suddenly felt a little wobbly and I felt butterflies in my stomach. I heard the click of loafers behind me as I sprinted ahead toward the athletic department. I forced myself not to look back at his tennis-player butt in denim.

Hanks was fishing in his pocket for his keys to the office when I came alongside. "You got an important meeting or something?" He shot me a quick look and pointed to my outfit.

"Yes, with you."

"No, you don't." He fiddled with the key until it finally turned and he pushed open the door to his office. I followed him, walking beside football trophies, boxes of jerseys, crates of water bottles and cans of new tennis balls. He set his briefcase on the non-cluttered corner of his desk, pulled a folded copy of today's Register from under his arm and tossed it onto the piles.

"I wanted to talk with you about—"

"Sorry, Coach, I've got bigger fish to fry right now." Preston Hanks dropped into his chair, picked up the phone and began to dial. He shooed me out of the office with his other hand, but I wasn't moving. I glanced sideways at the newspaper, creased in the editorial section, to read the headline: "New Stadium Proposal Wastes Taxpayer Dollars."

Hanks shook his head and slammed down the receiver. "I said, not now, Coach!"

I stiffened. "I'd like my team to do some fundraisers."

"Later, Wallace." He stood, his cheeks filling with color, the veins in his neck starting to bulge. "We'll talk about it later. Set it up with Mary. Now out!"

He was breathing hard and loud behind me while he followed me to the door and slammed it behind me. The crack of wood against metal shattered the otherwise quiet department. Mary had not yet come into work. Alone in the room, walls covered with team posters and schedules, I took in a deep breath. A tinge of stale perspiration crept into the air, the way smoke sometimes lingers in old cushions and pillows. I exhaled, reached for a cup of water from the cooler and gulped it. Then I crushed that plastic cup and threw it at the door that had just slammed.

I tried to avoid thinking of the two completely opposite encounters I'd had with men already that early morning, and then steeled my nerves for my English students as I walked to my classroom. It wasn't easy. But between preparing vocabulary lessons and introductory paragraphs, I managed to keep the emotions of the morning mostly at bay. At least until practice.

Kate and her teammates were stretching when I ran toward them from the coaches' locker room. They waved and I yelled for them to follow and we began a long-distance run around the school and through the sports complex. I needed the run. The girls kept up behind me, single file, even as we ran up the hill and down around the football practice field where Hanks was gathering his coaches and players. My pace picked up.

Soon, we were back at our own field, pushing through drill after drill, passing, juggling and throw-ins, then shots on goal. Hard. I said very little to my team except to direct them in their exercises and techniques. They exchanged a few glances and comments, but kept focused on each new challenge. Today, I didn't want anything but serious soccer. No conversations about malls or movies or boys. Just soccer. And for two and a half hours, I got what I wanted.

"Okay, grab some water," I finally said at 5:35. The sun was beginning to set and the air was cooling, just slightly. "Captains, lead the cool down."

They moved in silence, their bodies worked, one group of teenagers in a chain of athletes spread out across the athletic complex in the early evening light.

"Coach Rey, we've got some good stuff for the raffle already," Kate broke the mood while she leaned toward her toes. "Lots of people say they want to donate a prize or buy a ticket."

"Or both!" Maggie chimed in.

"Yeah, so we should be able to raise enough for championship rings!"

The girls high-fived one another. I remembered Hanks slamming the door that morning but I was determined not to squelch their enthusiasm. "Great work, Lions. That'll mean a lot to them. And guess what?"

"What?"

"You might even get to meet some of those first players at tomorrow's game. A few said they were going to try to make it when we play at home." I knelt beside a ball as the girls sat on the grass stretching.

"So let's talk about the game."

They nodded, drained and hot, and I wondered if I should have pushed them so hard the day before our first game of the season. But we needed to be ready.

And as I'd told them many times before, if they practiced hard, they'd play hard. So we talked about the lineup, who'd be in which position and what to expect from our opponents when they showed up at Claymont Falls tomorrow. They listened and drank their water, collected their bags and strolled back to their locker room just as the football team was also finishing practice. My players were tiny compared to the bulky boys they passed, lugging their helmets and sauntering so slowly they looked like their legs weighed a thousand pounds each. I was gathering up our equipment when I spotted a tall thin man in a white baseball hat and black sweats jogging the opposite direction of the young athletes and toward the football coaches.

Wally Knudsen stopped when he arrived at the middle of the field and raised his hand. Preston Hanks shoved a clipboard at an assistant and stepped toward Wally. The two shook hands and detached themselves from the crowd of coaches and trainers, who were loading coolers and first-aid kits onto the back of golf carts and riding down the walkway past the other fields.

Hanks and Wally walked toward a goal post, their backs to me and too far away anyway for me to see their interaction. Our storage shed was in the opposite direction, so I finished up, and left Wally to try his luck with Hanks. By the time I emerged from the coaches' locker room, Wally was leaning against a blue sedan, reading the sports section of the Register.

"Coach Rey," he said, tucking the paper under his arm.

"I thought that was you out on the field."

"Good practice?" "Getting there. What brings you here?"

"Like I said at Nelli's, I wanted to ask around, you know, see how the district could help with the team ceremony. Thought I'd start with Hanks." He sighed. "It's a great idea, by the way, one my sister and I have talked about before, but the timing was never quite right." His shoulders bounced as he spoke, his eyes full of the same energy and excitement that had filled Nelli's living room the night of the team gathering. It was not hard to imagine him as an elementary P.E. teacher, inspiring kids to jump vaults in gymnastics or run further than they thought they could on the track.

"How'd it go with Hanks? He can be a bit, um, . . ."

"Stubborn? Talk about bad timing. Preston wasn't interested in anything but getting the public to vote to fund that crazy new football stadium."

I leaned against my car and searched my bag for my keys as Wally continued. "But if you ask me, he's just using the stadium as another excuse."

Wally tapped the rolled newspaper against the side of his leg. His cheekbones were higher than Annie's, and his nose wider, but there was no mistaking the Knudsen resemblance. Then his words registered in my head.

"Another excuse?"

A whistle blew off in the distance at one of the sophomore football practices, and Wally's attention shifted. "It's still amazing to me to see all these fields and stuff," he said quietly. "I was just a kid when I was the ball boy, so I didn't understand how much that first team struggled. The older I got, the more I realized how wrong it was. I mean, I can't even remember the team practicing here. Of course, there were only two fields then and there was no way Preston's dad wanted anybody but football players using them." He gestured across the sea of fields. "And when I came to high school here, everyone thought I would play football like every other kid in town and I did think about it. But . . . "

He spotted something. I waited.

"I just didn't see the point of football if it was going to be like that, so I never tried." Wally opened his car door and shook his head. "Anyway, I struck out with Preston today, but I'll keep trying with other folks at the district office. You keep at it too, okay?"

"Will do. Thanks, Wally."

"We'll get there. That's what Coach Crawford always said: one way or another, we'll get there." He waved as he put his car in reverse, and I climbed into mine. We pulled out of the lot in different directions. I wondered how the coach of a brand new team, one who was up against so many obstacles, could have been so certain his team would "get there," or anywhere for that matter. I wanted his secret.

Preston Hanks was "out of the building" at meetings all day, his assistant told me the next morning. The soonest he could meet me, she said, was Thursday at 5:15 after practices. I considered my options as coaches and students hurried crowded the office.

"I'll take it," I told Mary, who typed in my name on her computer for our boss's electronic calendar. When she finished, she pointed at my feet.

"Love those. I've been looking for some pumps like that." She clicked "Save" on her keyboard.

"Kuebler's, on sale, over on Market Street," I said, clicking my heels. "They're my game day shoes. Let's hope they work."

A baseball coach dumped a packet of forms on her desk, cutting short both her enthusiasm and our conversation. I turned my stylish shoes toward the now bustling halls and got ready for a day of Mockingbird, word games and sentences.

Game day also meant dress-up day for my team, and though we didn't yet have official approval to honor Coach Crawford's championship, the idea itself seemed to have inspired my players. Every time I bumped into a player at her locker or in the hall, she not only looked classy in her skirt or dress pants, she was, "totally psyched" to play, she said.

Learning of that state victory seemed to instill enthusiasm and courage I hadn't yet seen in my players. Maybe they could relate to being an outsider, being on a team few kids in Claymont Falls even knew existed. The boys golf team got more attention than girls soccer, even in the Register. So whatever happened since we began dreaming of a recognition ceremony, my players found a spark they didn't have last year. They practiced hard yesterday. And I was crossing my fingers it'd pay off today.

By the end of the first half of our first game, though, I wasn't sure any of it had sunk in. We were down 0-2, and the girls seemed intimidated by the sheer number of players on the other team more so than by their abilities. We needed to rally. At halftime, I pulled them over to the sideline, passed around some water and pulled out my clipboard.

But we were interrupted in the middle of my pep talk. We looked toward a noise in the stands to see a total of five fans, four mothers and three additional women I recognized from a few nights ago. Annie, Nelli and Hannah were standing side by side, their fists in the air, and voicing a rising chant, "Li-ons! Li-ons! Li-ons! My players elbowed each other, until they, too, were on their feet, shouting with the women and mothers who had joined in, "Li-ons! Li-ons!" The referee blew his whistle, the teams sprinted on to the field and the second half began.

I hadn't finished my talk, but I didn't need to. Suddenly, the girls were playing with magic in their bones: bouncing all over the field, stealing passes from the other team, slide tackling against offenders and even taking shots on goal. Good ones. So many shots, in fact, that eventually the ball bounced off of one of the defenders on the other team and went into the net. The Lions—behind us and on the field—went crazy, cheering with extra force.

With fifteen minutes left in the game and the score 1-2, I screamed for Kate and Maggie to move up front and put the pressure on offensively. Soon we were camping out in our opponent's end of the field and hammering shots toward the posts.

But their goalkeeper was having a good game. No matter how many times we shot, she either caught the ball or punched it out of bounds. Our corner kicks, although close, had not shifted the score when the final whistle blew. Our first game of the season was our first loss.

I shook the opposing coaches' hands, waved my players over to the sideline and led them in stretches, silently. Both teams acted as if they'd just lost the

Super Bowl: The other team walked in a somber single file toward their bus, humiliated they did not win by a greater margin against a team like Claymont Falls. My players moped all the more.

"Well, that was one heck of a comeback, girls!" Nelli appeared on the field looking more like a corporate executive than a fan at a soccer match. Her slacks and blouse were perfectly tailored for her tiny frame and her earrings jiggled as she clapped. In jeans and blue shirts, Annie and Hannah stood beside her clapping as well, the team mothers joining like back-up singers.

"But we lost," Kate said softly.

Nelli scratched her head and looked at Annie. "Did these girls lose that game?"

"Only if they think that the second half didn't matter."

My players glanced at each other.

"Girls, meet Ms. Martinelli, Ms. Knudsen and Ms. Brown," I said.

"Green. I used to be Brown but I went and married a Green man. Isn't that a hoot?" Hannah said, flipping her hair to the side to correct an out-of-place strand. The gesture and the comment lightened the air, and a few of the girls giggled.

"These women played on that first team I told you about," I announced to my team. That got their attention.

"State champions!" Monica squealed.

"Ah, hon, we only came today to cheer you on and I'd say you made a real good comeback. You should be proud of yourselves." Nelli pulled the strap of her purse over her shoulder.

"She's right. You keep playing like you did in that second half, and anything could happen, believe me," Annie said, her arms out to her sides like she was waiting for someone to fill in the blank.

Hannah obliged. "She's right, Girls. Keep going like crazy women and you'll turn the other team . . . blue!"

A chorus of laughter erupted and the girls were slapping each other's shoulders. A few stepped toward the older women to talk, while the mothers helped pick up gear. Soon, we were moving toward the locker room, a blend of blue and green in motion, a single image of female capability.

At the edge of the parking lot, the women quieted the team and promised to bring back some other former players. They wanted to send representatives to each home game. The girls cheered and thanked their new fans for the support. For me, the exchange was like some out-of-body experience and I was watching two teams—who before a few weeks ago didn't even know the other existed— suddenly look like long-lost friends who'd just been reunited.

"Coach Rey, we have to get those rings for them," Kate whispered to me. "We have to."

"We will. One way or another, we'll get there." I patted her back. We were the only two left in the lot after an energetic rally of farewells. Kate smiled, her long braid flowing behind her as she tossed her bag into the trunk of her car and headed for home.

The phone rang just as I was walking in the door with a pizza. I heard Mom shuffle toward it.

"Oh, hello, Tricia . . . so glad you liked it . . . Yes, indeed . . . Great. Here she is now."

Mom, who was still in her cafeteria uniform, mouthed the word "Tricia" to me and handed over the phone. She took the pizza, glad she didn't have to cook, and shuffled toward the kitchen for plates.

"Hello?"

"Hi, Doll. Nice to talk with Jocelyn—it's been a while. Don't know how we get so busy. Anyway, how'd the game go?"

I relayed the score and the details of the first and second half, as well as the difference her friends made in supporting our team. She was pleased.

"Great to hear. You'll get 'em next time. Hey, listen, I've got good news and bad news, which is, of course, typical for a newspaper woman."

She laughed at her own joke and shifted gears. "I don't think I did our plan any favors with my editorial on the stadium. Preston was not happy about it."

"No, he wasn't."

"Sorry, Hon. But it's ridiculous to think we should pay more taxes and— oh, never mind. We won't let it stop us, right? So here's the good news. We've tracked down all of the girls from our team and it seems your last conference game—Saturday, November 5th—is the best for everyone's schedule."

"You mean everyone can come?"

"Well, that's the bad news. Kentucky isn't sure. She's out in Arizona these days, a lawyer on the border there, and thinks she might have to be in court then. Not sure yet but she's going to try. She was real glad to know about you and your team."

"She was?"

"You bet. Anyway, that means we've got 14 of the original 15, plus Wally, who've said they'd be there that weekend. Hold on—" Tricia was still in the newsroom, with shouting and clacking in the background. Mom set down a plate in front of me—pepperoni, extra cheese and onions—and picked up hers.

"Okay, I'm back. Listen, I'm on deadline, but let's touch base next week. We should know more then. Thanks, Coach!" Tricia hung up and I inhaled the first slice, and then grabbed a second and a third.

"Some day, huh?" Mom said, wiping the corners of her mouth with her fingers.

"A roller coaster."

"Nothing a Wallace woman can't handle." She reached for the television remote, studied it and then seemed to change her mind. "Some of those girls come to your game?"

I chomped on the crust and swallowed. "Which girls?" "Coach Crawford's."

"Oh, those girls. Yes, a few of them. How'd you know?"

"Heard you tell Tricia." Mom's eyes caught the living room light and I saw her weariness. She set her plate on the coffee table and leaned her head back against the cushion like she was remembering something.

"Whether it was raining or snowing or sunny, MaeMa and I would sit next to that field either in our lawn chairs or the car or whatever, and watch those girls kick that ball and run around with all their might. I never really understood it, but I didn't mind. I just liked sitting with her when I could." Mom's eyes clouded.

I slid the box of tissues her direction, and finished eating. This was a conversation we hadn't visited since we buried my grandmother. I hunted for something, anything, to say. "That must have been nice, Mom, being with MaeMa."

"It was. Made me glad to have those times with her whenever I could make it. Looked forward to them, really. And I was proud to sit with her, especially when those girls finished a game and Coach would walk them over—real gentlemanly like, you know—just to thank us for coming." A single tear slid down Mom's cheek, and she left it there. "He never said more than that, and MaeMa didn't either. And then we'd come home."

The lamp near the couch flickered

"Where was I?"

She ran her palm over her cheek and turned toward me. "What do you mean, where were you?"

"That was the year I was born, right? 1983. They started that August. So what did you do with me when you and MaeMa went to those games?"

Gentle laughter escaped the sides of her mouth and her shoulders rose slightly. "What do you think? You were either on my lap, or MaeMa's, or if we were in the car, you'd be in the back seat, usually asleep. Every once in a while, Cathy Crawford picked you up, too."

"I . . . was . . . at . . . those . . . games?"

"Most of 'em." Mom beamed. "I reckon that's where you first learned to love soccer."

She stood up suddenly and stretched. "Thanks for the pizza. I sure didn't want to cook tonight."

"But what about the next year? Did you go then too? And take me?"

My mother had just opened the first page of a book, and now I had to hear the entire story through to its ending. "What happened next, Mom?"

Her face grew tight. She sighed. "Well, after that championship game—which you slept right through—MaeMa and I didn't make it to another soccer game until you were a seven-year-old youth soccer player. What was your team's name?" She looked at the shelf with my team pictures. "Cubs, that's it. Anyway, I don't really know why. I think Coach Crawford kept on helping the girls the next year, but I got the job at the school cafeteria and, between that and taking care of you . . . well, things were . . . different." She stepped toward her bedroom.

"You know they never got any recognition, no trophy, nothing, for winning?" I leaned forward. "That doesn't seem right."

Mom rubbed her neck. "Lots of things aren't right, Rey. But I can tell you this: everyone in this town knew those girls were champions. Everyone." She looked at our plates and the empty pizza box. "Can you clean this up, Hon?"

"What do you mean, everyone?"

"Everyone knew who won that game. But not everyone liked it. That's all. Now you get a good night sleep, Baby."

No matter how many more pages I wanted to turn, Mom's story was effectively over for the evening. She closed her bedroom door and I went to the kitchen, my emotions still on the roller coaster that I couldn't control.

A team had won a championship, I'd been at their games as a baby, no one wanted to acknowledge their excellence, but everyone knew they were champions? The day ended as strangely as it began.

Sleep was a series of starts and fits that night, much like the rhythm of my next few days. I jumped between bad papers and assigned novels, led quick workouts and challenging practices, and offered hearty cheers every time my players announced they were making progress on the raffle. I wanted to believe it would do some good, even if I wasn't sure their work would amount to much. And I definitely avoided hallway conversations with Will in case I got too weird and he changed his mind about dinner. It was a week full of question marks.

Go back to your confidence, MaeMa used to say; if things got out of control, go back to what you can control. So I put on my best game face, focusing on coaching my girls and moving ahead with something that should have happened long ago: a ceremony for a bunch of former champions.

Hanks shuffled through piles of folders when I stood at his door. I rapped my knuckles against the wood and rallied some composure.

"Coach Hanks? Is this a good time?"

"No."

"I did make an appointment and—" He kept shuffling. "All right. Come on. Time's short."

I took the chair in front of his desk as he rearranged files and papers. I sat upright, my pumps firmly on the floor. It wasn't game day, but I had dressed to impress.

"Heard about your first game. Too bad," he said. "Next time."

"Next time is 5 p.m. tomorrow. Home game."

"I know." He leaned back in his chair like he'd rather be out fishing. Then he folded his arms across his chest. "Okay, what are we meeting about?"

"A few weeks ago you sent me to Coach Bailey Crawford's funeral, where I found out that he was the first coach of the program I now run."

"Hadn't I mentioned that before?"

I wiped my palm against my skirt. "Anyway, I met some of the women who were on that first team, the same team that went on to win the state title their first year in existence." I breathed. He sighed. "And guess what else I found out?"

His stare was his answer. So I continued.

"That they never received official recognition, as I think I've mentioned before. Can you imagine?"

"And your point is?"

"My team would like to do a raffle to raise money so they can buy championship rings for those players, as well as a trophy for the Hall of Inspiration. We'd like to make the presentations at our last game of the season to members of that first team, but we need official permission for the fundraiser."

Hanks did not move his arms. "No."

I coughed. "No? But don't they deserve that?"

"Oh, probably everyone thinks so these days. But I'll be honest with you, Wallace. A fundraiser of any kind would be a distraction from the work the Booster Club's doing to get the new stadium on the ballot. We can't just ask folks in the community to contribute to both. See my point?"

"No." I smelled a whiff of stale air, and considered my confidence level. "But having those women at our games, and honoring them at the end of the season, it's really good for our kids. It's helping them improve, knowing they have support and something to aspire to."

He pushed out his jaw, scratched it and then returned his hand across his arm.

"Tell you what I'm going to do, Reynalda Wallace. I can't stop that team from coming to your last game, or hell, to any of your games. And go ahead, say anything you want about them. I'm sure they'll be happy. But no fundraisers. No rings. No trophies."

The phone rang. He punched a button on it and ignored the call, still glaring at me.

Anger simmered in my stomach. "Wouldn't you want my team to succeed? This is giving them something to work toward, and a great opportunity to interact with the only championship team Claymont Falls High has ever had in its—"

Preston Hanks flew out of his chair and planted his fists on the desk so that he was almost falling toward me. The veins in his neck pulsed at full throttle, his cheeks turned redder than any human color I'd seen, and his jaw was clenched so hard the muscles bulged.

"You listen to me. That team should never have been allowed to play in the first place. Damn regulation meant my father had to make way for a sissy coach and a bunch of tomboys who should have stayed home. They just about took away football support that year. I ought to know—I was there. I was the quarterback who led our team to the state finals that year, in case you didn't know. But Crawford and those girls?" He said the word like he was spitting out sour milk. "Let's just say we've had to tolerate the program ever since, and the money it takes away from our real sports teams is ridiculous."

Hanks was breathing so hard his nostrils were flaring. I rose to my feet—a mix of shock and goalkeeper adrenaline teeming through my whole being—and adopted the same stance I used when about to face a penalty shot.

"Then why'd you hire me in the first place? I thought I was supposed to help take girls soccer to a new level, to make something of the—"

"Yeah, yeah. All that. But we needed diversity, Wallace. We don't meet our quotas, we don't get state funding. Plain and simple."

He nailed the ball so hard at me that I heard it zing right past me and into the net. I skipped back, away from the post, still facing the opponent, fumbling for balance.

"You hired me because . . . I'm black?"

"And a woman who could coach girls soccer and teach English. Hell, you're even one of our own highly-decorated athletes. It was a slam dunk." He stood straight up behind his desk, the flames now smoldering. "Are we finished here? No fundraisers. And no big deals. You understand?"

"No, I don't understand. Not at all." I shifted slowly, still wobbly. I reached for the door handle, swallowed back what else I wanted to say, and opened the door with a shred of dignity that came from somewhere I did not know.

Papers rattled behind me, but I did not look back. I hurried past posters, trophies and desks, each a flurry of fists in my gut.

Will again jumped out in front of me from behind a hall monitor. I dodged.

"Hey, Rey. How are you feeling about—"

"It's all a joke. One, big, shitty joke."

He stopped suddenly. "Whoa. What happened?"

"Hanks won't let us do the fundraiser, he's called my program a joke and he hired me to meet a quota." I was peering straight through the white guy in front of me.

"He said that?"

"And more. So forget it. I tried to help. But what good is it going to do? Might as well forget about it all."

"Wait, you're not giving up that easy, are you?"

"Why not?" I stepped around him. He adjusted his glasses. "Why would you care? Aren't we just a charity case for you, too?"

"Excuse me?"

"And while we're at it, let's just forget about dinner tomorrow."

"But—"

"I don't need any sympathy from you either."

I turned and sprinted away from Will, around the corner past the Hall of Inspiration—and that ridiculous photograph of me—as fast as I could.

chapter
15

1983

Eventually, Bailey Crawford found his hat. He picked it up from under the bench and pulled it squarely above his ears, adjusting the bill as he did. He tried not to laugh but he couldn't help it; one by one he watched his team emerge from a human pile, celebrating both their win over County Day Academy and something they never imagined. He sent them on a victory lap.

The satisfaction and joy over both feats ran deep, and Bailey laughed again, scooping up empty paper cups from the sideline and tossing them in the trash. A slight breeze tickled his face. He turned toward the field, a gorgeous green plot of grass beneath the perfect autumn blue sky. Right then, everything looked perfect.

The Lions girls soccer team jogged to where he was, passing the few soccer balls they had back and forth, their blonde and brunette pony tails relishing their victory in rhythm. Grass stains on their knees, baggy old jerseys swaying with each step, their conversations swirled with hearty cycles of "Congratulations!" They lifted up Wally as if he'd been the one to score the final goals, even though the ball boy had simply handed out water cups. When they set him back down, they huddled again for a group hug, and laughed and slung water on each other, gathering their equipment as they celebrated. Winning was sweet but being together was sweeter still. Bailey smiled again.

"Excuse me, Coach Crawford?" A skinny young man in jeans and a brown sweatshirt was trailing Bailey as he cleaned up the sideline. The man's chin revealed patches of black stubble that matched the color of his hair, and he held a thin white spiral notebook in his right hand, a pen in his left.

"Uh, I'm with the Register. Got a second?"

Bailey stopped. He thought he'd known most of the sports reporters from his tenure with the boys' team, but this face was new to him. He extended his hand for a proper introduction, but the young man clicked his pen instead.

"Let's see, did you ever expect to be here, I mean, you know, in this position?" The reporter's head bobbed as he looked at his notebook. "I mean, man. This is something else."

Bailey waited. The reporter shrugged, looked toward the Lions, who were still reveling in their state title, and then back at their coach, continually clicking his pen. "Uh, how'd you do it?"

"This team has played with a lot of heart all season, and at halftime I just reminded them of that, of how far they'd come, so that—"

"You can say that again. I mean, they're not sitting at home knitting anymore, are they?" An awkward laugh accompanied the statement, and Bailey took a step back. "So what's it like?"

"What's what like?"

He leaned into Bailey, like he was waiting for a secret, and whispered. "Off the record, you know, what's it like coaching girls? Must be pretty frustrating, probably can't do a helluva lot, right?"

Bailey blinked and glanced over to his team, who were bounding toward the bleachers as the small crowd of loyal supporters moved to meet them. He saw Cathy, Reyola with her daughter and granddaughter, B.J. and his friends, Freddie, Walter Knudsen and a few other parents laughing and hugging the girls and slapping each other on the back, pointing at the field and at each other, the scoreboard still ablaze with the final score.

"Did you watch the game today?" Bailey confronted the reporter, who simply nodded in response. "Then you'd know they can indeed do a helluva lot— obviously more than some people think they can. And for the record, I coached this team like I would coach any group of athletes—to do their best and play their best."

The reporter scribbled and concentrated. Bailey continued: "Maybe you didn't realize it, son, but this was the state championship game and both teams deserved to be here. They played hard. Both teams have a lot of talent, and the game could have gone either way at any moment. But the Lions managed to get the ball in the net when it mattered most, which is what's happened for them all season. As I said, they have a lot of heart and they play together really well because . . . they matter to each other."

Bailey paused to let his words sink in. He set down his bag and watched the reporter flip over a page of his notebook. The young man didn't look up when he asked Bailey to spell his name for him as well as the names of the two players who scored.

"A-d-e-l-i-n-e B-e-a-u-c-a-m-p and M-a-n-d-y C-r-a-w-f-o-r-d. Any other questions?"

"Crawford? Like your name?"

"Yes, she's my daughter."

The reporter stopped writing and looked like he wanted to ask a question about how a coach could let his daughter play, but he stopped himself short when he saw the look on Bailey's face. Instead, he threw Bailey a hard one: "Last question. Uh, what about next year?"

Bailey hadn't expected it. He picked up his bag and one more discarded paper cup, waving Wally over to help and giving himself a few seconds to consider the idea. "What about next year?"

"Uh, you know, how do you think you'll do?"

"Most of these girls are graduating in the spring, so I'm not sure what will happen. But the Lions always do their best."

His answer seemed to satisfy the reporter, who wrote one final scribble and jammed his notebook in his back pocket. "Okay, thanks, Coach."

"So will this be in tomorrow's paper?" Bailey asked.

"Uh, who knows? They've already got lots of other stories, football, mostly. I got stuck with this one. I'm the new guy, you know." His awkward laugh reinforced his comment. "But it's a start, I guess."

"Yes, it is a start," Bailey said, and again extended his hand to the reporter, who shook it this time. He then turned and jogged toward the parking lot just as Tricia skipped over to her coach.

"Did you just talk with a real reporter, Coach?" she asked, her eyes wide and her hair a wild mess of curls.

"I think so. Why?"

"I'm going to do that someday. Be a reporter."

"I thought you already were—with the school newspaper and the yearbook."

She rolled her eyes and shifted her weight to her left foot. "That's not the same."

"It's a start, Tricia. Just like today's game."

She looked out at the field, at her teammates, then at Wally and back to the father of her best friend. "Good point, Coach. I guess it is a start, a really good one, huh?"

Bailey put his arm around the girl as they walked side by side to join the rest of the team. Wally jumped piggyback on his sister, and after one final cheer, the girls drove home that afternoon just as they had come: in a few separate cars, but with far more confidence to unite them. B.J. and his friends piled into the car with his sister. They all planned to meet that night at Tricia's house for a pizza party, which, Bailey promised, would be compliments of the athletic department.

"It might be the only thing they'll get from the school," he said to Cathy as they pulled out of the stadium parking lot and onto the highway.

"Hon, they didn't expect to get anything, so pizza is a bonus," she said. She rested her hand on his shoulder and Bailey relaxed. He focused on the road ahead, as he listened to his wife's account of corner kicks and shots, as well as the excitement and reactions in the stands. It was all a bit surreal to Bailey, so he was glad to hear her perspective of what had just happened.

The phone rang as he and Cathy walked into the living room. Cathy got to it first, smiled and handed it to her husband.

"Hi Bailey, this is Reyola Mae. I didn't get a chance to talk with you at the game because we had to get the baby home. But I'm real proud of you, real proud." Bailey stared at his feet as he listened to his mentor.

"And Lars would have been too, you know. He knew you'd do right by those girls. And look at you! Coach Crawford and the Lions win state!"

"We had a lot of support, Reyola."

"No, you didn't. Nowhere near what you should have. But that's not why you do it, is it?" She laughed quietly, and Bailey shifted the phone to his other ear. "You did a great thing for your girl and her friends, Bailey. And you know what?"

"What?"

"I'll bet they never forget it. Even if everyone else does, they won't. Now you get some rest. Oh, and Jocelyn's making you a victory pie. We'll bring it by tomorrow after church."

"Thank you, Ma'am. Thanks for everything."

They hung up the phone, but Bailey just kept staring at his shoes, his thoughts a whirlwind of memories and emotions. He remembered Reyola's constant support of him when he started in the district, her words, her kindness, her gentle prods and expectations of his best over all these years. He remembered Lars and his contagious belief that all kids should get to play "the greatest game in the world." He wished Lars had been at the game today, but he knew the entire season had been touched by his presence, everyone shaped by his coaching.

Bailey's eyes stung at the thought, and he dropped onto the couch, flicking off his shoes and tossing off his hat as he did. He suddenly felt very tired. He closed his eyes and dozed into the summer practices Lars had come to for the girls, his suggestions for drills, and his constant encouragement about Bailey being the best person for this job. He drew in a deep breath and his memory flashed forward to the look on his daughter's face when she scored that final goal just a few hours earlier. He thought of Kentucky's selflessness in passing it off, of Nelli's spunk, of Annie's endurance and Wally's excitement, and how much they'd each overcome to achieve so much together.

And he hoped Reyola was right about what they'd remember.

Bailey rested his elbows on the pillows and sighed. A series of other thoughts floated through his head as he relaxed. He exhaled again. Cathy came from the kitchen and set a Coors in his hand. Bailey opened his eyes and watched his wife pull up a chair next to him. She clinked her glass to his bottle.

"Well done, Coach," she whispered, her eyes soft and inviting. He nodded at her, a man humbled by his wife's love, overwhelmed by more emotions than he could articulate.

"Cheers," he whispered back. Bailey took a long gulp and closed his eyes again, resting the bottle on his stomach and considered the games and faces, challenges and obstacles of the past six months. The colors of their hand-me-down uniforms suddenly melded into the blacktop of the school parking lot. Girls faces transformed into parents or referees. Soccer balls flew through the air and became one big plastic head that looked strangely like that of Harry Hanks, until it, along with a massive rectangle of white lines, scoreboards and grass, disintegrated into one deep black hole swallowed up by the earth. An imposing dark thundercloud with bright bolts of lightning hovered over the hole, waiting to strike. Bailey saw himself falling toward the pit, jumping to avoid the lightning, and fighting against a gust of wind that pushed him backward. He punched it, hard, again and again, until he saw his son's face, then his daughter's, fuzzy, but there was no mistaking who it was on the other side of the wind that kept him moving forward.

Bailey forced himself awake. He shook his head to push out the cobweb clouding his brain, looked around the room and realized his beer somehow was on the floor beside him. He finished it, lukewarm. He hadn't realized just how tired he'd been, and now the living room was dark. He was alone.

He reached for a lamp and sat up. Cathy had left a note in the chair beside him that read: "7:10. Didn't want to wake you. I'm dropping off pizzas and will be back soon. Love you." His head dropped back to the pillow and he lay still, listening to the sounds of the house, thankful to be here in the home Cathy had made for him and B.J. and Mandy.

By the time she returned, Bailey had forced himself into the shower and stood under the hot water for a long time. It felt good on his muscles and skin. He tried not to think about nothing in particular, even though Kentucky and Mandy's faces crept into his thoughts. He'd finish making those calls for scholarships for both of them and for any others he thought might have a chance, including players from the boys' team. B.J.'s grades had already landed him offers for an academic scholarship, but he thought his daughter might have a chance as well for some Division II or III team. Kentucky was Division I caliber, but that wouldn't be easy.

He dried himself off, grabbed a book and climbed into bed. But he was so tired that when his wife came in, she simply rested against his arm, close to his chest. He slept soundly, her breath easy on his neck, and neither husband nor wife moved until the sun shone through the window the next morning. Even then he did not stir.

When he finally got out of bed, Bailey Crawford was starving and very glad for the whiffs of Sunday morning brunch his wife was cooking. He strolled into the kitchen, and found B.J. helping his sister with blueberry pancakes and Cathy frying bacon. He reached for his coffee and sat down.

"Well, the champ has emerged," B.J. teased. "Really, Dad, you'd think you played that game yesterday, considering how long you slept."

"I feel like I did," Bailey said, dumping sugar into his coffee and pulling a strawberry from a fruit salad Cathy set in front of him.

"Hurry, B.J., turn this one over!" Mandy screamed to her brother who grabbed the spatula and slid it under a pancake in the shape of a very thick V. It browned quickly and B.J. served it onto a plate, which Mandy set before her father, beaming as she did.

"V for victory, Dad!" She hugged his neck and passed him the maple syrup before plopping into the chair next to him. B.J. flipped the rest of the pancakes into a stack, set them in the center of the table and took his seat across from his sister. Cathy sat down with a plate of crispy bacon and the Crawford household was lively and loud for a Sunday morning.

"We won, Dad. We got our state championship," B.J. said it with as much pride as if he'd brought the victory home himself. "You did a great job."

Bailey studied his son. What else had happened since he fell asleep?

"Really, B.J.?"

"Really, Dad. Great job. I'm happy for you—and I admit it, I'm happy for the girls. You were right: They're pretty good. And no kidding—the guys and I were super glad to be there." He paused to swallow his orange juice, set down his empty glass and elbowed his father. "Besides, it's about time!"

"Hey, what about me?!" His sister chimed in.

"Oh, yeah, I guess you did okay, too." He shrugged and then erupted into a fit of laughter which took them all a full five minutes to recover from. As they did, Bailey felt both pleasure and pride that these two young adults were his. And he knew his wife did, too, when he saw how her eyes sparkled in a way reminiscent of the first time she held their children just after giving birth. He wanted to reach across the table and kiss her right then, but he knew their children would protest. He indulged instead in another pancake and brushed her hand tenderly.

"The pizza party was fun, Dad, but don't worry, everyone understood why you weren't there." Mandy was talking and crunching a piece of bacon at the same time.

"Didn't intend to fall asleep. Sorry I missed it."

"That's okay," she said before launching into every detail of the party: how Tricia gave a speech and how Nelli taught them all some new dance moves and that even Kentucky came and ate four slices of pizza, as if she'd never seen such a banquet, and then Annie brought some cinnamon buns and lemonade, but Wally had had to stay home and go to bed. His daughter went on and on, with highlights interspersed from her brother who'd brought over his soccer buddies—"to support the girls"—and for some pizza and dance lessons as well.

Bailey just listened and smiled and listened some more. Cathy did too. And by the time they were done with brunch, they'd eaten everything on the table, Bailey winning the contest with seven pancakes, including the V, but realizing his twins had won something far greater than a morning feast.

The rest of the afternoon was quiet by comparison. B.J. watched the Cleveland-Pittsburgh football game with his friends, and Mandy babysat two little girls down the street. Except for a quick visit from the Wallaces, who brought a pecan pie, Bailey welcomed the slow, quiet day at home. He half expected the phone would be ringing a few times; not that he took Stan Gullen's threat seriously after Friday night's football loss, but Bailey wouldn't have been surprised had the Booster Club president called him with some other outlandish claim. He would have been floored, however, to receive a congratulatory call from Hanks or any school parents or fellow teachers. But surely, someone—anyone—would call to say something—anything—about the championship.

But they never did.

So while Cathy was in the kitchen, he sat back on the couch to read through the Sunday newspaper; first the news, then the business section. When he turned to the last page in the sports section, he found a tiny paragraph in the bottom right left corner about the game. The headline read: "Lions Girls Soccer Ends Strong." The story wasn't more than three sentences, covering who won the final game of the season, who scored the goals and what Coach Bailey Crawford expected for next year: "Claymont Falls High will always do its best."

Bailey closed the paper and tossed it on the table. He grabbed his hat and headed to the garage, found the rake and walked to the backyard. The leaves in their yard had been neglected for weeks. Even though today's sky was pale and gray, Bailey found the temperature pleasant enough for gathering all the leaves into one big pile near Cathy's flowerbed. It felt good to get some oxygen circulating through his body today, good to keep his feet moving forward, even against a small, annoying wind.

The next morning as Bailey pulled into the parking lot, he felt rested and settled. He pulled his briefcase and lunch bag from the back seat of the car and walked toward his classroom, passing the morning buses as students bounced off single file. He saw Kentucky up ahead and caught up with her. Her hair was neatly tied back, her jacket looked like it hadn't once been someone else's—just hers—and her step seemed to Bailey a little surer than the other times when he'd bumped into her.

"Good morning, Ms. Beaucamp. About those college applications—I've made some calls and so we should see the guidance counselor."

"Morning, Coach," she said, grinning slightly as she focused straight ahead. "Okay. Yes."

"Good. I'll check their schedules and get back in touch with you. Any ideas where you'd like to go?"

The girl's response surprised Bailey. "I've already been looking at Arizona and Colorado. They're good schools, a little far away, but maybe that'd be okay." She pulled her shoulders up and stood taller while they walked.

Bailey nodded. "They've both got good women's soccer programs, too. Colorado especially. Let's see what we can do."

Kentucky suddenly stopped, paused and looked intently at her coach. Bailey knew he needed to listen. "My mama used to tell me all the time it wasn't lady-like runnin' 'round and playin' basketball and soccer and sports outside all the time with the boys, that I should be helpin' her with the kids and chores and stuff. And she wasn't real happy when you got me on the team." Kentucky's eyes stayed gripped on Bailey's. "But after Saturday, you know what she's sayin'?"

"What?"

"She's sayin, 'Maybe, Adeline, you could do that at a college and get yourself an education.' And I said, 'Maybe I could, Mama. Maybe I could.'"

Kentucky reached out her hand to Bailey's shoulder. She nodded softly at her coach and turned into the hallway toward her locker, her pack firm and full across her back. It looked heavy with books. Bailey had always worried how she'd get her homework done at home. Now he knew he hadn't needed to worry at all.

He walked the other direction to his classroom, dropped his briefcase on his desk and prepared for the day's lessons. He approached the chalkboard to write the fact about "This Day in History" and considered writing about the history Kentucky and her teammates made on the soccer field on Saturday. It was small in comparison to a nation's milestones, to great political coups or scientific discoveries, but it seemed no less significant to Bailey on that particular morning. Hadn't he always told his students that history, after all, was comprised of a thousand little stories about groups of people and the steps they took together? What else was it, if not movements and challenges and victories? He sipped some coffee and reached for the chalk.

"Morning, Coach Crawford. Just thought I'd stop by real quick to say congratulations." Freddie Smith's frame filled the doorway, and he was leaning halfway into the room and halfway into the hallway. His wrinkled shirt was untucked, and his hair needed either a comb or a baseball cap. Bailey knew which Freddie would opt for.

"Thanks, Freddie. And thanks for coming to the game," Bailey said, rubbing chalk dust from his hands.

"Hey, it was a great game, Bailey. You should be proud."

"I am. We all should be."

"Yeah, about that." He sniffled and fidgeted, as if he had something else to say but couldn't quite figure out how. He rubbed the back of his neck, looking into the hall and then back at Bailey.

"What's up, Freddie?" "Stan Gullen just stopped by the athletic department, you know, the Booster Club president. No idea what he said because Hanks had the gall to shut the door so I couldn't eavesdrop," he tucked his fists into his back pockets. "But just in case it mattered, I thought you should know. Anyway, good job on Saturday."

"That means a lot."

"Yeah, it's probably going to be about as much as you get. You know how things are around here." He pulled his hand up to his heart. "But I mean it. I thought it was a great game. And I'll deny it if anyone asks." He laughed at his own joke before disappearing into the crowded stream of students and teachers arriving.

As the bell rang, teenagers filed into Bailey's classroom like they did every other day. For the next three hours in three different classes, Bailey led his students through discussions and filmstrips on American Reconstruction, Roosevelt, and Black Tuesday. Though they were unusually attentive for a Monday morning, Bailey noted to himself that not a single word was said about the weekend. About soccer or football, about championships won or lost.

By lunchtime he headed to the teachers' lounge for a cup of coffee. Three basketball coaches and one of Hanks' assistant football coaches saw him enter, picked up their trays and moved across the room. A biology teacher joined them, along with another history teacher who, Bailey recalled, had coached wrestling a few years back. They glanced at Bailey and leaned into one another with whispers. But Bailey just sighed, approached the coffeepot and topped off his cup. As he stirred some sugar into his mug, he heard a low rumble behind him.

He turned around. Delores Winston, Donna Sanchez and a handful of other teachers were standing at their tables, clapping in his direction. The basketball coaches began to laugh at what they saw, which only made the women's applause louder. Bailey took a sip of his coffee, considered his options and acknowledged his colleagues' salute with a nod. He walked back through the teacher's lounge, careful not to spill on the carpet. He pushed the door with his free elbow and when he looked back across the lounge, he saw Delores and Donna return to their seats, but not before sending murderous scowls to a table of bulky coaches, who shook their heads, killed their laughter and finished their meal.

The rest of the day was fairly routine for Bailey, as was the rest of the fall semester and into the winter. He taught classes, graded quizzes, met with guidance counselors, college coaches and players, ate dinner with his family, raked leaves or shoveled snow, and wondered when—or if—he'd hear from Hanks or Gullen or the Booster Club about their state title. Each time Bailey had stopped by the athletic department, the secretary told him Hanks was in a meeting. Freddie was probably right—Bailey and his team were not going to get much. Even so, the more Bailey thought about how hard his team worked, about their undefeated record, the more concerned he became that they might slip into obscurity.

They deserved recognition.

Bailey expected it might come that February day the yearbook photographer set up a backdrop in the gym for team photos and individual shots for all seniors. The athletic director was organizing team pictures with their trophies and Bailey seized the opportunity.

But Hanks approached him first and pulled him into his office, shutting the door behind him.

"Been meaning to talk with you for a while. But let's cut to the chase: I thought the expected outcome of your last game had been made clear to you," Hanks said standing behind his desk, loosening his sleeves. Bailey did not sit down.

"You mean to lose the state finals?"

"Yeah, that."

"Harry, it seemed pretty ridiculous, you've got to admit. It's just a—"

"Couldn't agree more, Crawford. But Stan's not happy."

"Because we won?"

"No. Because we lost. If you ask me it was a waste of his time to come after you at all. Hell, he's just upset because his kid didn't win, and probably more upset that it was my kid who lost it for us." He shook his head. "Preston will never amount to much, I know that. Can't handle pressure, and will choke every time."

Bailey swallowed at the incongruity he just heard. Did he just hear a father giving up on his son?

In the awkward silence, all Bailey could think to say was, "It was a tough loss." Then he noticed the second place state trophy, as big as his arm, glistening on the shelf.

Hanks saw him admiring it. "Sure was a tough loss. But we got that, and it'll go in the trophy case out in the front hall just after the team poses with it. At least there's some gold in our legacy."

He took an old T-shirt from a chair and rubbed the nameplate so that it was shone even brighter: "Ohio State High School Football Championship. Second Place. 1983. Claymont Falls Lions." Then he turned to Bailey. "The Boosters are happy enough about this, but you should know you made my job harder."

Bailey straightened his shoulders. "I couldn't have—"

"I knew you'd never throw a game. That's not the point."

"What is the point, Harry?"

"The point? That just because a bunch of girls runs a little faster than another bunch of girls, or happens to kick the ball in a goal more than the other side does not make them champions."

"Excuse me?"

"We're humoring them, Crawford, the whole ridiculous Title IX thing. It was a joke from the start; everyone knows that. So who cares if you win, when you're a joke to begin with?"

Bailey felt a sour taste slide down the back of his throat. He'd had enough. "You're wrong. They are champions."

Hanks laughed. "They're girls, Crawford! Wake up! Nobody in this town cares what they do or don't do, and they never will."

That was it. Bailey wanted to walk over, pick up the stupid gold football trophy and bash it over Harry Hanks' head. But as he looked out the window, he saw a group of girls running by, kicking a soccer ball, laughing in the sun. And so instead, he breathed deeply, exhaled and mumbled, "Are we done here?"

Hanks shrugged.

Bailey opened the door, and just as he was about to leave, Hanks called out: "I take it I can put you down to coach next year's girls, right, Crawford? Compliance and all."

Like he was in slow motion, Bailey reached for words that he'd buried since he saw his daughter's face the day she heard he'd be her coach. He found them, hard and real and cutting:

"It'd be my privilege to coach the girls again," he said, so quietly that the athletic director had to strain to hear him. "My privilege. They know more about being a champion than you ever will. And they deserve to be honored as champions."

Hanks stopped listening, a deep, eerie chuckle rumbling up from his belly and just about to erupt from his throat, when he saw Bailey's steely stare. Then he pushed it back down. Instantly. His eyes jumped toward the window, as he coughed and said, "That'll never happen, Crawford, believe me."

Bailey kept staring. The tension was both revealing and prophetic.

"We'll see, Hanks. We'll see." And with that, the girls soccer coach turned and walked out of the office. He did not even bother to close the door behind him.

He did, however, watch nine players from his starting lineup graduate in the spring, and sent two of them off to college on athletic scholarships. And he spent the next summer and fall practicing again in parking lots with beat-up equipment, and taking the Claymont Falls High girls soccer team to the first round of the regional tournament before they lost by a penalty kick.

Over the following few years, he repeated his training, practice and record to the regional tournament, until one summer, he decided it was time to step down and take the role of assistant coach. A new teacher had joined the district, showing both experience and excitement for the job. She was the best person to lead the Lions. Bailey knew it and he didn't mind saying so.

chapter
16

2008

The house was completely dark when my mother came home. She switched on a lamp and found me slung over the couch, occupying what she usually claimed as "her spot" in front of the television. But the TV wasn't on, so when she saw me, Mom jumped, startled by my presence.

My shoes were dangling from the tips of my toes. My skirt was wrinkled, my blouse un-tucked. My bag was on the floor surrounded by a pizza box, a plastic liter of Diet Coke, a paper sleeve off of a super-size serving of McDonald's fries and a pint of Ben and Jerry's peanut butter cup ice cream—all empty. The day's mail and a copy of the Register lay scattered beside them, unopened. It was only 7:45 p.m., but the scene looked more like I had pulled a college all-nighter.

"Good Lord, child, you 'bout gave me a heart attack." She bent over for a slice of pizza and was left disappointed. "What in Sam Hill were you sitting in the dark for?"

I grunted.

She picked up the mail and sorted through it. "Bills, flyers, nothing interesting."

"What time is it?"

"Almost eight. I stopped by that new Kitchen and Beyond store. They got some nice things." Mom sat down and pushed off her shoes. "Now, what's a matter with you?"

"Nothing."

"Oh, okay. Let me ask again. What's a matter with you?"

I shrugged and looked away from the lamp.

"Reynalda Lynn Wallace. You're sulking. What happened?"

My stomach hurt and I wasn't sure it was due to the junk food binge I'd just had or the conversation I was about to have. I shook my head.

Mom stretched her arms above her head and then let them drop in her lap.

"Haven't seen you look like this since that girl scored twice on you senior year."

"That about sums it up."

"Hmm, let me see. Some white administrator got on your case, but you didn't do anything wrong."

I pulled in my knees and jerked upright. "Something like that."

My mother chuckled as she rose from her chair, shuffled into the kitchen and returned with a plate of leftover macaroni and cheese. She settled herself into the cushions and took a bite. "Talk to me."

So I did. I rambled through the whole story, about how my players wanted to raise money so they could honor Coach Crawford's championship team, but Preston Hanks wouldn't allow it, calling it a "distraction" from the stadium proposal, and then he proceeded to inform me he'd hired me only because I fit the diversity quota for the district. Ever since he was a student at Claymont Falls High, he'd never expected girls soccer to go anywhere and especially not now that he was the athletic director and football coach. Only football made money for the school, he said, which is why it mattered most. As if any of that had anything to do with my current team.

I ranted on about power-hungry white men, and how backward people in this pathetic town could be, and then griped again about the fact that a group of champion soccer players had probably never even been congratulated, let alone given so much as a ribbon. All because they were girls.

"This place is messed up," I spat out. "And I just don't give a rip anymore." I kicked the pizza box for effect.

Mom was quiet. She'd lost interest in her plate, set it on the coffee table and was rubbing her feet as she listened. Her starched uniform was tight across her chest; tiny dots of yellow stains—as if she'd spilled her coffee—discolored an otherwise clean top. I wondered how she managed to keep working so hard in a job that never seemed to go anywhere, to serve as cook for a bunch of brats who probably never once said "thank you, Miss. Wallace." The mere thought incensed me—again.

"What are we doing here anyway, Mom? Why'd MaeMa ever think she should come to such a stupid little town where we'd be the only—"

"Stop right there." She pointed sharply at me, her voice a firm line of authority. "You may be mad at the world right now, but you will not disrespect your grandmother. Ever. You have no idea what she did for you or me."

Her hands were still, her eyes full. "It's because of her I could even get a job and—"

"As a lunch lady?"

My mother blinked, and whispered with a hiss: "This lunch lady brought you up, kept you safe, and helped you win all of those." She pointed to the shelves crammed with my trophies, medals and ribbons.

"I earned all of those."

Her lips made a slight upward motion and she nodded. "Oh, that's right. You paid for your own shoes every season, and for all your equipment, and youth soccer fees year after year, didn't you? And I guess you drove yourself to every practice and every game and every camp, and to every doctor's appointment or emergency room every time you got hurt, from the time you were seven until you left for college, right? Why, you even talked yourself into staying on those teams whenever you were losing or whenever you came in second, even when you really felt like quitting. You did all that all by yourself, didn't you, Baby Girl?" The mix of truth and hurt in her eyes stung.

I dropped my eyes.

"You need to remember that if MaeMa hadn't left the city to give me and Uncle Jimmy a better chance at things—and I admit I didn't do too much right before you came along—I'd never have gotten that lunch lady job—which I happen to love, by the way. And believe me, you'd never have spent one minute on a field or in a gym or on a court." She locked eyes with me. "And I can't think of anything sadder in this whole world than my baby girl not getting to do what she was born to do."

She picked up a photo of MaeMa from three Christmases ago. "Your grandmother was the first black woman ever to work in the schools here. And you know what? They did not want to hire her when she applied."

"Some things don't change."

"You can't imagine. She went through more than we'll ever know to put this roof over our heads and to make sure her granddaughter went to college. People threatened her, Rey, they called her all sorts of things, one lady even spit on her because she said she didn't want her son taught by a Negro. But MaeMa kept moving forward because people like Lars Lambert, and then Bailey Crawford, came alongside her, shielded her, helped her and, most of all, respected her. You know why? Because she was a good teacher and, in spite of all the craziness, she cared about what she did, the impact she could have on those kids. She wasn't perfect, but she did her best. Not anyone else's best. Just hers."

She drew in a deep breath and exhaled to regain her composure. "So forgive me, Baby, if I don't exactly feel sorry for you as you're moping in the dark because you didn't get your way at school and your boss offended you."

She picked up her plate, tucked it into my pizza box along with my other trash and took it all into the kitchen. I watched her balance the box like a waitress would her tray before I scanned the room filled with images of MaeMa or of me, of winnings from my sports career or my grandmother's favorite books on the shelves. Only a few small photos represented my mother's accomplishments: one of Mom in her high school graduation cap and gown, another of her wearing her white kitchen staff uniform.

I sat silently, each object around me a reminder of how the women in this house lived, always giving of themselves. For me. And for the first time since Bailey Crawford's funeral, I realized that it was not the number of wins or losses that made a good coach—no more than high test scores were a sign of an effective teacher. No, it was seeing the sacrifices of the people who cared for me so that I could care for others that finally hit me over the head. For someone who was an honor student in college, I was slow to comprehend things that mattered.

"So, Rey, you're going to have to make the best of a bad situation. Who cares why they hired you? Your foot is in the door now, which means you can show everybody what you're made of," Mom said as she wandered back into the living room. "And if Preston's going to be a stinker about the fundraiser, you'll just have to figure out a better way to do what you think is right. That's how we operate, you know."

"We do?" I slithered my sorry self off the couch.

"Yep. That's what we Wallace women do. We go on; we don't stop because of an obstacle, big or small. Besides, I'm pretty sure that if Tricia or Nelli or the others had really wanted the recognition, they would have pushed for it a long time ago."

"What do you mean?" "I mean, they weren't playing for fame and glory, Baby."

I looked around at all I had won.

Mom patted my shoulder. "I suppose it was nice that they won and all, but they knew that just getting to play was more exciting than a trophy."

"Then why'd you keep all of mine?"

She looked surprised. "Why? To remind me of every single minute that you ever got to walk onto a field or a court. You were our champion, the one who got to do what we never did." She hugged me tight. "Besides, we couldn't afford any fancy artwork to dress up the place."

"And all this time I thought it was because you were proud of me."

Mom swatted my head with her palm before pulling me close and squeezing me hard.

"When's your next game?" She let go of me as she asked.

"Tomorrow at five. Home game."

"I'll be there. Now, you show those girls what we do, okay?"

My mother held her cheek out to me, and I obliged with a good-night kiss. I watched her slide wearily toward her bedroom, shoulders high, steps slow but sure. When she closed her bedroom door, the sting in my eyes slipped down my face and onto my crumpled shirt. I dropped my head into my hands and let go.

Memories of MaeMa flooded in my mind, and I saw her and Mom sitting on the sidelines of my games, waving at me, cheering for me, welcoming me whenever the referee blew the final whistle, regardless of the score. I heard her voice reading stories to me, and watched Mom come home in her uniform, tired from working two shifts, but glad to make sure I had what I needed for practice or school. From their celebrations of my accomplishments, to their quiet embraces when I wasn't sure what to do, the memories of their tireless examples as role models made me whisper two words I now realized I did not say often enough, "Thank you!"

They were my sanctuary.

Sleep was short that night, not because I wasn't tired, but because my mind was so full of images and ideas and perspectives that I didn't want to put them to bed. I closed my eyes anyway and recalled my grandmother singing hymns to us on Sunday afternoons, or my mother baking cupcakes for me after school, or the trips we'd take into the city, "just because." Each memory took me to another place and time stored in some other room in my soul, each a well of strength to draw from no matter how weary I felt. Eventually, I did fall asleep, soundly, softly, so that every part of me—from my fingernails to my ankles and all of the muscles and nerves and emotions in between—finally found rest.

I was amazed that I had so much energy the next morning. I hopped out of bed for a quick three-mile run. By the time I came back, Mom had left for work. I poured a glass of orange juice and leaned against the kitchen counter. This was a good day already. I felt lighter, no longer "mad at the world," as my mother had put it, and eager even for the classes, conversations and competition that lay ahead of me. It didn't hurt either that I discovered a piece of blueberry pie on the table that my mother had wrapped and left out for me to take as a "good luck" charm for the game.

If I had been born an athlete, as she said last night, there was no question she had been born a baker. And I was the better off because of her gift, at least as long as I kept running.

Annie Knudsen was giving back change to a customer when I appeared in front of the cash register. As good of a morning as it was, a strong cup of coffee would make it even better.

"Thanks for coming to our game a couple of days ago," I said, reaching into my wallet for two dollar bills. "It meant a lot to my girls—and to me. An espresso, please."

"My pleasure," she said. "It brought back lots of good memories for us. Heck, I'm just sorry we haven't made it to more games before now. What time is today's game?"

While her assistant brewed my cup, we talked about how much quicker she thought the pace was now compared to when she played. In those days, Annie told me she had learned to anticipate more because the players were less skilled. But she also had to rely on her defenders to keep the front line from getting through to score.

"I'm not sure I'd stand a chance in the goal if I'd played on your team now!" She handed me my espresso. "I'm looking forward to the game."

"Me too. Oh, and we're working on that recognition night for your team!"

"Tricia tells me we are, too. Not sure everyone's going to make it, but we'll give it our best shot!"

We laughed at the pun, and I waved to her as I dodged the next wave of customers crowding in, a ground crew for the city parks service. And as I crossed the parking lot aiming for my car, oblivious to my surroundings, I walked straight into the path of a bicyclist dressed in jeans and a striped Oxford shirt.

"Will!"

He swerved his bike to the sidewalk and squeezed the breaks, his helmet latched beneath his chin, his messenger bag slung across his shoulders. He did not smile.

"What are you doing here?" I asked, immediately wanting to take back the dumb question. He pointed to my espresso. Will got off his bike and took off his helmet.

"Oh, yes. You're here for your morning cup of coffee." I raised my cup to him.

"That's it? That's all you have to say?" He shifted his weight. I looked down at my pumps and game day skirt and blouse.

"No, that's not it. I was an idiot yesterday. In the hall. When I saw you." I couldn't look away from the smudge on my shoes, but I made myself resist the powerful urge to kneel down and polish them. I kept talking. "Hanks told me I couldn't have the fundraiser and—"

"You said that last night."

"I know. And I let it get to me more than I should have."

Will didn't respond. I snuck a peek at him and saw him looking at his watch.

"I should let you go."

"Probably." Will started for the door.

"But I am sorry for being an idiot."

He stopped just short of the entrance as some of the parks guys came bounding out, slurping their coffees. Will adjusted his glasses and turned back to me. The morning sun cast a glow around his frame that made my knees wobbly. I sighed.

"Yeah, you were kind of an idiot. But, well, good luck tonight." He hoisted his backpack and walked into Knudsen's Bakery. I turned toward my car, amazed at how my insides could go from free and hopeful one minute, to brokenhearted and sentimental the next. On the drive to work, I turned up the radio as loud as it would go.

I'd blown it—again—with a guy who'd actually been supportive of me, of soccer, and, in fact, of the entire girls program. But I hadn't been able to see any of it, really see it for what it was. And now with a busy day ahead of classes and students and players, I could only hope that I might find another chance to talk with Will later. Maybe.

"Just give your best. Not anyone else's." The voice was clear in my head and I had to at least try.

Preston Hanks was waiting for me in my classroom by the time I unloaded my books and bag on my desk. He was wearing a stiff long-sleeved shirt and tie, black slacks and loafers, the kind of outfit he only wore for meetings with district administrators or Booster Club parents.

"Didn't realize you had an interest in English class."

He ignored at my comment and stood between two rows of desks not far from mine. "I didn't like how things ended with our . . . conversation."

"Uh huh."

"Yeah, well, I shouldn't have lost my cool."

"I'll take that as an apology. So you've changed your mind?"

He twisted his neck back and forth in an attempt to crack it. He swallowed, and I got the impression he was working on controlling his temper all over again. "See here's the thing, Reynalda. We have to get the new stadium on the ballot and the taxpayer support to pass it. When that happens, we'll get some other major financial gifts so we can break ground next summer. You know why that's a good thing? It gives all our kids what they deserve, a chance to be scouted by some of the big schools. And that could also mean some night games—and scouts—for your team."

"That's already happening. Our last game of this season is under the lights."

"This could give you more. The point is our department needs to have a unified voice on this, that's what the Boosters are expecting. That way, everyone wins. In fact, I'm on my way to a meeting right now and I want them to know everyone's on board with this."

I pulled some files from my bag and began organizing my desk. This line from Hanks, I realized, was one of those obstacles that Mom warned me about, one that would require me to stay alert. This morning, I was not going to give in so easily to his maneuvering.

"I understand, but I'd still like my team to be able to run a raffle so they can honor the—"

"No." He tugged the wrists of his sleeves to loosen them and adjusted his tie. "No raffle, no fundraiser. Nothing to distract from the campaign the Boosters are running."

I set a copy of Mockingbird near a pile of assignments I was passing back, and suddenly imagined my grandmother's classroom as well as my mother's kitchen. I moved forward. "Preston, it's wrong that this school has never honored that championship team."

He stepped back. "Excuse me?"

"I said it's wrong that this school, and the district for that matter, has never recognized the state title Bailey Crawford and his girls soccer team won. If it had been football, there would have been parades and banners and trophies in the Hall of Inspiration. Oh, and every player would have been given a ring, right?"

He clenched his jaw, and ran his hand across his forehead. His gaze seemed angry then distant, pained even, like I was picking at an old wound.

"But it wasn't football, was it?" I whispered. "The closest football ever came to winning a state championship was that same year, when you were quarterback, and it just didn't quite work out. I'm sorry about that, Preston. But that was a long time ago, and it still isn't a good enough reason for Coach Crawford and his team to be ignored all these years. I'd like to change that."

"No."

"That's not . . . right."

"It's the right thing today, for these kids."

The bell rang signaling first period class, and Preston turned toward the door. But I wasn't finished. "Before you go, you should know that I've been working with some of the women from that first team. We're planning a ceremony at our last game. To honor them."

"You might want to think twice about that," he stopped then grinned. "I wouldn't want a talented young coach like you to do something you'd regret later."

Preston's threat had a strange effect on me; instead of instilling fear, it freed me. "I'd regret it the rest of my life if I didn't do this—for them. So I hope you'll change your mind."

He gave no answer as he hurried out the door, nearly colliding with three pimply freshmen who looked like babies next to a giant. I welcomed them as 29 other students took their seats and class began.

It was odd that the rest of the day I didn't think much about anything but what was in my lesson plans. From the trial scene in To Kill a Mockingbird to subject/verb agreements to vocabulary lists, the subject of English somehow captivated me today and my students responded in kind. I'd been so absorbed, in fact, that by the final bell of the last class, I was stacking papers and writing on the board for Monday. If one of my student's hadn't wished me good luck on the game, I might have forgotten about it altogether.

Still in her cafeteria uniform, my mother was sitting in the bleachers near Annie Knudsen and a few other women from Coach Crawford's first team. Several families were in front of them, as well as some other students who'd come to support their friends on a Friday afternoon when the autumn air was still warm and crisp. They cheered each time we came close to scoring and were especially loud today whenever our goalkeeper came away with a save. Still, for all their support, we came away with an empty scoreboard: Lions 0, Bears 0.

We were more than halfway through our season, building on a better record from last year at this time, but still not what I'd like to see to help us qualify for district playoffs: three wins, three losses and one tie. Each game was closer than the last but it was still difficult to get my players to shoot, let alone score. It would take a while for them to gain the confidence and skills to be competitive in this conference, but I was encouraged at their willingness to work hard. They weren't giving up.

That's what I told the sports reporter Tricia sent over from the Register anyway. And though I'd seen great progress—in large part because of the great support of new fans, I added, making sure she scribbled that down in her notes—I knew we still had a ways to go. I smiled as she snapped my photo and then scurried over to talk with Kate and Maggie about being co-captains of this young team.

When all of the players in the locker room had iced their ankles and finished their showers, I gathered them together for a team meeting.

"Good hard work today, Lions. You just keep getting better and better, and it's not too soon to start thinking about next week's game. It'd also be good if we started shooting more."

A couple heads nodded. Ponytails swirled back and forth. I took a sip of water and continued. "But right now, I want to talk about the raffle and—"

"Yeah, Coach Rey, when will we start to sell the tickets? We're getting good donations," Maggie said. Her teammates shifted and smiled, eager for an answer.

"That's the thing. Coach Hanks has not given us permission yet to do any fundraisers. I'm sorry about that, really."

"What?" "How come?"

"Why not?"

They scooted into their circle more, some standing by their gear, others sitting on the benches under the Lions Girls Soccer sign that hung in the middle of our locker room.

"The Booster Club is running a campaign for the new stadium, and they don't want any competition to distract from their efforts." I tried to be upbeat but these girls were smart. They knew what that really meant.

"Man, we never get anything!"

"That's not quite true. The new stadium could be for us too, where more college scouts might come to see you play. Besides, look around you. We're in our own locker room with new uniforms and equipment and bleachers for our fans. And, unlike those first players, we don't have to worry about how we're going to get to the games or where we'll play for that matter."

"That's why we need to do something, Coach. For them."

"I agree. And we still can. We just can't do an official fundraiser."

"But what about their rings?"

"I guess those will have to wait," I said.

"So what will we do?"

"I was hoping you'd ask that, Kate." The players huddled in even closer, like we were little girls at a top secret meeting in the neighborhood clubhouse. Ideas jumped around, excitement grew palpable and, twenty minutes later, we knew exactly what would happen at the game we decided to refer to as, "Champions Night." Arms around each other, heads tilted toward the middle, the chant— "Li-ons, Li-ons"— raised a thunderous crescendo I'd never heard before from these girls.

"Champions Night" was just what we needed to look forward to.

Annie, Tricia and Nelli were waiting for me in the parking lot as I walked out of the locker room with my players. The three old friends stood talking and gesturing when we crossed over to them. And when they saw us, they applauded. My team bowed and giggled at the attention and quickly disappeared into their teenage Friday night fun.

"Good game, Coach," Nelli said as we watched them drive off. "They're getting stronger all the time."

"I think so too. Thanks for coming . . . again."

"We'll try to have somebody from our team at every game. And the good news is that most of us will be here for that last game." Tricia held out a list of names while Annie and Nelli looked over her shoulder.

"Listen, about the rings."

"Yeah, I'm looking forward to flashing mine around the newsroom! The sports guys will be so impressed!"

"I'm sorry, but we won't be able to get them . . . yet." I explained to them Preston Hanks' decision, and apologized for disappointing them.

"Typical," Nelli shook her head. "Some boys never grow up."

Annie jumped in. "Now, Nelli, he can't help it if he's got those Boosters breathing down his neck."

"Again." Tricia remarked. "Listen, Doll, I was just showing off with the ring thing. We didn't need trophies then, and we certainly don't need rings now. Don't you worry."

"But my team is still planning a special ceremony for you in two weeks, okay? It just won't be quite . . . as official as we'd hoped."

All three women sighed at the same time, as if this confirmed what they'd known all along.

"Listen, Sugar, someday this town will give us that big fancy trophy, or rings or whatever, but believe me, seeing you and those girls play with so much heart, that's about as good as it gets, right, Nell? Annie?"

"Absolutely."

"Right!"

They high-fived each other, imitating the younger players' enthusiasm, and threw back their heads in laughter. Trees rustled around us and a car honked out in the intersection. Tricia held out the list to me.

"Here's the 1983 team lineup."

"Perfect."

"Still not sure about Kentucky, but everyone else will be here, even Mandy, and her brother B.J. and Mrs. Crawford, so it'll be a real good night. I've already scheduled a photographer from the paper."

"Wally's coming too," Annie said. "It'll be a great 25th reunion! Thanks, Rey, for helping us finally organize something like this."

"Thank you. Really. For everything." I felt a lump of emotion in the back of my throat. My eyes filled, and Annie patted my arm, before Nelli interrupted.

"Okay, enough of this lovefest," she said. "I'm starving. See you next week, Coach." Nelli tossed a wave at me as she corralled her friends toward her car and drove off.

I was starving, too, I suddenly realized, and decided to stop by Thai Delight on my way home. I'd order takeout if nothing else. But when I walked in the front door, I knew I wouldn't have to order my dinner to go.

"Mind if I join you?" I asked slipping into a booth near the window.

"I was hoping you would," Will said, handing me a menu. "Good effort today."

"Thanks, but I wish we could have put it in the net and actually won—"

"I meant this morning. At Knudsen's. I'm glad you . . . said what you did." Will's smile was the perfect way to end this day. And for the next three hours, we talked about everything from "Champions Night" to college life to favorite movies, all the way through salads, cheap wine, Pad Thai, fried ice cream and tea, until the waitress hustled us out the door. Saturday night, we went to a movie, and Will joined Mom and me for Sunday lunch, which she fussed over more than she should have, but I was secretly glad she did. So was Will. The next week we talked each day, and were together so much that people at school began asking him if he was my new assistant coach.

"Sort of," he replied, winking my direction.

When "Champions Night" finally arrived, Claymont Falls High girls soccer— and every other fall team at school—had missed qualifying for playoffs. We had won four, lost six and tied two. The girls, though, had seen their skills improve, more than they'd expected. They knew that tonight's final game against County Day Academy was about more than their record. It was about their history.

But the forecast was grim. Thunderstorms were expected to start mid-afternoon and continue through the night. That'd make travel tough for Mandy and others coming from throughout the state. Hanks poked his head into my classroom at 2:45 to announce that he'd learn in the next hour if the district would cancel the game. He shrugged as he walked away, as if he'd already made his own decision about attending the event.

By 3:35, though, something happened that MaeMa would have called "a little miracle." The storm slowed, the lightning stopped and the sun popped out for a few seconds before sneaking behind some clouds again. It would be a soggy night, but not bad enough to cancel the celebration.

Under blue and green umbrellas, every player but one from the 1983 championship team sat together on our bench. My team had decided that when the stadium announcer called the names for the game's lineup, they would step out with the woman who'd once worn their number, or close to it. I'd given the list to the press box and they knew what to do.

After the marching band played our fight song, and County Day's lineup was announced, my team joined Coach Bailey Crawford's team on the field. With each name a current player in her soccer uniform was joined by an original championship team member, to whom the younger Lion presented a hand-made certificate and two roses. When the lineup was finished, Kate and Annie, Nelli, Tricia and Maggie and the others stood side by side, with Wally and Will in the center circle as well. A hush fell over the stadium.

"And now to celebrate Lions history, please welcome the family of the only coach ever to take Claymont Falls High all the way to an Ohio State championship: Mandy, B.J. and Cathy Crawford representing Coach Bailey Crawford." The family stepped forward and silence covered the field.

But not for long. The championship team began to clap, my team joined in, and soon everyone in the stands as well as County Day Academy was standing and giving their applause, cheering, whistling, and shouting "Li-ons!" I listened to the roar of their respect for what felt like fifteen minutes, and I knew that the praise Bailey Crawford and his first girls soccer championship team deserved 25 years ago had finally been heard.

The band started up again, and the newspaper photographer directed the older and younger Lions teams down the field in front of the goal for a group picture. He ordered my players to kneel in the front row and the champions to stand behind them. But just as he'd almost finished the choreography and was about to set up his camera, we heard someone yelling for us to stop.

"Hold on, hold on. Wait for me!" A tall, thin woman with short brown hair was rushing the goal in heels, black slacks and a purple jacket. She was hollering something about the rain delaying her flight and the craziness of the Cincinnati airport and how only Bailey Crawford and these girls could get her to fly through a storm for something like this.

The women let out a collective, "KENTUCKY!" and soon the photographer's careful alignment had fallen into disarray. Some of the women skipped and hugged each other. Others clapped and danced. I pulled my players to the side and explained that this was #10, one of the original team's leading scorers from that championship year. But before I could finish, Adeline Beaucamp stepped in front of me and extended her hand.

"If it hadn't been for Bailey Crawford, I wouldn't have played soccer or done anything else that mattered. But if it hadn't have been for the Wallace Women, I don't think we'd have accomplished much at all. Now where's your mama?" She looked toward the stands and saw Mom in the first row. She ran over to her, hugged her and escorted her onto the field. Cathy Crawford stepped toward my mother, Mandy waved Kentucky over to stand by her, and my team again assumed their kneeling positions.

"Now we're ready for that picture," Tricia said to the photographer. "The Lions are good to go!"

Ten minutes later, the referee blew her whistle to start the game. And an hour and a half later, she blew it again to end it. Kate and Maggie both had scored goals, but so had two players from County Day Academy. We walked off the field in what would go down in the record books as a disappointing tie to wrap up our season.

But by the time my players arrived at Nelli's house for a special reunion party with the championship women, I couldn't help but see this night as anything less than a beginning.